FORSAKEN

CURSED ANGEL WATCHTOWER 12

L.B. GILBERT

COPYRIGHT

DESCRIPTION

Years ago, he left her to die in the wastelands. Now his fate rests in her hands.

Cast out of Heaven thousands of years ago, Ash is given a chance to redeem himself. If he defeats the demon king and delivers the city from the curse plaguing it, his long exile will end. But raising an army and killing the king is only the beginning. Now, in the ruins of post-apocalyptic Paris, this fallen angel is struggling to keep Bastille afloat amidst a never-ending series of disasters. His only hope in stopping the relentless cycle of destruction rests in Kara, a woman he'd betrayed years before and leader of a mysterious band of scavengers who have somehow escaped the curse's influence. Ash needs to learn her secret if he has any chance of success, but is Kara their salvation or his downfall?

Forsaken is a standalone contribution to the Charmed Legacy Cursed Angel collection. Stories can be read in any order. To learn more, visit CharmedLegacy.com

PROLOGUE

Ash dumped the body in the pit, heaving it effortlessly. He listened for the satisfying thud as it hit the bottom before tossing the head in after it.

"Aren't you tired of this yet, Azazel?"

He pivoted on his heel, masking his surprise to see Raphael sitting on the burned-out wreck of an automobile.

Ash spared a moment to mourn the car, an old Mustang. Once upon a time, he had driven such a vehicle.

"Why are you here?" He was surprised to find his voice hoarse. It had been a long while since he'd spoken to anyone.

Raphael's lip curled into a familiar grin. Ash had always hated his former commander's air of perpetual amusement.

"That should be obvious," Raphael said, hopping off the hood of the car with feigned nonchalance.

He walked to Ash's side, sliding forward with that gliding gait that looked more like floating. It was a way of moving that he had always associated with angels who rarely left Heaven, and Seraphim in particular. The will to move like a human was there, but they just couldn't get the details right.

Ash continued to ignore Raphael as he went inside the dilapidated warehouse for the second body. The Seraph sighed impatiently, letting Ash know he was waiting.

"If you want to speed this along, you could help," he couldn't resist pointing out as he dropped the second corpse over the pit's edge.

Raphael's horrified expression almost made Ash smile. The Seraph sniffed, averting his gaze from the body covered in grime and blood as he absently patted the fold of his robe. Ash knew that was where the angel kept his jar of oil, which he carried like a child did a security blanket—back when children could afford such luxuries.

"I suppose this sort of thing was easier when cars worked," Raphael observed, seemingly unaware of the wound he was inflicting.

Ash, known to history as the angel Azazel, had been a thorn in the side of the Heavenly Host long before Lucifer had rebelled. Azazel hadn't understood why humans were denied the fruits of knowledge like agriculture or weapons to defend themselves. As far as he was concerned, they had a right to it—else what had been the point of expelling them from Eden for eating from the forbidden tree? Why then was some information denied to them?

Humans were no longer the cosseted innocents living in the protected shelter of the garden. They had spread across the world, eking a living out of the land as best they could, burying their children along the way.

Azazel had taken to visiting the humans, masking his angelic identity to move among them freely. He had admired the fortitude of the nomadic tribes, and the people living in the small holdings at the edge of the steppes. But his heart had broken every time one was wiped out. Their rapacious enemies would leave their bodies to rot in the open air with no sacrament.

How many times had he buried children with his bare hands? It had been too much for him. After the last massacre, he had flown back to Heaven to argue on their behalf. Humans should be given the means to defend themselves. As one of Heaven's swordsmith's, he could easily show them how to fashion weapons. How else could they survive in the wildness of *terra firma*?

His arguments had fallen on deaf ears. No matter what he did, how many examples he cited, the Heavenly Host was unmoved.

Most of his brethren were indifferent to humans. Some outright hated them. The latter had secretly been pleased when Adam and Eve had been expelled from the garden.

As his favorites kept dying, Azazel grew more and more discontented. That was when he'd taken it upon himself to do something. When another favored village had fallen under threat, he went down and taught them metallurgy. Together, they'd fashioned knives, swords, and shields, enough to repel marauders from the east.

The village had prospered. He'd watched with pride as they adapted the techniques he'd taught them to make ornamentation for their homes and even their bodies. He even taught them to make symbols of their faith as a show of gratitude to God, the source of all knowledge.

Azazel had gone home, confident the Lord would be pleased with his act. He'd been wrong.

The devil is in the details. He'd learned that phrase in the last century, but it immediately resonated with him.

The people he'd sought to protect had changed, evolving so quickly even he'd been taken aback. They used the craft he'd taught them to make bigger and more effective weapons, and they began to war for the resources of others in times of need. The strong rose, oppressing the weak or duping those less savvy than themselves.

Human society stratified because of his sin, growing alternately tyrannical and decadent. In most cases, the lower castes were no more noble than the upper class. Avarice and greed led to theft, graft, and murder in all levels of society.

Needless to say, the Creator did not approve. As punishment, the archangel Raphael had bound him hand and foot. He'd hurled Azazel deep under the vast desert, where only the fiercest Berber tribes dared traverse.

It had taken him days to dig himself out. That was when he'd adopted his new name. All his effort, his good intentions, were like ash in his mouth.

Cast out from Heaven, Ash turned his back on everything. He hadn't joined Lucifer's band of rebels. Instead, he'd shunned both sides when they came around to win his allegiance or gloat. He wasn't about to change the habit of a millennium for the jerk in front of him now.

"Azazel, we need you," Raphael said soberly.

"That's not my name anymore."

The Seraph's lips pursed. "It's the name God gave you."

Ash snorted. Wiping his hands, he put one foot on the carcass. He gave it a hard kick, sending it rolling down the steep hillside. Raphael waited until the corpse landed near its mate before speaking.

"Executing minor demons and their murderous human acolytes is a waste of time as long as King Amducious' curse grips this land."

"The curse isn't my problem," Ash said, tossing the dead imp's hat after him.

"Then why bother with all this?" Raphael scowled, waving at the bodies in the pit.

Ash ignored him, pretending to look around for more body parts.

"They killed a human you were fond of, didn't they?"

He bit his tongue. The Seraph knew him well enough to guess the truth by now. Why confirm what he already knew?

"This will keep happening as long as the king rules from over there," Raphael said, gesturing to the dark tower in the distance.

Despite his intention not to look, Ash's eyes gravitated to the demon king's stronghold before he forced them away.

But Raphael's presence stirred too many emotions. Unbidden memories of the time before the Collision played in his mind.

Though it had been difficult at first, he'd eventually achieved a sense of peace—or at least resignation—with his fall sometime during the enlightenment. From there, things had steadily improved.

As humans colonized the globe, they faced unimaginable hardships and challenges. To his surprise, they had risen to the occasion, inventing and growing in unexpected and truly brilliant ways.

Ash had a front-row seat for the invention of the wheel. Soon after that, it had been the internal combustion engine. He'd stood in awe when they left the earth and took to the skies in hot-air balloons, and then airplanes. Ash hadn't thought it could get better than that... and then the computer age had arrived. Once the exclusive property of the rich, the technology grew inexpensive enough for the average individual to carry the knowledge of the world in their pocket.

Many other immortals didn't respond well to those innovations. He'd seen angels and demons alike hold smartphones in their hands, puzzled as to how such a thing could connect them to another being, let alone the world. He'd mocked more than one of the Heavenly Host for shouting orders at the little rectangular marvels. They didn't realize they needed to use the buttons or screens to make it function.

All of that had been wiped away in one fell swoop. The walls separating this world and the Hell dimensions had collapsed when a demon possessed a powerful witch. Under his control, she cast a spell to let the demons cross the barrier, to end this world. But not everything had gone according to plan. The violence of the spell had overrun the demon's intentions. Instead of having free reign over the earth, the dimensional collision had split it into thirteen parts, each continent separated from one another by an impenetrable layer of magic.

Impenetrable to the residents of earth at least.

"I really thought the end of the world meant I wouldn't have to see you again."

"No such luck." The Seraph picked up a stone and skimmed it across the air as if it were water. The flat round rock bounced at least half a dozen times before sinking, falling into the pit, and landing on top of the bodies.

Show-off.

"And the world hasn't ended, not really," Raphael nitpicked. "His children still walk the earth...and they're suffering."

Ash didn't answer.

"You don't really expect me to believe that you're happy like this?" the archangel asked, turning to inspect the pile of rubble that had once been the Sacre Coeur Basilica.

Once one of the highest points in the city, the hill neighborhood of Montmartre was dwarfed by the watchtower Amducious, the demon king, built.

You're the only one who still calls this area by that old name. Once the demon tower was built and its infamy grew, the name of this once-vibrant neighborhood was perverted and appropriated. Now it was forgotten to everyone but him.

Montmartre was dead. Long live Montmeurtre.

Did it matter? This blasted hill was no longer the bohemian and eclectic home of writers and artists that Ash remembered. Now it was a sparsely populated ghetto called Eighteen, the name taken from the ancient arrondissements that had divided and organized the city before the Collision.

Paris had been his home when the Collision spell was cast. By then, it was no longer the cosmopolitan center of the civilized world. Like other leading cities, its importance had waned. But it still had a certain flavor, a zest for life that was reflected in its love of food and culture. Paris had been a bit arrogant at times, like an aging grand dame, but it had the best style.

Now it was his own little corner of Hell on earth.

"They're painting the tower again—Montmeurtre."

"Don't call it that," Ash snapped, rising to the bait. It was bad enough that his neighborhood and adopted home had been wrecked, but the usurpation of its very name completely got under his skin—and Raphael knew it.

"Why not?" The Seraph widened his eyes in mock innocence before humming contemplatively. "What does the name mean anyway?"

Ash rolled his eyes. "You know what it means."

"Only literally." Raphael raised his hands and dropped his bell-like voice to a grating imitation of human fear. "The *Tower of Death*. It's effective, isn't it? A bit ham-fisted, of course, but Amducious has always opted for the atmospheric, hasn't he?"

Ash ignored the reference to the demon king. "It's not the Tower of Death. Montmeurtre means Murder Hill," he corrected, turning to face the fortress.

Built from the ruins of the famous Tour d'Eiffel, Montmeurtre started with a wide foundation of twisted steel and stone that narrowed progressively as it went up. The tower itself stretched over nine hundred meters in height, taller than any pre-Collision manmade structure.

But what would have been an engineering marvel was a perversion in every sense.

Every stone in the tower came from Parisian churches, all of which had been razed to the ground. The rubble had been ritually desecrated and twisted with the melted-down iron of the city's most famous landmark.

Raphael squinted at the demon stronghold, its red-black stones climbing the dirty brown sky. "That's splitting hairs a bit," he said after a pause.

"It's not when you consider *why* they call it that," Ash said, his jaw tight.

"And that is...?"

Ash sighed, conceding defeat in the face of Raphael's superior acting skills. "Because of the paint. It's a mix of mud and blood—human blood. Lots of it."

Raphael's beatific features screwed up in an almost-human expression of disgust and pain. "I'd hoped that was a rumor."

The last thread of Ash's patience snapped. "Stop pretending you didn't know! You can see everything from up there. He knows all," he yelled, slashing at the sky with an angry gesture.

The Seraph's lips firmed. "I *wasn't* certain. The Collision has affected us up there, too. Things that were clear are hazy now." His voice lowered to a whisper. "I shouldn't be admitting this... but I don't believe His sight is infallible anymore."

Ash's head jerked in the direction of the other angel. He took a shaky breath, a bit of his internal foundation breaking and rearranging.

If God was no longer omniscient, then was he God?

Raphael narrowed his eyes. "Bastille has been afflicted by Amducious' curse for nearly sixty years. His children have suffered enough. We need your help to set things right. Bring down the tower, kill the king. You need to end the curse and free the people."

This was almost amusing. "Is it not enough that you were the one to toss me out of Heaven? Do you still want to get rid of me that badly?"

"I was under orders."

"A familiar song," Ash sneered before going for his shovel. "So how many angels have you sent to their final reward trying to take down Amducious? Three, four?"

He began to scoop dirt over the edge of the pit. Visitors were rare in these parts, but he needed to make a cursory effort to cover the bodies lest he give himself away. Few humans could have killed those two. Without food and clean water, they were too weak. There was no need to tip the demon horde to his presence. That was the last thing he needed.

"You will succeed where the others have failed," Raphael proclaimed in his 'heed this prophecy, lowly underling' voice.

Ash smiled involuntarily. "Your faith in me is touching, all things considered. But I have no intention of dying on my sword. In case you've forgotten, I don't work for you—or Him —anymore."

He pried the shovel deeper into the dirt, intending to knock loose part of the ridge down onto the bodies. Unfortunately, he applied a little too much force, and the ground fell out from under Raphael's feet. *More like fortunately*, Ash thought with a smirk.

Raphael glared at him with his arms crossed. He was levitating above the pit.

The other angel flew toward Ash, sending a draft over his sweat-dampened skin. Raphael snatched the shovel away. "Enough," he snapped. "I've been sent by Him with an offer."

"Not interested."

"You want to hear this."

Raphael hadn't changed. He was like a dog with a bone. "You guys must be getting desperate if you're coming to me. I've been beyond His grace since...well, I lost count of the centuries." Ash frowned at his former commander. "I've been here on my own for a long time, watching. I'm skeptical. You lot haven't shown much interest in the fate of humans. And that was true long before the Collision."

"You always did know how to cut to the chase, Azazel," Raphael muttered. "Look, we don't have to cover old territory. You've always advocated for more direct intervention in human lives, and that's what I'm offering you now. If you end Bastille's curse, you rescue all the humans here. They can go back to inventing all the knickknacks and technological marvels your jaded heart could wish for. Plus...He will take you back."

Ash's head snapped up. "Not possible."

"Anything is possible for Him." Raphael leaned over and put his hands on Ash's shoulders. "Azazel, you *can* do this. You know humans as few of us do. Say the right words, and they will rally behind you. Together, you can bring down King Amducious and end his curse. And then you can come home."

Home.

Raphael tightened his grip. "Az, please think about this. This curse needs to end. Order needs to be restored. It's not just lives at stakes. *It is souls.* And there are many in Heaven who want you back among our ranks. You've been missed."

Ash pushed him away. After all these years... Hope burned in his chest like acid. Home. He could go home.

"I've brought your armor. It's on top of that warehouse," Raphael said, pointing.

My armor. Raphael had stripped it from his body before Ash had been cast out. For years, he'd believed it had been melted down.

"What happens if I fail?" he asked.

The Seraph flew up to the roof. He came down with Ash's old sword. Raphael thrust the gleaming weapon into his hand.

"Don't fail."

ASH ROARED his war cry as he drove his sword through Amducious' chest. The demon king snarled and screamed, thrashing violently as he tried to push Ash away. The demon's efforts only drove the sword farther until it was buried up to the hilt in his chest.

The blood burned like acid, but Ash kept up the pressure,

twisting the blade until he severed the aorta. Black ichor pumped onto Montmeurtre's rough stone floor in spurts.

The hellfire in the king's eyes faded. Bubbles formed at the corner of his jaws, and his death rattle filled the air.

Suspecting trickery, Ash put his foot down on Amducious' stomach. Demons were so hard to kill that he refused to believe the evidence of his own eyes. Whispering an incantation, he lit his sword with Holy Fire. It cut through the demon's bone and diaphragm like a knife through butter.

He stopped at the neck, then withdrew the blade before swinging it in a wide arc, severing the king's head.

It landed on the floor with a wet thump. Staggering slightly, he picked it up, limping to the window. Taking a shaky breath, he spread his wings, launching himself into the open air before dropping in a controlled fall.

His ragtag army cheered when they saw him.

Despite his exhaustion, Ash lifted the demon king's head, hoisting it as high as he could while his men hooted and shouted to celebrate their hard-fought victory.

Marcus, the young human he'd chosen as aide-de-camp and right hand, wept. "Is it really over?" he asked. "Are we free of the curse?"

"The demon king is dead," Ash replied, tilting his head to rub a spot of gore off his cheek with his bicep. "If God is just, then his curse will die with him."

A great cheer went up in response.

Ash put the head down next to a pile of fallen demons, folding his wings back. He'd bury the head later. Checking on his people was the priority.

He walked across the battlefield, congratulating the men and women who'd survived. He blessed the wounded and prayed for those who'd fallen under the shadow of the tower.

Montmeurtre needed to be razed to the ground, but that was not his job. He'd done what he had set out to do, but he had renewed confidence in the humans of Bastille. Under his guidance, they had come together, mustering the courage to beat back the demon horde. Without their help, he wouldn't have been able to scale the tower and overthrow the king.

With Amducious gone, they could begin anew. Ash had faith in their industry. Human society would recover and rebuild.

But this time, he wouldn't be here to see it. He'd be in Heaven. *I can still watch over them. I'll just be doing it from a distance.*

Eagerness welled in his heart. He turned his face to the sky, searching for the signal that the deed was done, that he could go home.

But the Heavens were silent.

There was no clarion call, no shaft of sunlight breaking through the clouds. Ash would have even welcomed Raphael's obnoxious presence. But the Seraph didn't come.

It's okay. These things take time. How often was an angel restored to Heaven? It had to be a complicated procedure.

So he waited...and waited...and waited some more.

1

TWENTY YEARS LATER

S weat poured down Ash's chest as he sat up and tried to clear his brain from the image in his mind.

Those eyes. Why did he never dream of anything else? Humans got to see bucolic settings or the face of loved ones when they slept. All he saw was a child's face, with eyes that burned him down to the very core.

Nightmares. This kind of dream was called a nightmare.

He needed to give up this idiotic habit. Technically, angels didn't require sleep. He'd taken up the practice to blend in during his long years of exile. Now sleeping was so engrained he didn't know how to stop—but it was long past time he made the effort.

Why the hell was he suddenly having *this* nightmare again? It was understandable years ago, right after he encountered the child, but it had thankfully stopped after a few months. Now it was starting again.

The meaning was obvious. Over the years, there had been hundreds of casualties of Amducious' curse—or tens of thousands if the collateral damage from a building collapse or explosion was counted. Because that was what the Firehorse curse did.

It was a spell of ruination and death, one manifested through a single person.

Named after an Asiatic legend by an unknown soldier, the Firehorse curse was pernicious and unpredictable. A man or woman would be perfectly ordinary one day, and then the next—boom! Out of nowhere, it would strike. Those afflicted instantly became walking, talking magnets for disaster. Everywhere they went, destruction followed...until they were killed. Then another Firehorse would rise, and the cycle would begin anew.

The curse blighted the land, touching every citizen in Bastille. But the child was the victim who haunted Ash.

The little girl had been the youngest Firehorse in history, no more than five years old. She was the youngest person he'd ever killed.

Despite the circumstances, Ash had never attempted to deny responsibility for her death. He might not have murdered her himself, but she was still dead because of what he'd done...

It would have been kinder to strangle the life from her little body.

He squeezed his eyes shut tight, and focused on his breathing. The twin weights of guilt and regret pinned him to the earth, the bonds invisible but no less effective than adamantine chains. But Ash didn't try to block out the child's face. There would be no point to such a futile effort.

Denial was a luxury only humans could afford. Instead, he went deeper, focusing his photographic memory on the lines of her face and the colors of her eyes. The hazy image from his dream sharpened in his mind until it was like she was standing in front of him. Then he began to pray for his soul and for hers.

He didn't know anything about her beyond her name, but Ash would never forget her. To even try was sacrilege.

When he was done, he rose and bathed, dressing in his armor by rote. He had to get moving. Marcus was expecting him. His wartime aide continued to serve as his right hand. Today, they were overseeing the final construction phased of the Eastern aqueduct, the largest engineering works attempted in Bastille since the erection of the demon tower.

Amducious had intended the tower to be the last new building in Bastille. He'd built it using human slaves, mixing their bones into the walls when they died from exhaustion, and, as he'd described to Raphael years ago, painting the exterior with their blood.

The king had cast the Firehorse curse from the turreted altar room at the very top of the structure. No doubt he'd looked down from that room's windows, gloating over his own magnificence. From that moment the Paris Ash had known was dead, never to return. The curse would ensure it would never rise again.

But now the demon was gone, and Ash had to carry on. He had no choice.

After he killed Amducious, Ash had waited for God's light to shine on him. He fully expected the gates of Heaven to open and welcome him home. That hadn't happened. The skies had remained silent.

At first, he was furious with Raphael. Ash had been convinced the Seraph had lied to him, making promises he couldn't keep without His knowledge.

Then there had been a flood, followed by an unlikely fire that had wiped out an entire neighborhood in District Six along the banks of the Seine. That was when Ash realized the curse had not been broken. Overthrowing Amducious hadn't ended it. In fact, with the demon king gone, his chances of breaking it had dwindled to almost nothing.

Ash was still searching for a way.

If only I hadn't been so stupid, he thought, second-guessing himself for the thousandth time. He should have taken Amducious prisoner instead of killing him—not that the king had given Ash a choice. In that final moment, there had only been one option.

The king was dead, but the curse lived on.

In the beginning, it hadn't seemed so bad. During the years of demon rule, it had been only natural that death and destruction be the order of the day. The famines, earthquakes, and building collapses had all seemed par for the course when a horde of demons was in charge.

But in today's Bastille, the demons were all but extinct. Ash and his band had wiped most of them out. And still, the havoc continued. The curse was too strong. Its malevolence was soaked into the soil and into the air they breathed. It undermined everything they did, knocking down whatever innovation or stride they made to improve their lives.

If they made one step forward, the Firehorse would rise to send them reeling back.

Enough feeling sorry for yourself. Focus on the rebuilding. The routine kept him going. As of today, the curse hadn't struck in seven months, almost eight. With luck, he could finish the canal and aqueduct project before it did.

The people whispered that Amducious' gift, as the curse was sometimes perversely called, was beginning to wane. That perhaps without the energy of the demon king to keep it going, it would wind down on its own.

Ash wanted to rail at these fools. Though he'd never found the details of how the curse had been cast, he knew enough about Amducious to guess the demon would never make things so easy.

ASH WAVED Marcus and his team over to him at the edge of the construction zone.

"Get those supports ready to brace the structure while we pour the concrete," he ordered the group. "We have everything we need to complete this in a few days. Only use the materials

I've marked as safe. Don't leave the curse a foothold to undermine our efforts here."

The four men Marcus had chosen as overseers for the aqueduct project agreed with deferential murmurs before scattering to carry out their orders. Ash's aide stayed behind.

"Do you think we have enough blessed sand?" Marcus asked, taking a pencil from behind his ear and jotting down a few notes on a clipboard he'd made from the hood of a rusted car.

"I believe so, but—"

"Bring more for you to bless just in case," his aide interrupted with a smile. "Consider it done, my lord."

"Redundancy—"

"Is next to godliness," Marcus finished for him.

It was Ash's favorite refrain on the job.

He snorted and waved the man on, deciding against yet another reminder not to call him a lord. It never made a difference anyway. His human couldn't seem to break the habit.

He watched Marcus wander down the hill to tell the wagon drivers to bring more sand to the site, and sighed. Was that a bit of grey in his aide's hair? Humans aged so quickly...

Trying not to be downcast, Ash took a position at the top of the hill to survey the work.

Be satisfied the aqueduct will stand. It was the best he could do.

Water had been a scarcity in the days of demon rule. Most of the waterworks and purification plants had been destroyed years ago, first by the horde and later by the Firehorse curse.

When Ash overthrew the demon king, he was left in charge of a starving city with few resources. The little infrastructure that remained the pre-Collision era couldn't sustain the population.

He'd done the only thing he could. With Marcus' help, Ash organized a system to divide resources as fairly as possible. However, emergency rationing would only get them so far.

Rebuilding the city's infrastructure became his priority. The humans of Bastille needed food and clean water. Even the sewage systems of old Paris, once a model for the modern metropolis, needed to be rebuilt and reinforced.

To that end, he left governance to the council elders of the city. Each represented one of the old Parisian arrondissements, although only thirteen were populated enough to warrant a representative. The councilmen were mostly volunteers. A few had served in the ranks of his army as youths, but most were local leaders who'd managed to survive Amducious' rule with some influence intact.

The system worked as well as it could given the circumstances. Day to day governance in the arrondissements was handled by the council, whereas Ash oversaw the city as a whole.

After the horde was gone, he'd cleaned out the city center, making it habitable again. Reclamation of pre-Collision technology had also helped improve their circumstances. Though anything high-tech had been intentionally destroyed by the horde, a few engines and power generators had survived. Exhaustive tinkering had been necessary to make them run on steam power now that gasoline and oil were no longer plentiful.

One of the happiest days of Ash's post-Collision life had been the day he set up a small generator at the old Radio Notre Dame office. The station wasn't broadcasting yet, but with luck it would soon.

By focusing on reclaiming those hallmarks of modern civilization, Ash was able to glean a little satisfaction from his life. He was still barred from Heaven, but maybe his cell phone would work again someday.

The aqueduct he was overseeing was the third of four planned. This one lay on the east side of Bastille. The source was the springs of Marne-Chalons, the same waterway that had supplied old Paris with water. It had been believed the springs had been obliterated by the Great Collision. There was no trace of them aboveground anymore, nothing beyond a few trickles of tainted liquid that flowed in from the wasteland.

Hydrological inspection had saved them. The curse could ravage civilization, but nature was resilient. The springs hadn't been destroyed—they'd been driven underground. Wells had been dug to tap them again, but with the effort required to transport the water to the city, they were insufficient to serve the city's population.

After much debate with Marcus and consultation with the city's few engineers, Ash had implemented a rebuilding program based on a fluidity and reproducibility. To survive Amducious' gift, construction had to be modular and easily duplicated.

The aqueduct was an example of this. A lightweight mesh frame was encased in concrete to shape a hollow rectangular block. These connected to form a channel that ran along the hills leading into the city. They were easily patched and too heavy for floods to displace. If an earthquake destroyed a section, it was simply replaced with another standard-sized unit, one usually made on the spot.

Though the design was rudimentary by his standards, its very impermanence was its cloak of protection. And hopefully, with four geographically distinct channels, Bastille would still have water if the curse took one or more out.

Though there wasn't much of it yet, all new housing in Bastille was built along this same principle. Ash and his team drew inspiration from nature. All new homes and work spaces were built from hexagonal metal or wood frames shaped like the individual cell of a bee's honeycomb. If one or more cells was damaged or burned down, it could be replaced with another one. Ash also took the extra step of blessing every load of timber that was cut down and steel that was smelted before construction began. He did the same for all building materials reclaimed from pre-Collision structures.

One notable exception was Montmeurtre.

The watchtower was a ruin now. The much-despised monument of demon rule had been shunned for months after their victory, up until the point reconstruction began.

The tower had seemed like an obvious resource. But the cursed stone was uncooperative. Anything that used material from the ruin—whether it had been blessed by him or not—did not make it out of the first stages of construction. He stopped using reclaimed stones, leaving them in piles around the tower until the day came when he could have them carted to the wasteland or destroyed.

Ash also distributed knowledge equilaterally among the humans whenever he could. When one person could be placed in charge of a certain project or trained in a specific technique, he and Marcus chose four instead. It was Ash's way of ensuring expertise was not lost should the worst happen and one of the men or women fell ill or died.

Deaths by disease were thankfully less frequent. Urban farming and proper sanitation had cut down on the baseline death toll. A consistent supply of clean water would help reduce it further.

Ash continued to give out orders, pitching in and helping his team get a section of the aqueduct in place. When a few ropes snapped, the disruption was minor and quickly resolved.

Once that was done, he flew up high, checking their progress from a distance. He traced the line of the aqueduct taking shape as it snaked over the last ridge between the grassy fields east and the city's populated neighborhoods.

As if sensing his satisfaction, the mocking clang of the emergency klaxon sounded. Shouting to Marcus to stay and keep the workers going, Ash pumped his wings, following the sound. It led him to the center of the city where another disaster awaited.

A Firehorse had risen.

2

Place Vendôme was burning.

Ash's eyes swept the square, triaging from the sky. The earthquake had been small, but critically damaging. The steam-powered mill and a few of the apartments that survived demon rule were piles of rubble.

The twelve-story bronze-plated column that used to dominate the open space of Vendôme was long gone. It had been one of the first monuments razed by the demons.

At least I don't have to worry about the column landing on anyone. The massive structure would have killed many. The open space of the square was teeming with humans shouting and shoving each other.

He'd arrived too late. Hysteria had already set in.

A few people scattered and gave way when he flew down and landed among them, but the mob was mindless. Most didn't even notice his arrival.

"What happened? Where is the fire service?" he demanded, pulling on the arm of the man nearest him.

"They aren't here!" The belligerence in the human's face faded as he recognized Ash's armored form.

The weak sunlight bounced off his helmet and visor directly into the man's eyes. Blinking and squinting, the citizen pointed at the smoking pile that had been the Hôtel d'Orsigny.

"They say the old man who managed the building is the Fire-horse. He was cleaning the upper story when the ground began to shake. The place blew up, but he survived!"

Ash's jaw clenched. It was always this way now. Those fortunate enough to survive these disasters were cast under a cloud of suspicion—one that rapidly escalated into violence unless he intervened.

"You assign blame too quickly," he bit out. "Now go help the wounded or take yourself off. If the building exploded, it might have been a gas pocket igniting underneath it. There is still danger here."

He shoved the man away, herding him in the direction of safety. Beating his wings until he was hovering above the crowd, he felt their eyes on him.

"I know why you're here," he called out, muting the resonance in his voice to avoid driving the weak-minded mad. "You think the curse has struck again. It may have, but I shouldn't have to remind you that finding the Firehorse and passing judgment is my job—not yours. Vigilante justice cannot stand. If you kill, you endanger your immortal soul."

That speech, coming from an angel in full armor, should have been enough to cow the crowd. But the people of Bastille had seen too much.

"What immortal soul?" someone shouted as the mob shifted and the volume jumped up several notches. "Look around. God has forsaken us!"

"Yeah! What do we have to lose?" a woman cried.

"We need to stop the Firehorse before we end up dead, too!"

A man and woman with soot-streaked faces pushed a huddled form toward him. "We have him! We have the Firehorse. You need to kill him now."

The little man collapsed on his hands and knees in front of Ash. He took one look at the human and knew he wasn't the one.

All the Firehorses Ash had met had been younger than this. All had been strong and productive people. This small shell of a man was nothing like them. His best years were behind him.

Ash wanted to throw up his hands in frustration. Years of demon rule had warped the human moral compass and blunted their fear of judgment day.

This time, he let the unnatural resonance of his voice reverberate in his words. *"This man is untainted. Release him."*

He paused, studying the crowd, letting them feel the menace of his authority before continuing in a normal tone. "God has not forsaken you. If He had, I wouldn't be before you—and yet, here I am. Now, if you're not going to help the injured among you, please disperse! I will find the real Firehorse. Go back to your homes."

The people who had dragged the old man forward quailed and retreated. Relieved, the hapless human began to cry in earnest. A young girl ran out from the crowd, and helped him move away. Ash watched them go, making sure no others approached the vulnerable duo.

"Go," he growled at the stragglers, irritated they hadn't immediately obeyed.

His normally patient nature continued to fray as the last remnants of the crowd scattered.

At least they didn't throw anything at me. So far, no one had dared, but Ash knew that day was coming. He could feel it.

Landing, he adjusted the visor of his helmet as he moved toward the edges of the crowd to count the dead. How many had he lost this time?

A better question might be how many had been worthy?

A tipping point had been passed. If he hadn't appeared, the mob would have killed that man. The threat of the curse hanging over their heads was too much for the average human. If he couldn't find a way to break it soon, he was going to lose the entire populace. Shoring up walls here and there wasn't enough. People needed hope. Just a kernel would do—enough to ensure eternal salvation.

Unlike other angels, Ash didn't believe suffering magically transformed man's nature. Bury a human under a shit ton of strife... and the reality was that most of them broke. They lost their faith. It was hard to blame them. Not everyone could be Job.

Ash had finished blessing the injured when he felt a presence. Pivoting on his heel, he scanned, half-expecting to come face to face with a demon or one of the Host. Instead, he locked eyes with a young woman.

Her brown and gold eyes bored into his for a moment before he broke contact. Something about them seemed familiar...

It's a common eye color in these parts, he reminded himself. The girl was a stranger.

He shifted his gaze over the rest of the crowd in search of the source of his disquiet. No tentacled monster preyed at the edge of the square, no smirking Raphael mocked him from the corner of his eye.

Relaxing his subtle battle stance, Ash decided he had imagined the strange feeling. Even his kind could get stressed. A millennium or two of being barred from Heaven was enough to make even an angel daft.

A shout went up. Ash turned to see the fire service make their way down Rue de la Paix. They dragged their steam-powered fire engine through the thinning crowd at the edge of the square.

Ash flew to meet them. "Start here," he said, pointing at the modest two-story buildings on the opposite side of the square.

They were recent additions. The buildings stood in place of the Ritz Hotel, a favored haunt of demons when they'd been in power. So many unspeakable things had happened under that roof that the citizens of Bastille had demolished the Ritz themselves right after the overthrow of the king.

After the fire brigade began their work, Ash herded the few remaining humans away from the ruins of the Hôtel d'Orsigny. He still needed to check the foundations for cracks and toxic fumes.

It was one of the many topographical changes caused by the Collision. Once a safe and reliable source of energy, natural gas was now a threat—one that could ignite at any moment. Pockets of it were trapped under the streets, waiting to escape into homes and businesses to smother entire families or explode with a random spark.

Putting his back into it, Ash removed the debris from the explosion site, going over the foundation carefully for signs of another pocket. He'd just cleared the basements when he heard the second blast in the distance.

3

S moke and dust obscured Ash's vision as he dug through the debris of the St. Louis Hospital's collapsed second story. If he didn't miss his guess, this was where one of the old surgical suites had just been reopened.

So much knowledge had been wiped out with the Collision. All digital information had been destroyed. Electromagnetic pulses rendered computers inoperable, their data unrecoverable. Books were used as kindling by human survivors or burned in bonfires under the demon king's reign. Most of the population was now illiterate.

Getting back the medicine they lost seemed an impossible task. Antibiotics, painkillers, and surgery more complicated than stitching a wound were pipe dreams after the liberation. With basics like sanitation and food supplies scarce or nonexistent, trying to preserve anything more than rudimentary medical care was a low priority.

Only the most basic and brutal techniques of emergency medicine remained. Jagged stitch scars were commonplace among humans. Amputation had returned in force as a standard treatment. Many who would have lived died from infections that could have been cured with a few shots of penicillin.

But in the last couple of months, there had been signs, tiny seeds of hope. Scavengers had found an old repository of medical texts cached in a sparsely occupied tenement. His guess was that the building had once been overflow storage for a defunct medical school.

Marcus had the books copied and disseminated to the few field medics who'd survived the uprising. One—a woman named Madeleine Brès—had fallen on them with greater enthusiasm than any of the others. She'd made real strides since, using what she'd learned to remove an infected gallbladder. More recently, she treated a burst appendix successfully.

It was Madeleine who'd organized the reopening of the surgical suite, Ash remembered, a sinking feeling in his stomach.

There was something he was missing.

It was just a room. Ash hadn't thought it would make much of a difference. But he'd been wrong. *Too much progress and we're sent reeling back.* He cursed, picking his way through the rubble.

A foot wearing a rough leather shoe was sticking out from beneath the remains of a wall. Ash threw a metal beam to the side. He was relieved to discover there was still a leg attached to the foot of an intact male body. The victim was wearing makeshift surgical scrubs.

Ash pulled the man out, taking care to avoid further damaging the fragile human. The man groaned as Ash set him on the floor.

The nurse coughed, his lips parting. "She touched it, and it exploded."

Ash frowned, adjusting his helmet to better see the man's eyes. "Who?"

"Dr. Brès. She touched the oxygen tanks, and all hell broke loose. It has to be her."

The Firehorse. Unlike the old man at Place Vendome, this

made sense. Like the others before her, Madeleine was relatively young, strong, and capable.

Ash swore under his breath, picking up the man and cradling him in his arms. "Is she still here?"

"I don't know. The blast shook the room, but I was just past the doorway in the hall. I fell, and heard screaming inside. But when I tried to move the wall, it collapsed on me." The man grimaced, and his eyes rolled back into his head. He was unconscious again.

Someone had survived this blast as well—long enough to scream at least. Ash would lay odds on that person being Dr. Brès.

The mob wasn't technically wrong to look at the survivors of the disasters they were plagued with. It was the insidious nature of their burden. How else could the Firehorse continue to wreak havoc if they died in the first few instances of manifesting the curse? He'd probably find Dr. Brès had been at Place Vendome earlier that morning.

But Dr. Brès wasn't here now. The only body inside the room was crumpled next to the surgical bed. Judging from the hospital gown, it was the intended patient. There was no sign of anyone else.

I have to find the doctor.

Ash tightened his grip on the nurse and took to the air, flying them outside through a gaping hole in the wall. There he found Clement, the hospital administrator. A temporary triage center was in the process of being set up in the dirt courtyard in front of the building.

"How many are unaccounted for?" Ash asked.

Clement started and stuttered. He was an able man, dedicated to healing, but like many others, he was intimidated by Ash.

He waited quietly as the doctor stumbled over his words, missing the days when he could interact in anonymity. Now that humans knew what he was, he had to make allowances for their fear and awe. Being addressed by an angel—even one of the fallen—was enough to make anybody founder.

"We found all b-b-but the patient and the doctor," Clement finally said.

"N-nurse Addy was assigned to that floor, along with Julien, who was assisting Dr. Brès with the surgery," he added more clearly, gesturing at the injured man in Ash's arms. "Addy is dead. The blast crushed her when the ceiling gave way. Some piping knocked a hole through her head."

It spoke to the level of carnage they'd all grown accustomed to that Clement didn't even blink as he related that last bit of information.

"I found the patient," Ash replied. "He is also dead. But I can't find Dr. Brès."

Clement moaned, his hands flying up to rub against his receding hairline. "This is a disaster. The council will be furious. The patient was one of theirs—the overseer of District Four, Tulloch. He'd had a heart attack last year. He wanted Dr. Brès to operate. She was going to put in a stent."

That was news. Madeleine had made a lot of progress if she was conducting cardiac surgery.

The final piece of the puzzle fell into place, something Ash should have seen long ago. Madeleine Brès wasn't just important to him and her patients, but to progress as a whole.

That's why they were struck down. A Firehorse wasn't just a productive citizen who happened to be cursed. It had never been random.

Putain. He needed to deal with this revelation later. The council would have to wait as well. He had a Firehorse to find.

"They'll be here soon, Klein and the others," Clement said, looking at him hopefully. "They will want to speak to you."

"I have other matters to attend to," Ash said repressively, aware the director wanted him to break the news about Tulloch. "I will leave you to relay my message. Make sure they don't leave without offering aid. You're going to need to shift your operation. Tell them to allocate one of the new hive buildings for you."

Unless they were pushed, it could be days, perhaps weeks, before the council acted. The city needed this hospital too much for them to dally.

He scanned the rapidly filling lawn. Men and women were laid out by the able-bodied among them. Children, too, were part of the group. His eye fixed on a dark-haired little girl being helped into a bed and covered with blankets. His Firehorse—the one he thought of as his—she had been close to that age.

"The patients will need immediate assistance," he said flatly. "Tell the council I ordered it. I will find them later. And don't mention Dr. Brès is missing."

"Why?" Clement was genuinely puzzled. Then his eyes widened. "Oh no! Is she the one?"

"Unless you want a mob on your hands, I suggest you keep your voice down," Ash hissed, leaning over Clement menacingly.

Ash checked to make sure no others were in earshot. Fortunately for him, the other humans were giving them a wide berth.

"Help the survivors. Do your job," he continued. "And when the other council members come, tell them what I said about helping—and nothing more. Keep your nurse Julien quiet when he wakes up. No volunteering any details and no conjecture about the Firehorse from either of you. Even if the council members ask you directly."

The quailing man nodded, stuttering his agreement as he scrambled away. Ash watched him retreat, already regretting the act of intimidation.

Stop it. All his years alone on earth had made him soft. His place was above, not among humans. Getting too close to them, being friendly, undermined his authority. To maintain his distance, he used go-betweens like Marcus to pass on his orders, speaking directly to men like Clement only when he had to. And on occasions like this, threatening them.

It was a necessary and temporary stopgap. Even if Clement and Julien kept their mouths shut, the speculation about the Firehorse would continue. But hopefully, Ash had bought himself time. He had to find Dr. Brès before a mob rose and came for her.

It was better to die by his hand than theirs—much better.

The truth rent his soul to pieces, but death was inescapable for the doctor now. She was the Firehorse, the focus of the curse. Like the ancient Asian legend from which this curse took its name, the bad luck would be centered around her for as long as she lived. The chain reaction of death and destruction wouldn't stop until Madeleine Brès was dead.

The blasts at Vendome and the hospital were just the beginning. It could take hours or days, but more disasters would follow. It could be another explosion, a fire, or a flood. Regardless of the form the curse took, there would be no hiding that fact it had struck again.

Somewhere on the second floor of the hospital, the fire burned through a support, sending another section crashing down. Ash flexed his wings, spreading them with a snap. He shot into the air, scanning the ruins of the hospital with angelic focus.

Time stretched. The seconds between the beat of his wings lengthened as the figures below slowed to a crawl. Ignoring those on the lawn, he trained his ears on the building, listening for the telltale pumping of the human heart.

Nothing. Just the stain of freshly departed souls. If Dr. Brès was still alive, then she wasn't here.

She'll have gone home.

He didn't know why, but humans always went home when they were struck down. In denial about their state, they bolted straight for familiar surroundings, bringing misery and misfortune with them.

Ash sighed. He felt the greatest pity for the families. They were almost always the first to die when the Firehorse curse spread.

4

L ater that night, Ash watched over the city from the
balcony of his Belleville apartments, twirling his short
knife behind his back pensively.

Something was going on. He could feel it—a change in the
air. He wanted to believe it would be a change for the good, but so
far, the signs were not auspicious.

Dr. Brès was most likely dead, but he hadn't found her body.
The Firehorse's chain reaction abruptly ceased with the destruction of the hospital, leaving him little choice but to conclude
someone had gotten to the doctor before he could.

Ash tried not to think about the way Madeleine must have
suffered—or how her family had been murdered with her.

The entire Brès family, four in all, were missing, too. When
he'd gone to their home, the whole lot was gone. They were probably rotting in an unmarked grave somewhere.

In unsanctified ground. Ash buried his knife into the concrete
wall up to the hilt. He wanted to beat his fists on it, but the satisfaction that came with wanton destruction was fleeting. He knew
that from experience.

The demon king was gone, but the evil in man was just as

pernicious an enemy. His city harbored a band of murderers. But without the omniscience of God, he didn't know how to find those responsible. Blasted Raphael still refused to show his face, so Ash couldn't ask him who he had to punish.

He ground his teeth. *It's not like I can fly up there and ask.*

Didn't the Host know how tightly his hands were bound without their guidance?

How was he supposed to stop the humans from killing each other? As the resident angel, Ash was their moral guardian, the being responsible for their immortal souls. But he was flying blind.

Ash did know one thing he hadn't before. The cursed were important, necessary people. They were the movers and makers, the ones blessed with creativity and invention. Society was measured by its progress in the arts and technology. At least those had always been his benchmarks.

He didn't know what had marked each Firehorse as special, but he knew enough about some of them to know he was right. The designer of the hive house had been a Firehorse. Gaetan been studying how to earthquake-proof existing buildings when he'd been struck down. That had been a few years ago. Then there had been that woman, Livia, the one who'd found and repaired a guitar. She'd taught herself to play. Her music had been special, the sort that could influence people's moods—calming or alternately energizing them.

Every Firehorse had been significant in some way. Ash didn't always know how, but it made too much sense now that he'd seen the pattern.

He rubbed his head with rough hands. How could he have been so blind? Only an idiot would have missed something like this. *And I'm still being a fool,* he thought, doing some rapid math.

What if the curse struck people in inverse importance to their age? That way, they could never live up to their potential.

Which means...

Ash leaned on the wall for support. The child—the one he'd abandoned. What had been her destiny?

It was too late. She was long dead. Her bones were bleaching under the relentless sun in the wasteland.

"Katarina." It was the first time he'd said her name in fifteen years. He needed to know more about her. There was a reason she'd never left his thoughts. She lived in his dreams as a reminder—a missed opportunity that might have helped them all.

I should have protected her. Instead, he'd been the instrument of her death.

Don't think about. Don't. He couldn't allow himself to dwell on past mistakes. No, his path was clear—secure the future.

Maybe it wasn't too late to find out what Kara had represented. If he could glean some information about her, he might figure out more about how the curse worked. He knew where her family had lived. Most had been wiped out when the demon king reigned, but not all. Kara and her grandmother had survived. What if the old woman was still alive? In their society, that was almost an impossibility, but he'd learn nothing standing here, pondering what might have been.

Ash took to the air, heading in the direction of Le Marais.

HIS WINGS BRUSHED the dirt track that used to be the Rue Vieille du Temple. Ash turned and bit back a sigh. Years ago, he'd stood in this very spot. He could still see the crowd at the Carreau du Temple as he sat sipping espresso after a long day pretending to be human.

This part of the right bank had suffered more than most. Everything between the Republique metro and the Picasso museum had been laid to waste. His rebuilding efforts hadn't touched the area yet. All that survived were a few derelict apartment buildings interspersed between a ramshackle assembly of worn-out huts and shacks.

The street where Katarina had lived with her family was still there, but no one seemed to remember her. He was about to give up and head back to Belleville when a man in the crowd pushed a woman toward him.

The matron was little more than forty at best, but she could have passed for twice that. Bent, with cracked hands and deeply etched lines on her face, she held a suckling, near-skeletal babe at her breast.

"Do you remember the Firehorse who used to live on this street?" Ash asked in his softest tone.

The woman's eyes were unfocused. She probably needed glasses to see but her gaze sharpened nonetheless at the mention of their blight. "The cursed child?"

"Yes, her family name is Delavordo. She used to live here with her grandmother."

"Simone is in Hell."

Ash blinked. So the grandmother was dead.

The old woman didn't mean Simone had been a bad person in life. People no longer said someone had gone to their reward or were with their maker. No, since the Collision, the dead were all said to be in Hell. Heaven seemed too far a stretch for them to wrap their minds around now, no matter how often he described its perfection.

He eyed the hungry child, observing the way its sunken cheeks fluttered, working too hard for what little milk there was. *Maybe this is Hell.*

"Do you remember the family? They were here through the Collision, weren't they?"

The woman nodded, her rheumy eyes shifting to the apartments where Katarina had lived.

"I knew Simone well. Before the demons came, the Delavordos used to have money. The whole ground floor of this building was theirs."

She shivered, wrapping a torn threadbare wrap closer around herself and the child. "They even had fancy heaters in all the rooms, but they broke and poisoned half the family. At least four little ones died to hear tell of it, so they ripped the rest out. But you can still see the fittings."

Once upon a time, four deaths by carbon-monoxide poisoning would have been a tragedy, but he was too used to such tales.

"Is there anything else you can tell me about them? Did they have any other relations in the city?"

The woman shrugged. "No more people who I know of. Toward the end, they just had books. *Lots* of books. The demon king sent his servants for them." A shudder racked her skinny frame.

Really? Amducious had pilfered many family coffers for art and jewels during his reign, but as far as Ash knew, the demon never bothered to confiscate books. He'd just ordered them burned.

"When was this?"

"Before I was born. My mother told me. You hadn't come to us yet."

Ash nodded, wondering if anyone else might know more, but now he needed to get into that apartment. "If you remember anything else, or come across more information from your neighbors, send for me. It's important."

Nonplussed at the idea of being able to summon an angel, the crone stuttered her agreement.

"Who is your councilman?" he asked, scanning the near-empty streets for a well-fed face.

"Titouan, but he never comes here anymore. Spends all his time up at the Petit Palais with all the other nobs."

Ash hid his scowl, and dismissed the woman with a respectful bow.

That baby should not be starving. He'd made it very clear.

He waited until she was gone and stalked to the ground floor of the Delavordo family home. Ash went through the empty rooms, too angry to focus on his surroundings.

Innocent babes were a priority under his distribution plan. Yes, each arrondissement grew their own food, but the council re-allocated resources according to need. When a community was hit by a disaster, the others pitched in to help shoulder the burden. As far as he knew, Le Marais hadn't been struck in over a year.

The people here were no less able-bodied or aged than any other arrondissement. They should have bounced back by now, but the reason why they hadn't was obvious. This neighborhood wasn't getting its share.

Ash would have to a word with Titouan. He would have Marcus look into it to be sure, but his hunch was the meals these people were missing were being served at the Petit Palais...

First things first. Ash turned his attention to the abandoned apartment.

A few impressionist paintings were still intact on the walls, although most of the furniture had been broken up for kindling. The leg of a Louis XIV lay next to a fragment of a pink porcelain vase, a Ming if his guess was right. Across the room, the face of a shattered Empire mantle clock stared at the ceiling.

He found the library shelves bare and broken. Every trace of the collection was gone. There were no bits of torn paper or convenient catalogs listing the contents of the library in sight.

The old woman must have been right about the demon horde coming for them. But why take the books and leave the art? Demons loved defacing the old masters.

In the drawer of the remains of a delicate mahogany writing desk, he found a few abandoned miniatures. Most were tiny landscapes, but two were portraits, a matching set of a man and woman in wedding finery. The tiny face of the bewigged woman caught his attention. For a moment, the resemblance to the topaz-eyed girl in Place Vendôme surprised him.

What if...

Ash shook his head. He was imagining things again. Despite the deprivation, beautiful faces were still common in this land. Parisian women had been renowned for their grace and elegance before the Collision. It was still true, more so now that the demon horde wasn't going around disfiguring them for their own amusement.

That's it. She was just another pretty face. On impulse, he pocketed the miniature portraits in his robe before departing.

5

Ash flexed his wings, his brooding gaze sweeping over the city as he stood on his balcony. Marcus had arrived to give his report, but Ash knew what he was going to say.

"You were right, my lord. Le Marais has been getting supplemental aid from the council these last eight months, but it's not making its way to the people."

Ash's jaw stiffened, and he nodded curtly at his aide.

"What would you like me to do?" Marcus asked.

Ash stood and fixed his wings before reaching for his helmet. "Nothing. I will take care of this myself."

His aide blew out a long breath, his relief palpable. "I think that's wise. The last warning I issued about graft in our system was disregarded. The councilmen have always dismissed me." He leaned in and lowered his voice. "Between the two of us, I think certain members of the council need a reminder that they are serving at your discretion. Perhaps even a hint that we can start opening council seats for election. That always gets them back on track."

"Yes, but for how long?" Ash muttered, putting on his helmet with a scowl. There was no point in delaying the inevitable.

Marcus didn't answer. He didn't need to.

God save me from politicians. Ash paused, half-hoping a sudden break in the clouds would illuminate him in His radiance, but no divine providence was going to get him out of this meeting.

He headed for the balcony, but Marcus chased after him. "Don't forget this," he called, thrusting a slate with a series of numbers at him.

"What's this?"

"A summary of the accounting for Le Marais."

With effort, Ash summoned a grateful smile and nodded, taking the slate before flying over his beleaguered city, his destination the Petit Palais.

THE SLATE ENDED up making quite an impression. All the council members had their eyes fixed on it when he cracked it over Titouan's head.

Ash lifted the hapless councilman with one hand. The pudgy balding man coughed and kicked his feet.

"I think some of you have forgotten your purpose here," Ash said, letting a little angelic resonance infuse his words. "You oversee your arrondissement because *I* appointed you. Your sole purpose is to ensure the well-being of the people in your community. If you are not doing that, you can be replaced."

"But, Your Highness, all we have ever done is serve the people's interest," Klein protested with genuine affront.

Ash dropped Titouan in a pile next to the heavily laden table. "I am an agent of *God*, not a king," he said, his diction precise and clipped. He picked up a leg of pigeon. *Pigeon.* Even he didn't get to eat fowl anymore. "And pray tell, just how does a feast for you lot help the starving people of Le Marais?"

Titouan held up his hands. "But those people were given everything they needed after the last fire. It's not my fault if the seeds rotted and the grain molded."

Mazarin, the councilman for the first arrondissement, hastily waved Titouan into silence with a tinkle of his gold bracelets. Cowed, the sweaty little bald man scrambled up and sat down as far from Ash as he could.

"Surely you don't begrudge us a simple meal while we discuss our mutual business?" Mazarin asked in his most reasonable tone. "We work long hours on behalf of our people, discussing their needs and seeing what can be done to help as many as we can."

He broke off with a hapless little gesture. "Surely a light repast is not too much to ask?" His unctuous tone slid over Ash like a spray of noxious water from the Seine.

Ash eyed the man, weighing the sin of snapping his neck. Politicians did this to him every time. Even an angel had his limits...but as far as he knew, Mazarin's sins didn't warrant execution.

"I think it's time we opened council seats to a little democracy," Ash replied slowly, enunciating each word. "Next month, I'm calling for elections. Every man, woman, and child over the age of ten gets a vote."

Mazarin paled. "But what about us? No one understands the needs of our communities like us, its natural leaders."

Ash's jaw stiffened at the phrase *natural leaders*. Even after an apocalypse, the old order held on with a death grip.

"Some of you, the most junior, are welcome to run for your seats again. As for the rest of you—it's time to resurrect a lovely little rule tailor-made for situations like these. I believe they call it *term limits*."

Ash tossed the pigeon leg back on the table and crossed his arms, waiting for the inevitable argument. He didn't have to wait long for the explosion.

Everyone began talking at once. Klein was babbling, and Tucker was red and shouting.

Ash let their petty little arguments wash over him. Mazarin was the one he needed to watch.

This is my fault. He was about to call for silence when the klaxon began to sound.

Saved by the bell, he thought, wondering if he meant him or them.

He turned to Titouan. "You've been left to your own devices for far too long. See that your people are fed. Do it now." He lifted his gaze to encompass the rest of the council. "You *all* need to do it now. Local inspections will begin in every district without further notice. It will be an assessment of all of you. Consider the coming elections judgement."

Ignoring their responses and protests, he turned on his heel and left. Disaster was waiting, like always.

Morblue.

Ash had never used that particular swear in his long life, but it seemed appropriate now.

The sinkhole was massive, spanning the entire length of the Quai de Bercy. Worse yet, it had taken out the right-hand span of the bridge. The pre-Collision structure had risen in importance since Ash had decided to try and rebuild the tracks at the Gare de Lyon. He wanted to connect the city center to their fertile fields down south near the old Porte de Gentilly. Marcus was supposed to be at the station now with the survey team.

Merde. How many building supplies had they lost into that pit?

Ash flew down, circling over the gaping wound in the earth. It was like the entrance to Hell itself, only it was filling with the polluted sludge from the Seine. Derelict vehicles were bobbing on the greasy surface, along with one or two people. He plucked the survivors from the pit, flying them to the safety of the bank.

Marcus was heading toward him through the fleeing crowd, pushing upstream like a salmon.

"Did you see him?"

"See who?"

"Didier, from the engineering team. We were taking a break for a meal when word came that the axel of a lorry had broken. It was carrying a load of steel track for the railway."

Ash frowned under his helmet. "I think I just pulled him from the pit." That second survivor had looked a bit familiar.

"Thank the Lord," Marcus breathed, putting a hand on his chest. "Didier and the others have been getting the sewage system back in order. I'd hate to think we have to start over again."

Ash was getting a sinking feeling in his stomach. *It's always the ones we need.*

He didn't need divine guidance to know who the new Fire-horse was.

Didier and Marcus were friends. It wasn't much, but Ash could at least spare his aide some pain by not telling him until the deed was done.

"Go back to the train station. I'll fish what I can out of the sinkhole, but order more supplies to replace that shipment of track."

Marcus scribbled on his clipboard. "Yes, my lord, but I will have to check that we have enough ore to replace that steel."

"If we don't, then leave it be for the moment. We need to prioritize the canal and the sewage system."

"But what about this?" Marcus asked, waving at the pit.

The perfect roundness of the hole mocked Ash. Even in a disaster, he could see the stamp of the Creator.

Pi. Pi is perfect. I am not, he thought, hoping Marcus would understand why he didn't tell him about his friend.

"As long that foul water is pouring into the hole and not the city, we leave it be. At least until we can bring in enough filler material—things we can spare like the bad concrete batch."

"The one made using the sand from the wasteland?"

Ash nodded. "I'll find Didier. Go now."

Like the trusting fool that he was, Marcus saluted and waved goodbye as he headed back to the station.

Ash relaxed the fist he'd been hiding behind his back. His own nails had scored his palm, but the small cut sealed before his eyes.

Across the river, he could see the humans gathering on the left bank. *Speculating about which one of them is the Firehorse no doubt.* They were always so quick to turn on one another. In his mind's eye, they became a pack of wolves baying to the sky, hungry for blood.

He flew toward them. "This area is unsafe. Go home!"

"Shouldn't we find the Firehorse?" one of them shouted.

"It's taken care of," he promised with a heavy sigh. "They've been identified."

Didier would get the choice Ash had given all the others—all but the child. A quick death at Ash's hands or the man could take his chances in the wasteland.

Most of the crowd dispersed, though as always, a small handful stayed to gape at the new landmark in their city. He eyed one or two, searching for troublemakers, an unfortunate necessity. Experience had taught him how to spot them. Up in Heaven, he had been one of them.

Get moving. Didier had to be his focus. He had to find the man before something terrible happened. Ash glanced at the sinkhole. *Something else, that is.*

He will have gone home. Didier was covered in the poisonous muck of the Seine. He would need to bathe and change into fresh clothes. Ash would be able to find him there...if he knew where the man lived.

Marcus knows.

Ash swore. Dear God, couldn't he have one break? Just one?

The Heavens were silent.

6

M arcus was slack-jawed, a lost expression on his shattered face.

In the end, Ash had no choice but to ask where the Firehorse lived. One glance at his office confirmed his aide had mountains of records. Somewhere in the pile was a log with Didier's address, but he didn't have time to look for it.

He had never been one for the little details. He left the minutia to others, and so was beholden to them.

Ash cleared his throat, reminding Marcus he was waiting for an answer. If he didn't get moving, a fire could break out or a meteor could crash into his city.

Marcus blinked a few times, his voice distant. "Um, I think Didier still lives with his mother on Rue de la Santé."

"In Klein's district?"

Marcus nodded, looking down at his hands. "Do you really think it's him?"

"It makes sense," Ash muttered. "You praised him to me just the other day."

His aide looked up a wrinkle between his pale brows. "Excuse me?"

"I'll explain later," he promised. "I need to find Didier now."

Marcus jumped to his feet, touching his arm. "You'll make sure first, won't you? I mean, it could be someone else."

Startled, Ash patted his aide's hand. Contact—skin to skin— was considered a base indulgence to his kind. Marcus was scrupulously respectful, so he avoided it at all costs. Until today.

Ash nodded, his pity stirred. "I'll make certain first," he vowed.

It wasn't a difficult promise to make. The curse rarely left them guessing.

<hr />

DIDIER'S HOUSE in District Thirteen was a small but well-built thatch cottage. His mother was a widow with no other children. To make matters worse, she was mostly blind with severe cataracts.

"I haven't seen my son today," the woman lied.

Despite her infirmity, she looked hale and healthy, unlike so many others in this neighborhood. Her son had taken good care of her. Ash didn't want to think about how she would fare without him.

"I need to speak with him."

The woman felt around the kitchen table until her hand landed on the back of a rickety wire-frame chair. She sat down. "Is this about his work? Marcus was by the other night for the noon meal, and he was full of praise for Didier's efforts."

"I understand he's doing well," Ash confirmed. "But I think you know that is not the reason I'm here."

The woman blinked her sightless eyes. Her face crumpled. "He's a good boy. A son a mother could be proud of."

The impulse to spare her feelings was strong, but he couldn't lie. She had to prepare herself. "I've come to realize the curse only takes our best," he said.

His words of comfort only made her sob louder. "Is there anyone else you can stay with?" he asked. "Someone no one here knows?"

Shaken, the woman wrung her hands. "Why?"

Because if the people learned Didier was a Firehorse, her neighbors would probably turn on her. *Guilt by association.* Ash could no longer trust in man's better nature anymore...maybe he never could.

"If you don't know of anyone who can take you in, go to Marcus. Do you know where he lives?"

"His quarters are in Belleville...with you."

"Yes." That was close enough. He lived in the top-floor apartment of a three-story building, while Marcus kept rooms on the bottom. None one lived in between. Didier's mother could have one of those apartments.

"I don't want to go," she whispered, running her hands over the scarred table.

"It's temporary," Ash said, hoping it wasn't a lie. "Take what you need for a few days. Maybe you will be able to return here soon."

He couldn't promise more. It was time for him to leave. He'd given Didier enough of a head start.

With a murmur of thanks, he departed, blotting out the woman's suffering as soon as he exited the building.

Ash felt the chill autumn air rush around him. He embraced the cold, letting the icy touch freeze him inside and out. *War is easier than this.*

A sneaky little voice asked him why was he bothering anymore. For every Marcus and Didier, there were a dozen or so members of the mob or worse—a Titouan or Mazarin.

Forcing his feet to move, he breathed deeply of the tainted air. It tasted like grease, and not the good kind. He closed his eyes, aching for the fresh tang of clean mountain air and blue skies.

He frowned, looking back at the cottage as a thought struck

him. The woman inside hadn't been surprised to see him. Sure, she'd been upset, but not shocked. *Almost as if someone had warned her he'd be coming.*

Which meant Didier was aware he'd been cursed, and, somehow, he'd accepted it.

Most Firehorses were in denial even as entire buildings fell around them. And so far, only one disaster could be attributed to Didier. His sudden departure—his mother lying for him—was too strange.

Flexing his hamstrings and glutes, Ash crouched before launching himself into the air. He began to scan the neighborhood from above.

His eyes followed each male of Didier's age and height, the few who were out at this hour. There was no sign of anything unusual until he flew higher.

There. A fast-moving pair was making its way up Boulevard Saint-Jacques. He recognized Didier's sandy-blond head. The other figure was smaller and hooded. They rounded a pile of stones and dry brown shrubbery, disappearing from sight.

Mystified, he streaked down, landing a few paces from the stones. There was nothing behind them. It wasn't until he pushed the dry branches aside that he saw the hole.

Ash curled up his wings, folding them so they tucked in and melded with his body. No longer encumbered by the huge appendages, he squeezed through the narrow opening, dropping lightly onto the ground below.

He made his way down the tunnel until it opened into a wider passage. He was in the catacombs, he realized with a start. The subtle glow of bleached bones was unmistakable to his superior night vision.

The network of tunnels and passages had run underneath most of pre-Collision Paris. When the cemeteries overflowed in the late-eighteenth century, people filled the spaces with the bones of their dead.

People had taken tours and snapped pictures, he remembered. Death was always fascinating when it wasn't a part of everyday life.

But given the instability of the terrain in the last decade or so, this subterranean network was unofficially a no-man's land now. No one in their right mind came here for fear of being buried in a cave-in. In fact, Ash would have bet most of the entrances to the underground network had been obliterated in this part of the city. A small quake near the Paris observatory a few years ago had done a lot of damage.

Except you never bothered to check.

A winking in and out of retreating torchlight ahead stopped his self-recrimination. The part of Ash that was created for battle rose to the surface, his every instinct sharpening for the hunt.

His feet pounded the dirt floor of the narrow passage. A blur of winking skulls laughed at him as he streaked past.

The noise of his pursuit alerted the people he was chasing. Ahead of him, footfalls sped up, but they were no match for his preternatural speed. He gained ground and was almost on them when they turned, banking left. Ash was forced to slow down as the tunnel narrowed unexpectedly.

Even without his wings, he could barely manage. His shoulders brushed the wall, their breadth dislodging femurs and rib bones in the skeleton-lined passage. Ash turned to his head, continuing to push forward in a crab-like crawl until he couldn't anymore.

He was caught at a bottleneck, a space where the tunnel almost closed before opening wide into a small pocket cavern. At the opposite end, an arch was partially blocked by debris. The opening gap appeared too small for people. Nevertheless, his quarry was managing just fine.

"Go!" The hissed whisper rang in his ears with a strikingly high melodic tone.

The hooded one was female.

Ash squeezed past the constriction trapping him. He jumped, spreading his wings for a few heartbeats. His body sailed over the open space of the cavern. He landed on the opposite side with a thump.

Ash was too big to fit through the narrow arch, even turned on his side, but he'd managed to get one arm through. He was holding the cloth of a hoodie in his hand.

Someone screamed—Didier was shouting, but the hood Ash had grabbed hold of wasn't the man's. Ash had caught the female.

She twisted to face him, trying to wrench away from his grasp. It was the girl from Place Vendôme, the beauty who'd stopped his heart.

The wide brown eyes of his mystery woman were flecked with green and gold. They flared as the sound of her pounding pulse reverberated through his ears. For an instant, his heart and hers pulsed in unison until she wrenched away. He was left holding the discarded black sweatshirt. She'd sacrificed the garment to get away.

His last glimpse of her was of her wide eyes staring at him, fear shifting to confusion before she pivoted and fled, melting into the darkness.

7

S he had vanished into the deathspace of the catacombs. So had Didier. They'd evaded him.

That was almost as shocking as the fact he was lost. Ash had tried to force his way past the arch, only to bring it and part of the ceiling down on top of him. Using his superior strength had only made the cave-in worse.

Ash forced himself to breathe shallowly and slow his heart rate with a calming chant. It was only when he was utterly still, his movement molasses slow, that he was able to wiggle one hand, and then the other, free. Sliding on his belly, he crawled out from under the rubble. By the time he was free, Didier and the mystery girl were long gone.

He'd tried to follow their trail, but the catacombs were a warren. The interconnecting tunnels used to stretch hundreds of miles in length in the Pre-Collision era. He wasn't sure how much of the network was still intact, but clearly it was more than he'd thought. It had only taken a few dozen turns before he'd lost any trace of them.

Unbelievable. How had this happened?

Ash was made to hunt. Angels possessed superior strength

and hearing. He could detect minute disturbances in the air, an ability that allowed him to track demons fleeing from God's wrath. But the air around him was confused. Whatever ripples he could sense were faint and came from too many different directions. He tracked one after another only to find small human nests, abandoned nooks, and small chambers with old clothes, broken dishes, and trash. He even found the remains of an old rave—a pre-Collision event that used the grinning skulls and bone-lined ossuary as a backdrop for parties.

The demon horde hadn't bothered much with this space. What novelty was there in skull-lined passages and monuments when Hell was literally paved with them? Entire buildings in the internal regions were built of bone and blood-soaked cobb. To a demon, this French curiosity was a pale imitation of home, so the abandoned network—*deadspace*—was left intact by them. The same could not be said for humans.

In the immediate aftermath of the Collision, the demons laid waste to the population. The tangled web of ossuary tunnels had expanded exponentially as legions of the dead joined their ancestors in eternal rest, at least until the curse made the area unsafe. Then it had faded from memory.

This subterranean world had always made Ash uncomfortable. He was a creature of wind and sky. Even the perpetually tainted air above was preferable to the closed stillness down here.

His route took him past one of the elaborate crosses made of human skulls. Stepping past it, he tried to ignore the macabre display, but his overheated angelic brain kept processing the bone, fitting teeth and ocular orbits into the proper configuration until they were recognizable human faces.

He was doing a better job of ignoring them until he turned a corner and came face to face with the bleached pate of Robespierre, a ringleader of the revolution and an instigator of the Reign of Terror.

Ash narrowed his eyes at the skull, impulsively using the one-fingered salute humans still favored for total dicks.

Time dragged as his search continued. He had no idea how long he'd been down in the catacombs. *I need to start carrying a watch.* Digital ones still didn't work, but the classic wind-up ones did, although their best still lost minutes a day.

If he'd been human, this would be around the time he would start panicking. Thousands had lost their lives after becoming lost down here. In fact, he'd already passed a few of those poor souls. They were easy to distinguish from the other remains. The bones lay as they had fallen, not in the orderly piles and arrangements made by humans past.

Starvation or death by dehydration wasn't a concern for him, but he could spend ages lost down here. In the meantime, his city would suffer. He had to find Didier and the girl before the council leaders inflicted lasting damage.

Ash needed to get his bearings. He shouldn't have lost them so easily. *I'm rusty,* he thought with a scowl. He'd lived in secret so long his powers had atrophied.

Remember your training. Angels were created by the Maker with their abilities intact the way a robot was programmed. But Ash's kind were supposed to practice and hone those skills.

Quiet inside, quiet outside. Raphael's voice echoed in his head without his trademark smirk. The archangel was an ass, but he'd been an excellent commander. He'd been the one to teach Ash the deep meditation techniques that were the foundation of his hunting and warrior ability.

He let go, relaxing again. His mind scanned the air for those little ripples that would indicate human movement.

Nothing...except. He opened his mouth, the coppery tang so faint he might have been imagining it.

Magic. It was only a trace, but it was there.

Magic had a half-life close to the lifespan of a snowball in hell. If he was detecting traces of it, that meant a spell had been cast recently.

But all the witches were dead. They had been hunted down after the Collision by both demons and humankind.

His stomach tightened in apprehension. A witch had been, albeit indirectly, responsible for the end of the world. But Ash had seen too much to believe that all were the unholy evil creatures rabid priests and prophets painted them as. They were the scapegoats of the apocalypse.

We hunted them, too. He couldn't name an angel who would hesitate to kill a witch on sight.

He had to get moving. The hint of copper in the air was fading even now. Time was running out. Spurred by the reminder, he began to run.

THE TRACE LED him to another nest. Blankets and tin cans were folded neatly next to a lantern with a little oil left in the reservoir. He studied the water-tight space. The entrance to the small cavern was a few feet above the ground, protecting it from the periodic flooding that plagued many of the other passages around him.

Ash squeezed out of the entrance, his boots covered to the ankle in water. The trace of magic was still there, prodding him forward.

Signs of human habitation weren't rare down here. But most of them were old—pre-Collision. The vast majority of people were too close to death as it was. They avoided this place. But over the centuries, there were always exceptions.

This nest had something the others didn't. Not only were the blankets clean and the tins in a neat row, but it was *spotless*. No dust. This space was used, even organized in a minimalistic way.

The only thing out of place was a medical reflex hammer.

It was lying on the floor next to one of the blankets. His immediate thought was of Dr. Brès. Had the doctor taken refuge down here after she realized she was a Firehorse? How else could the hammer have ended up here?

It could be nothing. It wasn't as if the hammer had been carved with the doctor's initials. Until he found the people who frequented these catacombs, he could only guess. Tucking the hammer into his belt, he resumed his hunt.

He finally found what he was looking for outside the catacombs, in the wasteland near what used to be Vanves.

There were people. Not just one or two, but *many*. At least two score. Ash knelt behind a pile of boulders, trying to hold in the exclamation trying to burst out of him.

Dr. Brès was down there. A small child clung to Madeleine's leg, looking uncertain. Her daughter. The rest of Madeleine's little family was here, too. They were in a basin at the bottom of the cliff. There was a fire going, and someone was cooking what looked to be a wild hare. An aromatic stew was boiling in a large pot.

They had *food* in the middle of the wasteland.

Ash nearly jumped out from behind the stone when he saw Theo Faure and Demetria Long, Firehorses from the last few years who disappeared before he could track them down.

I thought they were dead. In fact, he'd been certain Theo had been done in by his fundamentalist family. But he was alive. And so was Didier. He was down there, too...talking to *her*.

Ash watched his mystery girl move among the crowd at the fire's edge. She appeared to be introducing Didier to her little band. And it *was* hers. He studied the group from behind his rock for some time. No one else had the same easy air of authority. All the others looked at or spoke to her deferentially.

The beautiful brunette was the leader of this band of survivors.

The girl turned abruptly, scanning the hillside as if sensing his intent gaze. Ash ducked behind the rock, sliding to crouch on the ground. He waited. There was no sound of footsteps, either running toward or away from him. He hadn't been seen.

Ash's mind reeled. How was this possible? This was the wasteland. Nothing survived here. Except for these people...and whatever they were cooking on that fire.

Merde. This was impossible. How had so many Firehorses escaped not just him, but also the mobs? And why hadn't the earth swallowed them up?

Something was going on. Unchecked, the curse had the power to level Bastille. By rights, this basin and the surrounding hillsides should be a smoking crater. *Seriously*. He wouldn't put it past Amducious' blasted hex to call down a meteor to strike them all down. It was what God had done with the dinosaurs when he'd tired of them.

But there they were—Firehorses who lived, walked, and talked. True, they didn't seem all that healthy. They were far too thin. Unless Ash was mistaken, several were showing signs of scurvy, too.

So does half the city. What mattered was the fact they were alive. Somehow, the power of the curse had been checked.

Sweet Jesus, was this the miracle he had been waiting for? If the curse had been broken, he would have known. There were survivors down there who had been struck down years ago. And Didier had just been cursed...

Was it possible for the afflicted to be cured? Could he bring Didier home to his mother?

But what if it wasn't permanent? What if he took Didier and the others home only to have the destruction resume? *What am I supposed to do?*

He needed to learn more. And Ash couldn't do that as he was. To the people of Bastille, he was a guardian, the savior who had delivered them from demon rule and now from the threat of the

Firehorse. But to those who were afflicted, he was the angel of death.

Those people wouldn't tell him anything. If only there was a way to win their trust before revealing his identity...

There is. Ash could go as one of them. Without his armor and helmet there was a chance they wouldn't recognize him. He could tell them he was looking for his blood, a relative he suspected was afflicted.

There was only one problem with that. If they even so much as thought he was lying, then they'd try to kill him. They wouldn't have a choice. If they let him go, he might tell someone in the city, and if that happened, it wouldn't be long before the mob came after them.

If he was forced to fight them, chances were he'd kill one or more while trying to protect himself. And then he'd be right back where he'd started—watching a miracle from the outside. Either way, the chance to break the curse would slip through his fingers.

And that's the best-case scenario if I'm discovered. The others he'd considered were far worse. But what other choice did he have?

8

A sh pulled the hood of his sweatshirt closer around his head as the band of survivors gathered supplies at the outskirts of the city.

He had taken off his armor and helmet and folded his wings until they melded seamlessly into his back. Then he'd donned his old pre-Collision clothes. Marcus had even found him a beat-up pair of tinted eyeglasses that would mute the slight luminescence of his eyes.

Ash hoped his disguise was good enough to fool his quarry. He needed to win their trust long enough to learn how they were evading the curse.

Rain began to fall, making the fabric stick to his skin. Already these clothes felt strange. He'd spent the better part of the last decade wearing full angelic armor on a day-to-day basis, ever since he'd accepted Raphael's bargain.

Now the armor is sitting in the back of my closet in Belleville, a shining symbol of God's might gathering dust.

But sometimes, might failed. Centuries of observation had taught Ash that. Kingdoms rose and fell like the tides. And it wasn't the ones with the biggest armies or fiercest warriors that persisted. That distinction fell to the ones that valued peace and prosperity. Civilizations that prized knowledge and art over the sword—those were the true immortals.

Knowledge and understanding were required to win this battle as well. Somehow, he had to convince those people down there to give him both.

It's a good thing I didn't throw out my human clothes. He'd kept them in part to remind himself of the goal he was working toward. But Ash hadn't anticipated ever wearing them again—not until this undercover mission.

For the last few weeks, he'd tracked the band of survivors, studying their ways and piecing together their structure. He confirmed his mystery girl was their leader. He could see it in the way the other members deferred to her, always seeking her approval before striking out to gather supplies. Another woman, a wizened and wiry crone, appeared to be her lieutenant. That made the entire group distinctly matriarchal in bent.

There were over forty in all, but the survivors rarely congregated in one place at the same time. They were typically split into smaller groups of four to six. Some hunted in the catacombs, looking for rats and other vermin, while others moved at the fringes of the wasteland, scavenging whatever they could to survive.

And somehow, against all odds, they were making it.

Okay, here goes nothing. Ash climbed down from the pile of rubble he'd been using to spy on the group who scavenged in the outskirts of the former commune of Bagnolet.

In the demon days, anyone blundering about out at the edge did so at their own peril. Humans attacked humans for whatever supplies or valuables they had. Unspeakable acts had soaked the soil with blood and bile. This was still considered to be a no-man's land. Only thieves and killers lived here.

Can't come off as one of those. Ash waited until his quarry was around the corner of a burned-out building before running out at a jog.

They stared and started, but not as badly as he. His eyes widened, and his mouth parted in feigned terror. Pivoting on his heel, Ash ran a few steps, tripping over his own feet and face planting into the dirt with a loud thud.

Scrambling, he turned again as if afraid to keep his back to a potential threat.

The others had begun to run away, too, but when one of them saw him fall, he turned back. It was a teenage boy—Theo Faure if his guess was right. He stared at Ash as the others ran.

Ash held out his hand, palm out defensively. "I don't want trouble," he called out. "I'm just looking for someone."

He thought the boy wasn't going to answer, but the youth's curiosity got the best of him. "Who are you looking for?"

Slowly, Ash got to his feet. He dusted himself off, careful to keep the movements slow and unthreatening. As an angel, he could never look as emaciated as a human even when starved. Here the appearance of being well-fed and fit was a mark against him.

Once he was sure the boy wouldn't run, he pulled out a sketch. He'd made it himself. The rough picture was of an average-looking young woman. "This is my sister, Helena. She was at work in the canning factory, but disappeared a few days ago. It was just before the glassworks had a meltdown. I'm...worried about her. She has brown eyes and hair my color," he said, pulling his hood back to reveal his head before drawing a line at his shoulders. "She's this tall. Have you seen her?"

The boy's head drew back as if he were thinking, but he was eyeing the bulging muscles on Ash's forearms.

Ash could see the youth's suspicion, but also concern and sympathy. The latter was the sentiment he needed to exploit—carefully. Someone in his position didn't come right out and admit they had a relative who was a Firehorse. That would only put a target on their loved one's back, and their own by extension.

The boy knew that. He was wary. Though this area was not as dangerous under Ash's rule as before, traps were still common enough. The kid would be a fool to take him at his word. Ash needed to prove himself trustworthy.

"Look, I don't know if you've seen her, but if she's anywhere, it's here at the fringe." He kept his hands up, palms out, to demonstrate his weapon-less state.

The boy shook his head. "I don't think she's out here, man."

Ash took a shaky breath. "Maybe she is, and you just haven't run into her yet." He paused, trying to figure out how to convey his honest desperation. The sentiment was real—it just wasn't about a missing relative. "I would like to give you something in case you find her."

He opened his knapsack and took out a few of the ration bars he'd packed, making sure the boy saw the rest. Made with oats, cereals, wild nuts, and honey, the bars were a highly sought-after source of nutrition. Packed in dried maize husks, they could last for almost a year if stored properly.

After fastening the sketch to the bars with a string from his pack, Ash held them out. "I realize you're going to eat these instead of her, and it's all right. But if you see my sister, maybe you can help her out if she needs it. It would only be long enough for me to get to her. I would owe you a favor then—a big one."

The boy shuffled his feet, maintaining his distance, but still taking what was offered. But he couldn't mask the calculating expression on his face as he weighed the bars in his hand. "Can you get more of these?"

"I can," Ash said. "I used to haul grain at the factory that made those. The foreman promised to hold my job because I can haul the most bags at once...I have almost a case hidden at home. It's how he paid me when he couldn't afford my wages. I can bring them, but only if you pass along my message and sketch to others out here. The more people willing to help my sister, the better."

The boy appeared to think about it. Then he offered his hand, careful to tuck the ration bars into his pocket first.

Ash clasped the teen's hand and shook. "My name is Ash."

"I'm Theo," the boy said, withdrawing.

It is him. Another confirmed Firehorse—alive and well. Ash hid his excitement, biting the inside of his cheek to keep from saying anything that might betray the storm of emotion roiling in his breast.

The boy glanced over his shoulder. None of his compatriots were in sight, but Ash knew they hadn't gone far. He could feel their eyes on him. They were hiding behind the ruined cars, watching and waiting.

"Thank you," he replied, his gratitude genuine. "I'm sleeping in that building over there while I search this area, but will move on in a couple of days."

Theo nodded. "I'll pass the word along, but you may want to rethink keeping that food on you. People around here kill for less."

That was part of the plan, but Ash nodded anyway. "I'll keep that in mind."

Later that night, Ash threw together a makeshift shelter in the corner of the empty ruin he'd pointed out to Theo and settled down to wait. After night fell, three people approached, climbing the stairs.

They are making enough of a racket to wake the dead.

It wasn't the smooth operation it would have been under his command, but hey—humans. He suppressed a sigh and rolled over, giving his back to the trio.

At least they didn't hesitate when they saw his vulnerable position. One of the men came at him with a piece of a broken pipe. A second carried a piece of timber. Ash could tell what their weapons were when they struck his body.

Covering his head with his hands, he rolled to see one man rear back to bring the pipe down on Ash's shoulder. The other landed a lucky hit with his wooden bat. While a blow from a human was nowhere near as painful as one from a demon, the strikes still hurt. He fought to keep his warrior instincts from reacting, letting let them get two or three more good blows before spinning forward and putting his hands up.

Once on his feet, Ash feinted right and threw himself left, avoiding a hard blow that would have broken the ribs of a human. Reacting a beat slower than his inclination, he threw his gear pack at one of the attackers hard enough to make them lose their breath. The last man, who had stood by and watched throughout, snaked forward to grab the bag. Only it wasn't a man at all. It was a little girl of about nine or ten. Hugging the pack to her skinny chest, she ran out of the room.

Damn it. If he wanted to pass as a desperate human, he needed to go after the bag, but what if the little girl hurt herself trying to get away from him? With a growl, Ash shrugged off another hit from the first attacker, whipping out his hand to knock the weapon out of the man's grip. Then he rushed the second man, giving him a little shove to clear a path to the stairs.

Ash ran down two before intentionally tripping over his own feet. He cried out as he tumbled down the flight of stairs. A broken step at the bottom added the finishing touch, a jagged shard of wood impaling his side. It wasn't a deep wound, but it bled—or at least it did once he shoved the six-inch splinter in hard enough to break his preternaturally tough skin.

Picking himself up with bloody hands, he limped across the floor, making it down into the open area in front of the building before collapsing.

9

A sh peeked out from beneath his lashes to where Theo and the crone named Sij were arguing about whether to help him. Each was pleading their case to their leader Kara.

That was his mystery girl's name. *Kara*. And she was even more intriguing up close. Not that he'd been able to take a good look, pretending to be half-conscious the way he was. But the few glimpses he'd snuck had been so intriguing he regretted feigning an injury. If he'd chosen some other tack, he could be on his feet talking to her now.

Of course, those other options might not have worked. His gut had told him this was the tactic with the greatest chance of success. And he'd been right. A few minutes after his attackers had run away, Theo had come back with Kara, Sij, and two other men.

"I'm so sorry about this." A near-tearful Theo knelt in front of him. "I told our people about your ration bars. Some of them wanted to come and take them, but Kara told them not to. They disobeyed, but they didn't mean to hurt you."

I knew it! Ash was triumphant. He hadn't lost his touch. His assessment of Theo's character had been spot on. Even the hapless thieves hadn't seemed evil, just desperate. Apparently, Kara didn't surround herself with bad people.

He'd murmured something suitably indistinct to Theo, keeping a hand over his bloody wound so no one would notice it was almost closed. As soon as the others began to argue about him, he reached under his shirt and reopened it again with a hard yank.

"We should dump him in the desert," the old crone argued when he let his head droop as if he'd fallen unconscious. "Look at the size of him. He'll snap our necks in our sleep."

"He's *injured*," Theo protested. "And it's our fault. We need to help him. You never know; he might even be able to help us when he gets better. He's so big and strong. He could help defend us when the raiders attack."

Raiders? What raiders?

There was a soft snort. "We haven't seen any raiders in over seven weeks. They're probably all dead. Not that this man would be of much use. If Saul and Gaspard were able to do this to him, a raider would tear him apart."

Ouch. For some reason, Kara's judgment stung. He peeked, trying to get another glimpse of her face. She was standing with Theo and Sij just a few feet in front of him. He thought he read reluctance in her expression, but her voice was too low to be sure.

Finally, after what felt like an eternity, Kara was done hearing arguments. She approached and knelt in front of him. The hard planes of her face were chiseled, carved out by life in the fringe, but her lips were still soft and full.

I want to kiss them.

Ash blinked in confusion as that unbidden thought ran through his head. Despite spending over a millennium on earth, he'd never felt desire so strong. It was bewildering, which perhaps was fortunate timing because Kara's face softened as if she'd been undecided. His temporary disorientation had worked in his favor.

Had she suspected him? His helmet and visor had covered most of his face during their encounter in the catacombs. Only his lips and eyes had been visible, but was that enough to recognize him? He hadn't spoken to her, so she wouldn't know his voice.

The longer she stared at him, the more he squirmed. It was inexplicable, but he felt exposed under her arresting hazel-eyed gaze. He felt as if she could see into the very depths of his soul.

Ash parted his dry lips. "I will never hurt you," he vowed, surprising himself.

He'd surprised her, too. Kara's eyes flared for the briefest of seconds before darkening.

"You stay long enough to heal and not a second more," she said in a stern voice that didn't succeed in masking its natural honey and butter tone.

She called the two men who still waited nearby. One of them blindfolded Ash before helping him up. He was too big for them to carry, but with his assistance, they dragged him behind the others.

They had only gone a few hundred meters before the quality of the air changed. He didn't need them to remove the blindfold to know he'd been taken down beneath the surface—into tunnels that should not exist. According to every map he owned, this part of the fringe didn't connect to the subterranean warren of the catacombs.

This location is impossible, he thought, reaching out with one hand to touch the damp stone wall. If someone had built this, he would have known.

And yet, here I am. Ash was underground now, deeper than he'd ever been before.

How close to Hell are we?

Just then, a blow landed to the front of his head, dulling out his final thought.

10

T he knock to the head wasn't hard enough to render Ash unconscious, but it was strong enough to leave him dazed.

"*Damn it*, Roget," Kara said. "Watch where you're going or you're going to brain him before we get back to base."

"Perhaps I could just remove the blindfold," Ash suggested in a pained voice, guessing he'd been walked into a stone overhang.

Technically, he could move well enough with one using just his hearing, but so long as the humans were guiding him, that wasn't an option. He went where they walked him—even if it meant straight into a wall.

Be more helpless, he reminded himself.

"No," Sij snapped from somewhere behind him. "You take that off before we get where we're going, and I'll run you through with my blade. Can't let everyone and their mother know where our top-secret base is..."

The last was a near-indecipherable mutter. Sij was clearly not on board with Kara's decision to let Ash stay.

She wasn't the only one. By the time they took off his blindfold, he could feel the collective gaze of a dozen suspicious people like tiny daggers all over his skin. Rather than try to converse, he decided to tug open his wound a bit so it wouldn't close.

Confident he was safe in Kara's care, he closed his eyes, feigning sleep so convincingly he drifted off.

When he woke, his wound was being treated by none other than Dr. Madeleine Brès. Kara was standing next to her, overseeing his treatment.

Ash grimaced with genuine discomfort as the doctor poked and prodded his wound, remarking on the speed of his recovery with an air of wonder.

"It may not even leave a scar," she added with a bright smile. Ash smiled back and thanked her with a murmur, grateful she did not seem to recognize him despite having met twice in as many years.

He'd never been around her or any other human without the helmet that obscured his face. Only Marcus was familiar with his features. But his voice was distinctive. All angels had a little extra resonance, a vibration that tweaked human nerves, even in their daily speech.

But Madeleine didn't even blink when he repeated his thanks more loudly. Nevertheless, he was relieved when she packed up her medical bag and moved on.

He hoped Kara would stay and converse with him, but as soon the doctor was finished with him, Kara walked away, too, called to duty by her many followers.

The flaw in his plan was exposed in the days after. Kara came and went, delegating tasks and leading groups of scavengers in the fringe or hunting parties down here in the catacombs. He wanted nothing more than to join in and help provide for the others, but whenever he tried, he was sternly told to sit and heal.

"The sooner you do, the sooner you can get out of here," Kara said, rubbing salt in the wound.

Forced passivity made Ash's skin itch. He was chafing under

the restraints of his disguise, but he made the best of a bad situation by pumping those who stayed behind for information.

He learned a lot by proxy. Theo and several others, the newest arrivals, were happy to brag about their leader when she wasn't around.

It was obvious Kara knew the wasteland and how to survive in it. But how she'd acquired this knowledge was a matter of some debate.

According to one of her acolytes, she had been born on the fringe to a Firehorse mother, who taught her everything she needed to know to survive. Another one said it was actually her father who had been the Firehorse. The pair had been forced to flee from the city when he'd been struck down. By the time the man died a few years later, Kara was an expert hunter and scavenger, more than capable of surviving on her own.

No two people had the same story about her. The only common thread was Sij—the scrappy little woman who hated him. It wasn't until after Kara teamed up with her that they founded their refugee community. Everyone here was related to a Firehose. They were always very clear on this point. Their little band was composed of relatives of the afflicted. None of them confessed to being cursed, nor did they point fingers at anyone else. Their solidarity on this point was unassailable.

A few days into his subterfuge, Kara left to lead a scavenging party with a reluctant Sij in tow. As soon as they left, Ash was on his feet, pitching in to help the group wherever a hand was needed.

"Can I help clean that up?" he asked when Dr. Brès came in one day. She was holding her daughter, who had a long scrape along one arm.

"I don't want you exerting yourself," Madeleine scolded, rushing toward him when he stood up.

He waved away her concern, patting the wound with a slap to indicate how well he was. "I'm fine now," Ash assured her.

When he didn't flinch, Madeleine threw him a suspicious glance. But her daughter was crying so she dismissed him, opting to care for her child instead.

Theo approved of his eagerness, assuming Ash was auditioning for a spot in their band. "We could use your help clearing passages," he said, signaling Ash to follow him. "If you want to stay, you have to convince Kara and Sij you're worth feeding."

They reached the blocked tunnel a few minutes later, and Ash got to work. The tunnel was cleared in no time.

"I can't believe we're done," Theo said a bit later as Ash tossed the last boulder out of the way. "Thanks so much. It would have taken twice as long without your help."

"Not a problem." It felt good to use his strength again after days of forced inactivity.

"Do you think you can help me with something else?"

Ash grinned with genuine satisfaction. "Of course," he said, putting a hand on Theo's back as they walked back to meet the others.

That had been the beginning. When Kara returned to the catacomb hideout a few days later, she found Ash nearly indispensable. He'd ingratiated himself far more deeply than she would have suspected. And she was not happy.

But things could get worse. Much worse. Which was exactly what happened when the ceiling above them collapsed.

11

A sh tried to delay the inevitable confrontation with Kara off for as long as he could. He'd thrown himself into the hard work of surviving in the wasteland, joining whatever group he could to avoid being alone with Kara or Sij.

This morning when Theo asked for a hand, Ash rushed him through first meal so they could be out of Kara's way before the band started their day.

"Where is this tunnel we need to clear?" He hopped from one stone to another in a partially flooded cavern.

His internal chronometer told him they'd been traveling for almost an hour.

Theo leapt with the dexterity of youth, landing on a loose rock and balancing automatically. A ripple disturbed the oily surface where he landed.

"It's still some ways out. We're in the eastern branch of the catacombs. The tunnel we want to clear caved in a long time ago. It leads to Masséna. We hunt there."

"*Oh.*" The Masséna plains were where Bastille grew most of its grain.

Though they weren't exactly plentiful, wild game could be

found in those wheat and maize fields. It wasn't enough to sustain the city, but Marcus had started an initiative to have some of the meat served at the local schools. The rest was traded, but the area was off limits to the general population. Ash hadn't wanted Bastille to exhaust what little game there was.

It's a good thing I stopped the council when they wanted to make poaching an illegal act punishable by death.

Not that any council guard could have gotten the drop on one of Kara's people. From what he'd seen, they were too well trained for that.

They arrived at the blockage shortly after and set to work. Ash was still marveling over the industry of the band when he realized Theo had started speaking again.

"If we clear the tunnel, we won't have to cross overland or through the old metro and train tunnels," Theo was saying. Ash's head snapped up. "Kara has us avoid those whenever we can."

Finally, an opening. He picked up a heavy boulder, taking advantage of Theo's turned back to heave it out of the way with one arm. "Why don't you cross overland?" he asked, lifting another boulder almost half his weight.

"Why do you want to know?" Kara replied from somewhere behind him.

Ash spun, dropping the stone on his foot. It would have crushed every bone in it if he'd been human. Suppressing a wince, Ash dragged his foot back before Kara noticed and wondered why he wasn't screaming in agony.

The woman was breathtaking in a faded brown tank and torn cargo pants.

His mind flashed back to the scenes of the court of Louis IV with the women in all their finery. Kara didn't have a silk gown. She wasn't wearing makeup or any of the fine jewels he'd seen females adorn themselves with. And yet, none of those women could hold a candle to her.

Damn it, this is the last thing I need, he thought as she picked her way through the debris from the last cave-in. Why were these thoughts plaguing him after so many years? A millennium on earth without a problem like this, and now all he could think about was how soft her lips looked.

Why her? Kara was literally the last person in the world he should fixate on.

"Theo, can you go help Sij in the west tunnels?" she asked, rounding a pile of stones and fragments of ancient powdery plaster.

"But we already cleared those..." Theo trailed off, noting the dark glance she gave him. He touched the leather thong around his neck and nodded. "Unless there's more to do now, and there always is down here. Excuse me."

The youth nodded at the two of them, backing away with a *you-have-this* gesture at him Kara couldn't see behind her back.

Kara turned, her thick sooty lashes flickering as Theo disappeared around the bend. Once he was gone, she dropped the civil mien.

"I see that you're feeling better. Well, enough to lift at least four stone."

"I heal quickly," he supplied, crossing his arms.

Kara narrowed her eyes, reaching over unexpectedly to snag the hem of his shirt. "Very fast, I see. There isn't even a scar."

He smiled haplessly. "Dr. Brès is a very skilled physician."

His tone was as blasé as he could make it, but Kara didn't appear to buy his. She backed away a few feet, studying him like a bug under a microscope.

"Why are you still here?" Her voice was flat and unwelcoming.

He opened his hands, holding them low at his sides. "As I told you and the others before, I'm looking for my sister."

"You already know she's not here."

"Not yet, but—"

Kara held up a hand. "*Save it.* I've heard the story about you buying our goodwill on the off chance she turns up. Not that she ever will, because we both know she doesn't exist."

"Of course she exists," he scoffed. "Why would I be here otherwise?"

The hazel gaze didn't waver. "That's a very good question."

They stared at each other. Ash searched the right words to allay her suspicions, but the only ones that came were the truth. The impulse to tell her everything was riding him hard.

"Why don't I ever know what to say to you?" Maybe it was because he always got distracted. Even now, he could barely focus on their conversation. Instead, he was lost studying the texture of her skin and the graceful curve of her neck.

She's not wearing anything around it, he thought, tilting his head to one side.

The survivors wore a leather thong with something at the end. Theo had been fiddling with his just before he left. Madeleine wore one as well. The outline of what it held—a small cylinder—was visible just under their clothes.

All of them wear it. Even Sij and the children. But Kara's neck was bare.

Ash gestured to his neck. "Why aren't you wearing one those thongs with the cylinder at the end? Everyone else has one but you. Is it a charm or something?"

Kara's lips firmed, but she didn't say anything. The only answer was the snap of a holster opening. Ash eyed the blade that had suddenly appeared in her hand from a hidden sheath strapped to her back.

Either she had just lost all patience with him or he'd just touched a nerve.

She held up the knife, backing away slowly.

Her stance reminded him of the time he tangled with a trained *Mossad* security officer in Cairo at the end of the twentieth century. That woman had been a highly rated assassin. But there was no death in Kara's aura. How she'd come by such ease with a blade was mystifying.

"Consider this the official end of your stay here. Go back to whatever council member you're working for, and *don't come back*," she said, spitting out the last words like bullets. "You can tell them whatever you want. It won't matter. We'll be long gone before you can bring the council guards here."

"I don't work for the council." *They work for me. Or at least, they're supposed to.*

"*Right.*" Skepticism and contempt were in every line of her body, but she didn't lower her guard. The knife remained raised, ready to strike.

"It's true," he insisted, holding up his hands. His covert operation was officially in the crapper. "I wish there was something I could do or say to convince you."

She shifted her weight. "Well, there isn't. You've overstayed your welcome. Go back to Bastille. Leave the fringe to us. We're not hurting anyone."

"I know that. All I want to do is help." He infused his words with all the truth in his heart.

It almost worked. She hesitated, checking her step as she began to walk away. But then she shook her head, slipping her knife back in its holster. "Sij and Theo will be waiting in the main chamber. They'll show you the way back to Bastille. Make sure you're gone before I get back."

"Wait, please!" He needed answers. What were those things around their necks? Was it spelled amulets or tiny vials of some kind of potion? Was that how they were evading the curse?

Kara didn't stop. She turned a blind corner, disappearing from his sight. By the time he rounded the bend, she was gone.

"*Kara?*"

Swearing a blue streak, he pounded after her, calling her name. This time, he tracked her easily. She wasn't moving fast. At first, he assumed she wasn't trying to get away, but after a few minutes, another explanation presented itself—in the form of a chunk of stone hitting him on the head.

"Kara! This passage is not sound," he called out, careful to keep his tone muted. He didn't want to shout in case the vibrations of his preternatural voice caused a cave-in.

A quick scan confirmed his worst suspicions. They were descending deeper under the ground in what was barely a tunnel. The ground moved under his feet. If it wasn't stable, then neither were the walls or ceiling. He went through one crumbling passage after another, tracking both Kara's movement and scent.

A glimpse of golden caramel skin up ahead told him he'd finally caught up with her. Shadowy movement indicated she whirled around.

"Are you fucking kidding me?" she spat. "Get the hell out of here. This area is not safe."

"Then what are you doing here?" He walked closer, picking his way through the labyrinthine space. The walls were close. Ceilings were too low for him to stand without crouching, but he kept going until he reached Kara. Her scowl was blacker than an archangel's on a bender.

The urge to envelop her in his arms and carry her out of here was overwhelming.

Do it anyway. Even if she resists. In the distance, a falling chunk of rotted plaster or concrete fell with a wet thud as if it landed in a puddle or mud. Unable to stop himself, he reached out for her, but she backpedaled, her back hitting one of the grey pebbled supporting walls.

They both looked up as a sickening crack sounded over their heads.

Kara's eyes flamed gold with accusation before the ceiling began to fall. A large chunk struck him in the back of the neck. More was raining down, coming down on them.

Ash unfurled his wings with enough force to make them burst through the back of his thin T-shirt. He flew toward her. In the space of one heartbeat, he reached her.

He took Kara in his arms, wrapping his wings around her just as he registered the expression of abject horror in her eyes.

12

A sh could taste Kara's fear. Her too-rapid breath fanned his neck as he tried to flex his wings to shift some of the stones burying them.

His body was a cage around hers, protecting her from the weight of the stone ceiling that had toppled down on them. A hint of copper teased his nose, but it was only a trace. Kara was bleeding, but it was just a scrape.

He stroked her hair with the hand pinned closest to her, hoping it would calm her racing heart. The rapid pulse filled his ears, its thrumming beat against his chest.

Her whimper of fear was like a dagger to his heart. "Kara, I'll get you out of this," he promised.

She must be terrified. Hell, he was alarmed, and he was an angel.

She started to say something, but he cut her off. "Don't speak," he admonished. "We need to conserve air."

He couldn't see anything in front of him, but the crash had been thunderous. Most of the ceiling in this chamber had come down on top of them. He prayed it was only this room. If the ceiling and walls of the adjoining spaces and passages had come down, too, Kara didn't have a chance—and he'd be buried down here with her body.

Determined not to let that happen, he redoubled his efforts, trying not to audibly grunt as he strained the muscles on his back. He was trying to lift his wings up to dislodge the stones pinning them down, but he only succeeded in pressing his body more fully against hers.

He'd never been this close to a human female before. Did they all smell this good? And she was so warm and soft. It was like she was made to fit against him.

"*Hey!*"

Heat coursed through his body, a combination of embarrassment and arousal he'd never experienced before.

"Sorry," he muttered, lifting his hips to get a critical part of his anatomy as far from Kara's body as he could.

"*You better be.*" That was followed by a series of curses worthy of an eighteenth-century sailor—a detail Ash was grateful for. Anger had replaced fear in Kara's mind, and that could only be a good thing under the circumstances.

It would be another story when they got out of there. *If we do.*

Ash crushed the negative thought. He *was* going to get Kara free, even if it killed him.

Wrenching his wings, he strained, forcing them forward. It felt as if his pectorals were going to burst through his skin, but he managed to dislodge some of the rocks pinning him down. Finally able to move, he crawled, holding himself up to give Kara enough space to shift and wiggle in his wake.

The next hour was the most excruciating of Ash's entire existence. He did his best to stay a gentleman, being careful not to brush against the beautiful woman lying underneath him any more than he had to.

He should have tried harder. Her scent and heat were

imprinted on his brain now. It was all he could do not to strip her down and bury himself inside her.

Except for the occasional swear, Kara held her tongue, not speaking to him. Instead, hot liquid gold burned him up every time they locked eyes. *She'd castrate me. Or worse.*

Ash was starting to wish he didn't have preternatural night vision when the floor suddenly gave way under his right knee. Chilly air drifted in. It wasn't fresh by any reasonable standard, but it didn't have a toxic taint.

"Do you feel that? There's a chamber underneath us. Air is moving down there, which may mean there's a way out. Can you wiggle to my left? I need more room to kick the hole wider."

"All right." Her words were clipped, but he didn't stop to soothe her ruffled feathers. An apology for his deceit, necessary as it had been, was going to have to wait until they were free.

That happened moments later when the hole was wide enough to accommodate his broad shoulders. Tucking his wings in, he dropped down a few stories into a tunnel so narrow it scraped against his sides. In the distance, he could hear running water, enough for an underground river.

Ash turned to the side and looked up, scanning and gauging the distance. "Kara, there are no footholds. Just a clear drop. You'll be all right. I'll catch you."

Kara appeared at the edge, staring down at him for a long time. It was too dark to see her eyes at this distance, but he knew she was weighing staying up there and trying to find her own way out. But she knew better than to try.

"You better not let me fall." It was almost a growl, but delivered in husky tones, it only succeeded in arousing him further.

"I won't, I promise." Ash held out his arms, sparing a thought to regret his attire. The soft human clothes he was wearing didn't disguise his painful condition as well as his armor would have.

Her long, drawn-out sigh spoke volumes about the confidence she had in him, but Kara had no other options. One long leg appeared at the rim of the hole, then the other. She perched there for an endless moment, staring down at him with barely concealed irritation. Then, with an audible swear, she let go.

She landed in his arms with a thump, her slim muscled form a natural weight in his arms. Adjusting his grip, he held her close.

"You can put me down now," she hissed as he crab-walked down the passage in the direction of the running water. "It will be easier if I can walk."

That was probably true, but it wasn't safer. "Not until we're in the clear." He gestured above them by heaving her up an inch. "If that ceiling gives way, I can protect you by wrapping my wings around you."

At the mention of his wings, Kara tensed. He took a deep breath, expecting a string of recriminations and accusations, but she stayed silent, no doubt waiting for him to release her before berating him.

A few minutes later, the narrow tunnel turned into a crawl-space before suddenly opening into a wide cavern large enough to fly in. He vaulted into the air, taking flight with Kara in his arms.

She sucked in a breath, her head whipping around to look at him and back at the chamber as they flew through it to the other side. He followed the sound of the water and slight breeze until they burst out the warren of catacombs and into the open air.

He recognized the uneven horizon. They were only a few kilometers from the edge of Bastille, along the southeast near Ivry-sur-Seine.

Unwilling to let Kara go, he pumped his wings hard, flying them high into the air, savoring the light of the full moon. They crossed the barren desert, heading west to the cliff basin where he'd seen the survivor clan for the first time. But he didn't hurry.

"It feels good after being down there for so long, doesn't it?" he asked Kara over the wind.

She didn't answer. He tried to read her expression and failed. Kara averted her eyes, fixing her gaze on the distant lights of the city. They were much dimmer than the glittering carpet of diamonds he remembered from his memory.

"You should have seen it before the Collision," he murmured as they arrived. "It was breathtaking. Only Heaven itself could rival it."

Kara's head whipped around to look at him as he made a soft landing on the gravel-filled dirt. "You lived here?"

Ash nodded. "For many years," he said, slowly sliding her down his side—fighting his inclination to hang on to her every inch of the way.

Kara had no such reservations. The force with which she pushed away from him stung his pride, but Ash understood.

A lot of people hated him. In addition to the religious extremists who put him on the same level as the demon horde, there were the relatives of curse victims he'd been forced to execute or abandon to the wasteland.

Who had it been? Which of her loved ones had he killed? Her mother or father? A sibling?

Her face could have been carved from the stones lying on their feet. "You were here before the Collision? So you're not the warden of Bastille—you're one of the fallen."

The relief in her voice was crushing.

For the first time in his life, he was tempted to lie, but that wasn't his nature. "I'm both," he said softly.

Her hands fell to her sides. She shook her head, sniffing loudly. "No. The fallen are outside His grace. He wouldn't come to you. You can't be the warden."

Ash wanted to take her in his arms, to soothe her fears. One move toward her, however, and she stepped back.

"He did send others," Ash confirmed. "But all the emissaries failed to kill the demon lord. They died in their attempts to bring him down. Raphael, my former commander, begged me to try."

"The Seraph?" Kara's voice was hollow. "Your commander was the *archangel* Raphael?"

"He's a total git, really." He held up his hands. "I didn't want to accept the job. It was a suicide mission, even for a seasoned warrior of the Heavenly Host. And after what my brethren did—expelling me for helping humans—well, let's just say I didn't feel much allegiance to my Lord or my commandeer. But the people were another story."

He shifted his weight, trying to gauge her reaction. All he saw was more of that careful blankness.

"I was banished from Heaven over a millennium ago because of humans. People I loved were dying. I wanted to help them. It was forbidden, but I did it anyway. Unlike others of my kind who were cast out, I survived because I admired people—the way they could grow. Their adaptability. Humans have a great capacity for change. It's not always for the better, but wait long enough and society leaps forward. Watching that progress kept me sane. Raphael knew that deep down, I was invested in my life here. There was only so much time I'd be able to watch the horde abuse and terrorize the populace. So I accepted his bargain. Against the odds, I succeeded in killing Amducious."

"But the curse didn't end," she whispered.

"No." He stepped closer, grateful when she stayed in place, staring up at him. "Kara, I deserve your worst for lying about who I was. But when Dr. Brès disappeared, and then Didier left with you, I knew something had changed."

Kara raised her sleeve, dabbing her eyes. "I knew something was off with you. You were too nice, too helpful. I can't believe you're *him*—the one who takes the Firehorses out to the wasteland. The one who leaves them there to die..."

Her voice was a hoarse thread.

The weight of those deaths rose, choking him. "You have to understand," Ash began. "My duty was to save as many lives as I could. Every time a Firehorse rises, it threatens the lives of thousands. I did what I had to do, but that's all changed now."

Impulsively, he took her in his arms. "Kara, *you* have changed everything. The cursed are shielded somehow under your care. I don't know how you're doing it—or even if you know how the shielding works."

Desperate now, he wrapped his wings around her, lifting her chin with a gentle hand to make her meet his eyes. "I never wanted to hurt anyone. It goes against every fiber of my being. Angels protect the innocent. Having to hurt them, to abandon them—"

He broke off, blinking. His throat was too tight to continue.

"Some say the Firehorse are cursed because they're not innocent," Kara said in a mechanical voice. No trace of emotion betrayed what she was thinking. "The cursed hold a seed of evil deep inside. It's why they're punished."

Ash shook his head vehemently. "That's a lie the extremists spread. Believe me, I should know. Every Firehorse I've ever met has been good, blameless." His voice dropped to a whisper. "And that's not all. It's taken me years to come to this realization, but I believe Firehorses are humanity's most precious gifts. Or they would have been had they not been struck down."

Confusion flickered across her expression. "What do you mean by that?"

He beat his wings involuntary, so great was his excitement. "Haven't you noticed the cursed were significant in some way? Like Madeleine and Didier. They are both skilled and innovative in their vocation. I now believe the others were all gifted in some way. How exactly, I can't say for certain. All I know is they're important. More than any of us realized."

Unable to resist, he ran his finger down her soft cheek. "You have no reason to trust me. Because of me, you lost someone." He let his hand fall away. "I'm not asking for absolution. I have no defense because what I did is beyond forgiveness. That's why I'm here. It's my purpose—to do the unforgivable in His name. But you can help me find another one."

Kara's scowl was immediate. "How can *I* help the warden of Bastille? And why would I want to?"

How could she not see they needed each other?

"Because we want the same things—to save the Firehorses and end the curse."

The weight of her stare felt like the judgment of Heaven.

"And what about—" She broke off, waving her hand between them. "What about us? About the way you look at me?"

"I..." He looked down at his feet. "I apologize for making you uncomfortable. Being interested in someone is something new for me."

"*Really*?" The sarcasm alone could have flayed him open. "You fell from Heaven how long ago? A millennium, you said? And there's never been a woman in all that time?

"No, I told you. I was cast out for helping humans, not for bedding a woman."

"How about a man? Have you *bedded* one of them?" She held up her fingers, forming quotes around the word.

The corner of his mouth lifted, but he didn't dare smile. "No."

Kara stared at him. She closed the distance between them with slow deliberation. He waited for the slap he knew was coming, but when she reached him, she put her hands on the either side of his face.

The kiss that followed rivaled every wonder he'd ever seen in his long life. Her lips were softer than he imagined, the pressure sweet and hot at the same time. Every muscle in his body relaxed before blazing with sensual fire.

And then... she stabbed him.

Ash sucked in a breath and drew back, looking down in shock at the thin, bone-handled blade sticking out from between his ribs. He fell to his knees, blood pouring down his front, the T-shirt sticking to his six-pack.

He looked up to see Kara rearing over him with a large rock in her hand. "If you had been anyone else but the warden, I could have forgiven you..."

Her arm swung down, sending the rock crashing against his skull. Blackness claimed him.

13

Bloodied, his head throbbing, Ash stumbled into his Belleville apartment. The knife wound was closing, but the injury to his spirit was going to take much longer to heal.

"My lord!" Marcus sprang from the wooden table in the antechamber that doubled as his office. "Are you all right? What happened?"

Ash stripped off his bloody sweatshirt before throwing it on the floor. "I failed."

He'd been so close. Up until the moment Kara decided to play Judas—only she'd stabbed him in the front.

Except that wasn't fair. Ash had gone undercover, knowing he'd be perceived as the enemy. To the people who'd lost a loved one to the Firehorse curse, he was worse than the devil.

I would have stabbed me, too, in her place...

When he'd regained his senses at the edge of the desert, Kara had been gone. Closer investigation revealed two underground entrances to the catacombs within walking distance.

He'd decided not to go after her right away. He'd needed to regroup. And bathe. He was a bloody mess.

Marcus scrambled to pick up the sweater. He winced at the garment's condition. "This must have been painful. How did it happen? Did you find the people you were looking for?"

"I did."

"And?" Marcus gripped the soiled sweater in front of him like a talisman.

Ash waved at his fresh scar. "It did not go well."

Marcus waited for more. For a second, Ash considered elaborating. He would, eventually, but for now, he couldn't share. Truthfully, he was ashamed of himself.

How much of his failure had been due to his untoward behavior to Kara?

She kissed you. How unwanted could his attention have been?

You're forgetting about the part where she stabbed you. Ash should have paid closer attention to all those romances humans were so fond of writing before the Collision. Then maybe he would have seen that move coming. Not that it would have changed the outcome.

Ash couldn't lift a hand against Kara. Not only did he need her help with the curse, but...he might be falling in love with her. Stab wound notwithstanding.

Merde. Centuries upon centuries of watching humans fall in love hadn't taught him a damn thing. How many had he seen make complete asses of themselves in the process?

Apparently, that capacity for soul-wrenching humiliation wasn't strictly a human trait.

Ash turned to see Marcus still watching him expectantly, waiting for the dirty details. "Can you get a few buckets of hot water up here?"

His aide nodded, his lip drawing down, betraying his disappointment that Ash wasn't sharing. "Is there anything else I can get you? Food, wine?"

He nodded. "Something quick. And lay out my armor. I'll be

heading back out as soon as I'm finished." Ash traced the new scar and tsked. "I need to try again."

And again and again, if the knife wound was any indication.

That didn't matter. He had to find out what was going on with those people. He'd go back to the wasteland as often as it took to convince Kara to trust him.

Just keep at least two paces away from her while you do.

Marcus' face fell. "Oh, I see. I should mention a few things before you go. Perhaps I can debrief you while you eat?"

Ash murmured his assent. He washed while Marcus gathered his notes, and they broke their fast together on steel-cut oats mixed with yogurt, honey, and fresh fruit. He briefly described what had happened in the wasteland without going into too much detail about places and names.

Every bite reminded him of the survivors. *I wonder if Kara has enough to eat?* Not to mention Theo and everyone else. Ash even spared a thought for Sij—the hateful old crone. She probably did a jig when Kara told her about stabbing him and clobbering him over the head.

Marcus went over the progress on the canal project—only one unexpected disaster. A batch of concrete had been ruined by a drunken bricklayer. The man had been so inebriated that after he added the required amount of water, he'd repeated the process over and over again. A section of the Northwest canal had collapsed as a result. Along with a few other problems similar in scale, things had been blessedly uneventful in his absence.

"And the radio station?" Ash asked, taking a final bite.

His aide shook his head. "Nothing yet. Sorry."

Ash shrugged, giving Marcus a second look. There appeared to be a few new lines around the corners of his mouth. Something else was wrong.

"What's troubling you? Is it the council?" Ash guessed.

"Yes. I don't know what they're up to, but there's something off with them lately. "

Ash rubbed his forehead, irritated he had to deal with bureaucrats when something phenomenal was happening in the desert. "Well, it would have been too much to hope they would take the news of the elections well. What's going on?"

Marcus pursed his lips, looking at the ceiling as if searching for the right words. "Actually, they're *too* cooperative. Since you saw them last, all eligible to run have been preparing for the elections and actively campaigning. The senior leaders who can't run have handpicked successors to throw their support behind."

That was news. Ash sat back in his seat, scratching his head. Under other circumstances, he would have said the coming threat of elections had its intended effect—that Mazarin and the others had been scared straight. But he'd known too many politicians to believe that.

"You think they're trying to rig the elections?" Technically, picking a successor wasn't against any established rules for a democratic election, but making sure they won definitely was.

If I'd known I'd have to worry about a group of middle-aged overweight men stuffing a ballot box when I ran my sword through the demon king's heart...

It shouldn't have come as a surprise. His short-sightedness had a solution, however. It wasn't too late to put safeguards in place before the elections. After all, he hadn't chosen a date for them yet.

Ash wiped his mouth and threw his handkerchief aside. "We need to choose observers like the U.N. did back in the day."

"The what?"

"The United Nations," he clarified.

Marcus stared at him blankly, the gulf between them highlighted like never before. His aide had no concept of a nation beyond the borders of this one city. The idea of a nation made up of many such cities was alien enough. But the concept of *multiple* countries, each with its own identity and language acting independently or in collaboration, was too radical a concept for today's conversation.

"I'll explain what that was later," Ash said. "For now, let's focus on ensuring that every citizen of Bastille has the opportunity to vote, privately and free from intimidation. More importantly, we need to make sure those votes aren't tampered with."

Marcus' expression cleared. "The observers will do that by watching over the counts. So we must choose men who can be trusted to act for the people's good, not the politicians'."

"Exactly. But more than that, these safeguards should have a certain degree of redundancy." An image of a burning gold gaze rose in his mind. "We need women."

The comical confusion on his aide's face almost made Ash laugh aloud. "There *are* trustworthy women in every district, are there not?"

"Oh...you mean as observers. Of course there are!" Marcus laughed shortly, wiping his face to conceal his embarrassment.

Ash pretended not to notice his aide's chagrin. "Pick the *least* likely person—male or female—in each district to observe in secret. The politicians can't bribe them if they don't know their identity."

His aide puffed up. "None of the people I choose would dare to accept a bribe, I promise."

Ash loved Marcus' optimism. But he'd been a student of human nature for too long. "I'm sure they wouldn't, but how far would Mazarin or any of his ilk go to keep their fingers in the pot?"

Marcus deflated in his seat.

Ash clapped his aide on the back in response to the man's crestfallen expression. "I'm also going to need you to pick an appropriate venue in every district, one everyone has access to. If the old or infirm can't make it to the designated polling place, a representative of our election team will go to them to collect it."

"Yes, my lord. I take it you'll be in the wasteland while I make these arrangements?"

"On and off. I'll keep my trips shorter this time around." There was no point in longer ones now that his identity was exposed. "If anything big happens, I'll hear the klaxon, even deep underground. If there's an issue you think is significant enough to require my personal attention, send up our signal. I'll come straight back."

The bulk of his time would probably be spent trying to find the group again. No doubt they had decamped to parts unknown, but maybe he'd get lucky and find Kara with a team of scavengers. He needed an audience with the lady herself, although it wouldn't hurt to get some of the others on his side if he could.

That's a big if. Theo probably hated him. The thought made guilt flare in his breast. Angels just weren't cut out for subterfuge.

Marcus nodded, checking the notes in front of him before pressing the pad to his chest and rising. "I think that's all I needed. I wish you luck, my lord. I don't envy you your task."

"Really?" Ash smirked. "Stab wound aside, you're the one with the unpleasant job. You have to deal with the council."

Marcus' expression clouded, but then he grinned. "You may be right. I should ask for hazard pay." The moment of levity took years off his aide's face.

He should always look like that. Which made Ash wonder. How much had Marcus given up to devote his life to him, and to Bastille?

Ash put a hand on Marcus' shoulder. "All joking aside... when I said we needed women, the look on your face told me you hadn't thought about such a thing in years. You're not a priest, and I don't require your vow of chastity. Don't let the work we do get in the way of your other needs and desires."

Was that a blush? With Marcus' tan, it was difficult to tell. "I'm not—not intentionally," his aide said. "But the work we do is so important I never seem to have time for socializing. With my hours, it's hard to imagine finding a partner who would accept seeing me so little."

"The right woman would understand," Ash assured him. "And might I add, quite selfishly, that Bastille will need more people like you if it's going to flourish. Say the word, and I can delegate some of your tasks to another if it means having a Marcus Junior waiting in the wings."

Marcus dropped his gaze. "I'm...I'm not sure I would choose a *woman* if there was anyone."

"*Huh.*" Ash blinked stupidly before finding his tongue. "Believe it or not, the powers that be don't really care what your family looks like or who you build it with. That's just something the interpreters of His word have added to further their own agendas. As for children, it's what you teach them that counts. Whether they're your blood—that's not important."

Marcus huffed a laugh. "Yours isn't a popular opinion. There are some who say we brought the demons and the curse on ourselves because of the sin of pederasty."

Ash growled. "Yet another thing I've been lax about. I hate the idea of policing other people's interpretations of His word, but anyone spreading that kind of divisive rhetoric is going to answer to me."

"Shall I add that to your list?" Marcus teased.

Ash closed his eyes. In his mind's eyes, that list now stretched to the horizon. "Yes. Please do."

Once the city was free of the curse, he'd redouble his efforts in education. By the time he was done, Bastille would be a beacon of freedom and learning in the world.

Then reality set it. The minute this land was set to rights, he'd be recalled to Heaven. The city would have to manage without him, or any angel interference. That was His design.

It could still work out. Whoever ended the Firehorse curse was going to deserve more than one boon as reward. After his exile was officially ended, he could demand visitation rights from Raphael.

And as long as Kara is around, it will very likely be denied.

The Heavenly Host wasn't stupid. They'd wonder why he'd want visitation rights after going to such lengths to end his exile.

Yet another thing I'll have to deal with later. He hadn't broken the curse yet—and if he didn't get moving, he never would.

A few minutes later, he parted from Marcus. He struck out for the wasteland. This time, he was resplendent in angelic armor. He didn't plan on engaging in combat, but he wouldn't put it past Sij to greet him with an arrow to the heart.

His concern was unwarranted. The catacomb chambers previously occupied by the band were empty. They'd had plenty of time to clear out, but Ash was still surprised not to find a trail to follow.

Something about that was off. An angel's tracking abilities were second to none. He should have been able to pick up any trail, no matter how cold it had grown.

And yet, he wasn't picking up magic, at least not in the quantities he would have expected for a bonafide concealment spell.

He wandered the tunnels, stumbling on an ossuary damaged by an earthquake. Picking through the bones, he wondered if the remains of so many dead were messing with his senses. Even a demon would be affected by this many skeletons.

The dead had their own power.

Cutting his losses, Ash left the subterranean passages to search from the air. Hours went by as he scanned the edge of the wasteland for signs of the group, checking every steam vent for traces of cooking smoke. Aside from some unpleasant sulfur vents, there was nothing of note.

He was close to giving up for the day when he saw it. A splash of olive green interrupted the monotonous beige and rust of the wasteland soil.

Ash swooped down, his heart somewhere around his knees. It

was a tree—an unexpectedly lush one. And it was *growing* in the wasteland.

This part of Bastille, the region beyond the makeshift border wall, had been devastated by the original Collision spell that divided this continent from all the others. But Amducious had wanted to make sure no one could survive out here on their own.

If they'd had the means, his minions would have salted the earth. Since that hadn't been possible, the demon horde had despoiled the land with a series of earth-shifting spells so no food could ever grow here again.

To add insult to injury, this area became a toxic dumping ground for their waste. It was totally barren, devoid, and incapable of supporting life. Not even fungus or lichen could grow, and those resilient organisms could thrive in the most extreme environments.

The tree stood in complete contradiction to everything he knew. Ash knelt, touching the rough bark almost as if he needed to convince himself it was real.

"*Etz haChayim.*" It meant the *Tree of Life* in the old tongue.

The trunk was bent and slightly gnarled, but it arched in an elegant conformation, brushing the sky with a graceful sweep of limb and boughs. It was crowned with a carpet of thick leaves like the bonsai trees he cultivated before the Collision.

What was it doing here? How had it survived?

Still unclear about the meaning of it, he bowed his head and prayed. He may have been an angel, but it wasn't all that common to witness a miracle—especially when exiled on earth for a few millennia.

Crossing himself, he kissed his fingers and rose, tears stinging in his eyes.

Wait.

Ash stood slowly, pivoting on his heel. He knew where he was.

The line of the horizon and the boulders just to the left of the ravine were unchanged. The tips of his wings brushed the rusty soil at his feet as he spun in a slow circle, his throat tightening.

Years of seeing it again in his nightmares had imprinted this hellish spot in his mind. He was back where he'd committed his greatest sin. This was the exact spot where he'd abandoned the Delavordo girl all those years ago.

14

What was that old definition of madness? Doing the same thing over and over again and expecting a different outcome?

Ash had traversed the same twenty or so square miles repeatedly since finding what he now referred to as the *Arbor Vitae*.

The tree was not the only plant growing in the vicinity. He'd found a stunted little cactus with a deep red fruit crown over its spiky and thick fleshy lobes. There was also something that resembled mesquite beans. They were growing in a shadowed crevice near a trickle of water running between two stones halfway down the slope.

The plants resembled flora native to France, but they'd evolved from their pre-Collision form into a useful edible. They had somehow adapted to grow in the barren environment of the wasteland.

But there was no explanation for this dramatic change.

Lord in Heaven, what does it mean? He cast his gaze upward, willing his maker to send him some guidance—a sign, anything. But there was nothing.

He kicked a rock. *Why is there never a burning bush when you need one?*

Ash was so engrossed in his search for clues that he almost missed Marcus' signal.

It was a system they had rigged up years ago. As the warden of Bastille, Ash was required to traverse the length of the city and the fields they'd cultivated to the west, just inside the border walls. A klaxon was well and good for a disaster, but there were other non-life-threatening emergencies requiring his attention.

The signal itself was simple. Bastille had many foundries. One of the oldest and least used was in the city center. It was still active enough to have chimneys billowing smoke every day, but there was one that was never lit for metalwork. It was a small one that belonged to an unused office, one that, for reasons unknown to anyone but Marcus and himself, was well-stocked with kindling. Only the fuel they burned wasn't the standard used across the city. This was weed gathered specifically for its distinctive smoke. It burned white with a blue tinge. The color wasn't dramatically different, not enough for anyone unaware of the difference to take note.

Ash inhaled hard and took flight. He hadn't been making any progress anyway.

He met Marcus on the roof of the foundry. His aide had been pacing a track in the worn shingled roof.

"What's wrong?" Ash asked. The lines on his aide's face were deeper than normal.

"We have a situation. A very serious one. Only, I can't prove it —or I've lost my mind." Marcus rubbed his face with his hands. "I really don't know anymore."

Okay, Ash was definitely overworking the poor man. "I trust your instincts," he said. "Tell me what you do know."

Marcus took a deep breath and cleared his throat. "I've been preparing for the elections. I put together teams of observers, both the public and covert ones, and began to search for places where everyone can vote."

He stopped, waiting for his acknowledgment. Ash waved him on, trying not to betray his impatience.

"I was looking at a few buildings in the ninth arrondissement."

Hmm. "Tulloch's old district." A factotum had taken over council duties there temporarily, until the elections, but the man was also a baker so oversight was minimal.

"Yes. One location I scouted was a former community center. I thought it would be a good place because it's central, but the air was unhealthy—too much mold. The second possibility was an abandoned *lycée*, a former high school. Though it was not as convenient, the building was in better shape. It even had a working water pump. I decided on the school and sent a few people to clean the old gymnasium, but over half asked to be reassigned. They kept hearing strange noises from under the floorboards. Rumors of it being haunted began to spread. When I investigated further, I found this was a widespread rumor and not a new one at that."

"The citizens of Bastille are a superstitious lot." It was an unfortunate side-effect to having a populace who knew angels and demons existed.

True ghosts were rare. The vast majority of human spirits were eager to leave this plane for Heaven. Those souls headed in the other direction were swiftly claimed by reaper demons. The latter were responsible for most of the mischief associated with hauntings.

There was a certain class of sub-demon, ones too low to have a body, that amused themselves by scaring the piss out of anyone who came across them. Most were too weak to do real damage, but the highly intelligent ones could trick people into hurting themselves.

Marcus, aware of the truth of this, nodded emphatically. "Yes, well, I know how important your negotiations in the wasteland are, so I went to take a quick look on my own. I planned on asking you to come and bless the building if I confirmed a haunting."

Comfortable with the knowledge Marcus could handle himself, Ash nodded in appreciation. "And?"

Marcus tapped the table. "Apparently, this school had a basement. The front end was full of debris and old unused furniture, but the back..."

He looked at Ash and squeezed his eyes shut hard. "It was dark, and there were voices. Human voices—not some weak lower demon whispering obscenities. It was people. But I couldn't get to them. There was a heavy iron door in between."

"You couldn't pick the lock?" Ash had found that such a useful skill, he'd made sure the men under his command could open a basic padlock.

Marcus shook his head. "It was too complicated to open without proper tools. But the noise I made attracted their attention—at least, I think they could hear me."

"Who was it?"

His aide threw up his hands. "I don't know. My knocking got a faint response. But I could have sworn one of the voices was calling for help." He passed a hand through his hair roughly. "I hurried back here for my tools. But when I returned to the school, the door was open. The room behind it was small and empty." He broke off, his brows drawing together. "And that is confusing. If a person had been speaking, they would have been behind that door as close to me as you are now. I would have heard them clearly."

"It could be a lower demon after all," Ash suggested. Though most were stupid, there were always exceptions. A crafty one could have turned Marcus around.

"I would have thought so, except for one thing. The door," he said. "It was old, but the lock was new—as if were added recently."

ASH KNELT to examine the lock. It was just as Marcus said. It was one of the sturdiest made in town, the kind used to protect their grain silos and the livestock barns in the Pigalle area. It was also new, manufactured within the last year or two.

There was also something Marcus hadn't noticed about the door. The hinges looked out of place. The edges didn't match the grooves in the doorjamb, as if the whole thing had been moved from another location. They had also been oiled.

A careful examination of the room beyond with his excellent night vision revealed a hidden access panel in a dark corner. Ash squeezed through it to find himself in a rough sub-basement room.

Great. Back in the catacombs, was his first thought.

But he was wrong. The sub-basement didn't lead to the warren beneath the city. Instead, it dead-ended in a midsized room down a short hallway.

One glance was enough to kindle a cold anger in his gut. Not wanting to believe what he was seeing, he knelt, picking up one end of a pair of manacles. It was attached to the wall with a crudely hammered spike.

There were two other pairs.

Someone had turned this room into a prison. And judging from the fresh excrement in the corner, it had been recently occupied.

ASH TORE through the city like a man demented. He'd never experienced rage like this. Not even in battle, when his blood lust had taken over, enabling him to mow down large swaths of the demon horde.

No, this was different. This was *people*. They may not have been the same ones he'd fallen to protect, but since taking up Raphael's cause, he'd devoted everything to the people of Bastille. He'd *bled* for them. And now, they had betrayed him. Someone had been keeping captives without his knowledge or consent.

It's not all of them, he reminded himself. That prison had been in a secret basement room for a reason.

His immediate thought had been to raze the council's chamber at the Petit Palais down to the ground. But he didn't know if one or more of the council members were behind this.

Despite his best efforts, violence was still a part of Bastille. When people were hungry and supplies were scarce, fights inevitably broke out. Theft and other crimes still plagued the city, particularly in the poorest arrondissements. They did keep a small handful of prisoners, but never for very long.

Murders were rare, and the perpetrators were executed as soon as he had proof of their crimes. It was the only capital punishment in the city, one he hadn't carried out in years.

I may have to change that. Keeping prisoners without his knowledge or consent was the deepest betrayal. But first, he needed proof. He had to know if there were other prisoners.

Ash began to hunt in earnest, tearing in and out of abandoned buildings. He targeted the out-of-the-way places people could move in and out of without being seen.

In a city with thousands of abandoned and derelict buildings, the possibilities for hidden prisons were legion. Deductive reasoning might have saved a few hours of search, but self-righteous anger fueled his wings. It took hours for his brute-force technique to yield results.

The captives were being held in a small attic room at the edge of the Bercy neighborhood close to where the Bois de Vincennes used to be. There were two of them, a young man and much older woman, grey-haired and painfully thin.

The young man was terrified to see him. He crawled away,

pressing close to the wall and gibbering nonsensically when Ash entered the room. The frail old woman was too weak to react.

He went to the female first, breaking the thin shackle that fixed her to the wall. She blinked cloudy opalescent eyes at him. Cataracts must have obscured most of her vision, but she still recognized him. A deep shudder racked her skeletal frame.

"Please. Have mercy," she begged.

"I'm taking you out of here," he said, careful to keep his voice low and even despite the rage burning in his chest.

How dare anyone do this to one of his charges?

He lifted the crone. She was too light, as if her bones were filled with pockets of air, like a bird. If she had been given food, it was barely enough to keep her alive.

"Who did this to you?" he asked.

Did they think the wrath of Heaven was a joke? Someone was going to answer for this.

The rheumy eyes clouded further, with confusion. "*You did.*"

15

A sh was back on his Belleville balcony, brooding as he fixed his gaze in the direction of the Petit Palais. He fingered the broken manacle Marcus had just handed to him before crushing it to dust. It fell to the floor in a little river of gunmetal grey powder.

"How many more?" He turned around, helmet in hand.

Marcus, who'd been standing behind him, waiting, eyed the dust on the floor a touch nervously.

"Seven, including the two you found. We found the rest in Bel-Air, in a blind old man's basement. He rented it out in exchange for food to a woman calling herself Mary. Other than her voice, which was new to him, he has no way of identifying her. He never bothered to ask for a family name."

Ash banged the helmet on the balcony ledge. "It wouldn't have been the real one, anyway. They had covered their tracks well," he said, turning to face his aide. "And it's what we thought?"

"Yes, they are all related to a victim of the curse. The woman and young man you found are both maternal relatives to the same Firehorse—Sarafina Ducatte, the one who took down the Pantheon in the Latin Quarter."

Ash nodded, remembering. "That was one I lost to the mob."

Marcus shuffled on his feet. "We can't be certain of that. Her body could have been crushed by the pillar. The entire neighborhood was in shambles after the earthquake. It could have been the curse itself."

Ash appreciated Marcus' ability to give his fellow man the benefit the doubt, but it was more likely the pillar had been pushed on the girl. Now her relatives were being hounded and imprisoned by their fellow man.

In my name. His hands formed fists.

The fiery vengeance of the Old Testament was too distant a memory. The people of Bastille had forgotten what he was. They needed a refresher. But he didn't know who to give it to.

"None of the prisoners saw anything useful?"

Marcus threw himself down in a chair, resentment and frustration driving him to break his self-imposed formality. "All the assailants wore masks, and none of the victims could identify them by their voice. Most of them were taken from their beds. They were confused and disoriented during the kidnapping. We can't be sure the council was involved."

He was right of course. There wasn't a tie to them directly, but Ash was done playing the fool. He turned, putting on his helmet and spreading his wings.

"What are you going to do?" Marcus asked, his voice uncertain.

Ash looked back at him. "What I should have done a long time ago."

He shot through the air, beating his wings with the force of all his anger. The fading sunlight bounced off the shining metal of his armor. He didn't usually move this fast. Below him, people stopped in the streets and pointed. He must have looked like a comet streaking through the sky.

The long windows on the west wing of the Petit Palais had been one of the few pre-Collision glazing works to survive the dedicated destruction of the demon horde. The glass had survived hundreds of years intact, a testament to the glaziers of the early twentieth century. Their hard work stood—right up until the point Ash burst through the central window of the council chamber in a blaze of fiery sunlight.

The frescoes on the arched ceiling above them buzzed and vibrated, raining dust on the remains of the meal littering the long table. He noted the food was simpler than the decadence of days past, but it was too little too late.

Reaching underneath, he flipped the table, hurling it with such force it shattered against the marble and plaster walls in an explosion of splintered wood.

The council members present, eight in all including Mazarin and Devos, scattered, running for the exit as fast as their human feet would carry them.

It wasn't fast enough.

He flashed in front of them, grabbing the one closest—Ragot —by the neck.

"You have broken faith with me," he bit out, shaking the pudgy man like a rag doll. "All of you."

"My lord, we've done everything you asked," Ragot sputtered. "The elections—"

"The elections are off."

As usual, it was Mazarin who recovered first. "Why, my lord? I don't understand what possible reason you have to remove us with such little civil—abruptness," he said, catching himself before making the grievous error of outright insolence.

"All we've ever done is serve our people," he added, infusing just the right touch of injured pride to his unctuous protest.

"You count false imprisonment among your accomplishments?" he snarled, dropping the greasy Ragot in a heap on the floor. "Seven innocent citizens locked away and left to rot *in my name.*"

Dust rained down as the ceiling vibrated with the force of his bellow.

Ragot scrambled away, rushing behind the knot of others rooted to the floor a few yards in front of him, cowering to hide from his sight.

"But, my lord, we have nothing to do with those prisons! We just learned of them ourselves when you did," Klein said. "It's a tragedy and misguided, but it's not fair to hold *us* responsible when we weren't even away it was going on. Clearly, some of our people have gone rogue."

He drew himself up to his full height. "Fear of the Firehorse is too deeply ingrained. It permeates all levels of our society and is why the mob murders those unfortunate enough to be tainted by the curse. Some could argue this is more humane—not that I ever would. Imprisonment of innocents can never be justified. But I do understand why some of our citizens have acted on this fear, particularly when you've been absent for such lengthy periods."

He broke off, glancing at Mazarin, who was frantically signaling him to stop. His crafty black eyes turned back to him, waiting to see if he would swallow their excuses.

Not this time.

Ash advanced on them. "How dare you presume to lecture me on the Firehorse? Me—the one who freed you from demon rule, who is doing everything to break the curse."

"So you still believe there's a way to undo it?" Jolly, the most junior member of the council, asked, hope lighting his eyes.

"I do."

"And the answer is in the wasteland?" Mazarin questioned, genuine curiosity in his eyes. "The whole city has seen you flying away, leaving to roam the outskirts. We're curious. What could be so important when there's an entire city beckoning for your aid?"

Putain. He knew his movements weren't secret, but Ash would be damned if he was about to share his motivations.

"What I do and where I do it is not for you to question, *mortal*," he snapped, raising his voice an octave. The broken glass on the floor reverberated. He'd had enough of being dragged into pointless discussions, enough of politicians entirely.

"Even if the kidnappings can't be tied to you, it is still *your* failure. This crime was carried out in your arrondissements. As their representative, you were responsible for the lives of all your followers. By allowing these people to be scapegoated, you abdicated that responsibility. Now pick up this mess and go home. You won't be coming back."

The more intelligent council members began to scramble to the table's wreckage. Even Mazarin shuffled over, leaning to pick up a token amount of debris.

When he felt he was a safe distance away, he called out to Ash. "My lord, what about the elections?"

Furious, Ash closed the distance between them with a snap of his wings. He stopped so suddenly Mazarin was startled into falling on his well-padded arse.

"*I said they were off,*" he said, his voice resonating with a trace of angelic resonance. "None of you are eligible to serve. Nor are your acolytes. *I* will appoint the next representatives for each arrondissement." His wings beat the air, sending it into their faces with the force of a slap.

He hovered, clearing the floor by several feet. His furious gaze passed over them with a blistering sweep. "Believe me, God would not be so forgiving. You get to keep your lives."

Too furious to trust himself not to act with violence, he flew out the hole in the window, shooting high into the sky. The city dwindled in the distance, but he kept going, breaking past layers of soiled air until he was flying a few kilometers under the ionosphere.

There was almost no air here, not enough for a human to survive on, but Ash felt cleaner here than any space down below.

If only he could keep flying straight up to Heaven. But the gates were not only barred, they couldn't even be seen. If he kept going, the curse would bat him back down to earth like a gnat. He knew that because he'd tried before.

It had been right after he'd abandoned the child in the wasteland. Broken and defeated, he'd tried to go home, only to be hurled down into the desert a second time.

Things are different now. The tree was proof. *Kara* was proof. He needed to continue his investigation in the wasteland and to talk to her about what he'd found.

Now was not the time to lose faith. His sentence on earth could be over soon.

It wasn't the pep talk to end all pep talks, but it calmed Ash enough to accept he had to return...in a minute.

An hour later, a resigned Ash folded his wings, allowing himself to drop down far enough to see the tops of Bastille's highest buildings. A few strokes later and he was over Belleville. The crowd surrounding his apartment building came into view.

I should have expected this. The council wouldn't let power slip from their greasy fingers without a fight. They must have run home to their districts, stoking the fires of discontent with stories of his wrath.

Below him, the rabble had spotted his wings. Fingers pointed. The crowd of almost four hundred rumbled and roared, giving voice to their discontent.

That this many people were so easily manipulated into open defiance against him stung his pride. He had to remind himself he had other things to worry about.

Think of the tree. His ill-disciplined mind threw up an image of Kara instead.

He landed on the high ledge of his balcony three stories

above them. Ash spread his wings before jumping down, landing on the steps of his building with a thump.

"I know why you are here. I disbanded the council for their failure to protect you. You should be thanking me, not laying siege to my home like whining children."

A few people in the crowd quailed appropriately, but the mob had been waiting long enough to feel its power. It snarled and rumbled in response. "The council are our people! They protect us," someone yelled.

Ash snapped his wings. "*No*, I protect you. They've been in power too long, and have grown corrupt. It's time for a change."

That was met with silence until a woman found her voice.

"The council *is* our people, our leaders," she called out. "Who will represent us now? Who will speak for us?"

What nonsensical trash was this? "*I* am your leader. I speak for you."

"No, you speak *to* us. It's not the same. My counselor said he had nothing to do with the prison! Mazarin hasn't failed me."

Of course, she didn't believe that. Mazarin's people were the most brainwashed. He could steal food from their very children's mouths, and they would thank him for it.

"Then why is he so fat while you are so thin?"

There was another silence.

"If the council had been doing their job, I wouldn't be seeing so many gaunt faces here today. Now, tell me," he snapped. "Who delivered you from Amducious' grasp? Was it Mazarin? Or was it me?"

His hot glare passed over their faces when they didn't answer. "Who helped you rebuild your city and plant your crops?" He lifted his arms. "What hands rebuild your fallen buildings—mine or Mazarin's?"

"But the curse hasn't ended!" a man wailed. "And you keep leaving the city instead of waiting here for it strike again. What will happen when the next Firehorse rises and you're not here?

We can't deal with it on our own—you declared it a capital crime to kill a cursed person!"

"I am never so far I can't return to deal with one," Ash pointed out. "And know that each of my absences will be brief but necessary—my goal is to end the curse once and for all. Murdering its victims won't do it, and neither will killing or imprisoning their innocent relatives."

"But they aren't innocent!"

"Their sins condemn us all," another cried out. "It's in their blood. We have to lock them up so we can watch them for signs of the curse."

A rock flew up from the left, moving with enough speed and force to kill a human. Ash reached out, snatching the offending stone in a blink. Closing his fist over it, he crushed it, the fragments falling and rolling down the steps.

Reaching deep into his soul, he spoke as one of the Host, using the angelic resonance at full force—a first in his long years on earth.

"Now hear this! I am the warden of Bastille," he shouted, making the ground tremble under their feet.

All around him, men and woman clapped their hands over their ears, but he showed no mercy. He needed every man, woman, and child in Bastille to hear his decree.

"I am your leader. I hold your lives in trust in the name of God himself. And when I say the Firehorse must be left for me to deal with, you *will* obey. Their friends and relatives are equally off limits. *Now go home!*"

Screaming in terror, blood running from their ears, the crowd surrounding his building splintered as the people ran away.

16

I t was too bad therapy had died out with the Collision, because Ash could really use someone to talk to.

He was back in his Belleville rooms, trying to come up with a new system of government to replace the ruling council. He'd hoped Marcus would have been full of suggestions, but things had drastically changed between him and his aide.

Everyone in the city had heard Ash's true voice a few days ago. It had been necessary. The people couldn't continue to disrespect him the way they had been. He'd allowed the council too much rope to hang him with.

But he hadn't considered the consequences. The image of hundreds of people running in terror from him kept replaying in his head on a loop.

"Is gullibility a sin?" he wondered aloud.

Next to him, Marcus jumped, making the hole in Ash's stomach yawn into a bottomless pit.

Ash was used to being a helpmate, a leader, and a guide. Now the fear in his aide's eyes was painful to see. His only friend had been brutally reminded that his boss wasn't a man, but a disciple of Heaven.

I needed the reminder, too, he thought, stifling the urge comfort Marcus.

"I need the daily reports from the southeast foundries. Have they arrived?"

Marcus scrambled to his feet. "I'll go see, my lord."

Hiding the reports under a stack of papers, Ash watched him go with a heavy heart.

It was temporary. Eventually, Marcus would grow comfortable with him again. He'd seen Ash in battle, cutting down demons and their acolytes with a burning sword, for pity's sake.

That memory had faded. This one would too as long as they continued to work together.

As for the population at large, they didn't have to like him. They just had to accept he was in charge. No politician was going to build an empire on their backs on his watch. This would be a communal effort. He just hadn't expected it to be such a personally disheartening one.

Ash had given up his grace, becoming an exile to help people. It was a painful truth he was facing. Some of them weren't worth it.

Corrupt politicians are men, too. Avarice, greed, selfishness. Those were an integral part of the people he sought to protect. His father had designed them that way. The gift of free will was both a blessing and a curse.

It didn't help that deprivation made people desperate. Desperation was the seed of many a sin.

And I laid the groundwork for the situation I'm dealing with now, he admitted to himself. After living hidden among them for so long, Ash didn't just think like a human, he acted like one, too.

From the start, he'd negotiated and compromised when he should have bellowed his declarations from the rooftops without a go-between. Instead, his abhorrence of dictatorships had led him to found the council.

Now that he'd disbanded them, he was forced to do the work of ten men. Over the past few days, he'd been all over the city. Ash had taken charge of the council's chief task, food distribution. Food and clean water were their most precious resource.

At Marcus' prompting, Ash examined the chain at every step, assessing it for graft. He was working on reorganizing it to ensure the resources went where they were needed most.

There was an ulterior motive to his actions. Ash wanted to stay visible in the aftermath of using his true voice. Keeping a distance from the people—even if they were frightened— wouldn't help his cause now. He wasn't about to give Mazarin and the others enough wiggle room to hammer at the wedge between him and the rest of the populace.

But Ash couldn't keep running the whole distribution system indefinitely. His labor was needed in the reconstruction efforts. And sooner or later, the curse would reassert itself. He'd have to drop everything to go and attend to whatever emergency it caused.

Maybe there can be a regular rotation of supervisors in each district? They could be chosen at random for the task. But first, he would need to make the network foolproof.

Engrossed, Ash leaned forward at his desk, blowing a lock of hair out of his eyes. He took out a sheet of paper, beginning to lay out plans for a better distribution system.

Scratching out the few lines he'd jotted down, he crumpled the paper and tossed it across the room in the direction of his waste bin.

It hit Kara in the chin. She caught it neatly on the rebound.

Startled, Ash stared, his tongue trapped somewhere in the back of his mouth.

Kara's dark hair was tied back in a ponytail. She was wearing a simple sleeveless top and dark pants with a lot of pockets.

"How did you get in here without my noticing?"

One fine eyebrow lifted in question. "Honestly, I have no idea. I wasn't quiet coming up the steps. You might consider having a guard posted."

He shrugged. "I don't need one." At least, he hadn't before.

The knife Kara always carried slid out of her sleeve into the palm of her hand. "Are you sure about that?"

As threats went, it was effective. But Ash wasn't scared. There was a glint in her eye he didn't recognize. Could she be teasing him? Who teased an angel?

She does.

Two could play that game. "Does this mean I get another kiss to distract me? Because in that case, I might be tempted to let you try."

Kara flushed, her lips twitching as she sheathed her blade in a narrow pocket at her hip. She cleared her throat and unfolded the ball of paper, her eyes moving from right to left a few times as she scanned the lines.

"You can read," he realized.

Kara scowled. "As can you."

"Sorry," he said lamely. "Not everyone can."

He'd done his best to keep the schools open, but not everyone was able to take advantage of them. Too many children gave it up to work and provide for their families.

Kara nodded, indicating the paper in her hand. "Apparently, you can write, too, in our language. I didn't think an angel would bother."

"An angel can read and write in any language, but it's true. Most don't bother. They find it beneath them. But I like human languages. They're inventive."

Curiosity seeming to get the better of her, Kara leaned on the wall a few yards away from his desk. She folded her arms. "How so?"

Ash leaned back. "My native tongue is simple and quite bare. You can describe so many more things with English or French, or any of the others. Each language has its own nuance and subtlety. Most of my brothers and sisters never take the time to appreciate that."

Kara sniffed. "That doesn't surprise me. Angels are known for their arrogance. Funny how God doesn't come down so hard on you for the sin of pride," she said, gesturing to the balcony behind him with a languid wave.

"This blight on the city isn't an act of God," he reminded her. "It was a very enterprising demon, with the help of a witch."

Kara bristled. "The witch didn't *help* him," she spat. "Not willingly. She was possessed by the demon. Then *he* cast the curse. Or have you heard differently?"

"I haven't," he conceded with a nod, wondering why she was so passionate about a witch who died hundreds of years ago. "I take it you have business in Bastille? I didn't think you ever left the wasteland or the catacombs."

If she was the child of a Firehorse, walking openly in the city was risky. She might be recognized.

True, there were many comely girls in Bastille, but Kara's features were distinctive. Strength and delicacy were blended seamlessly in her face and form. People would remember her. They wouldn't be able to help themselves.

Kara stiffened. "I heard your proclamation— or rather, I felt it. We all did. You caused a cave-in shouting like that."

Ash cursed.

She held up a hand. "Relax. No one was hurt. We're prepared for minor tremors. But it was a good thing you kept it short or it might have been a lot worse."

"My apologies," he mumbled.

She shrugged. "Your shouting served its purpose. There's no more council leaching off the fat of the land anymore, right?"

"Fat is a bit of a stretch. Bastille is more akin to a starved goat."

Kara coughed suddenly, as if choking back unwilling laughter. "I'm here for the prisoners," she said after recovering. "I'm here to take them off your hands."

"The *prisoners*?" He leaned forward in his seat with a frown.

"Yes. We rescue those the curse has struck down," she said as if stating the obvious.

"Because you've found a way to circumvent the spell..." he finished.

At first, it appeared she wouldn't answer, but after a pause, she gave him a curt nod.

Ash released a breath he hadn't been aware of holding. Hope blazed in his breast. He had to actively restrain himself from rushing to her and sweeping her up in a jig.

Focus. This was just the beginning. He still had to convince her to tell him how she did it, but he needed to talk her out of this crazy plan.

"I understand taking a Firehorse. However, the prisoners are free of the curse's taint. They aren't immediate family to any of your people, are they?"

The only close blood ties they'd been aware of had been to deceased Firehorses of years long past.

"It doesn't matter," she countered. "If someone has pointed the finger at them, they should come with us. It isn't safe for them here."

"But it's mere superstition that the curse runs in families," he said, standing up.

Kara moved back instinctively. He checked his progress, moving to mirror her earlier easy pose by leaning against the front of his desk.

"Your resources in the wasteland are stretched thin." He should know. Two of her men had attacked him for a bag of food. "There's no need to add to your burden. I've put a stop to the problem."

Kara put her hands on her hips. "I realize angels are supposed to be omniscient and all-powerful up in Heaven, but your magic fairy dust doesn't work for jack shit down here. Despite your terrific shouting match with the mob, you can't count on the people to do the right thing. Next time, they won't imprison the suspects. They'll just kill them. It's the way people are."

"No, it's not," he protested, feeling the irony bite deep. *She's stealing all my lines.* "And angels are not God. They do not see or know all."

He didn't bother to add that Heaven's view was obscured, or that the angel with answers—Raphael—had been steadfastly ignoring him for the last few decades.

"If another Firehorse rises, I'll be there, knocking at your door, or tunnel entrance," he promised when she continued to stonewall him. "But adding seven extra mouths to feed—none of whom show symptoms of falling prey to the curse—is crazy, even for your resourcefulness."

She wasn't swayed. "Why don't we let the prisoners decide how they feel about staying in the city?"

Ash narrowed his eyes. "Tell me, what will Sij have to say about adding seven more people to the fold?"

Kara smirked. "She'll grouse about extra foraging duties, but as long as you're not one of them, she'll accept them easily enough."

He huffed. That was probably true. Sij was not his biggest fan. But Kara hadn't been either. Yet, here she was, offering to help him when it should have been the other way around.

Ash opened his mouth. He was about to promise to ask the rescued prisoners what they wanted when she clapped her hands over her ears. The emergency klaxon on the roof was vibrating the entire apartment.

"Come with me," he shouted to Kara over the din. He held out his hand and waited as she stared at him openmouthed, her hands still over her ears.

"*Hurry*," he pressed.

Snapping out of it, Kara closed the distance between them at a run, taking his hand a split second before he took flight.

17

Ash pleaded with Kara to stay out of the burning building, but short of tying her to a tree, there had been no way to prevent her from following him.

"At least stay behind me!" he shouted, pulling her back before she ran around him in the foyer of the manor house.

The space had been renovated last year to function as a temporary textile mill. It was supposed to be a temporary situation after the original building had developed an aggressive case of black mold. They'd been forced to shutter the structure. He was waiting for the wet season to burn it down himself. He didn't trust anyone else to flaunt the city's fire laws, metaphorically spitting in the curse's face.

Instead, flames were consuming the mill's provisional home.

"Damn it, I told them to move to new quarters last month," he growled, following the smoke to the back chambers. That was where the seamstresses worked their looms and pedal-powered sewing machines.

He dragged Kara along with him, not trusting her to stay with him of her own accord. Pausing at the bedroom that had been turned into the manager's office, he ran in to yank down the fine muslin curtain that had been hung on the windows.

"Here, tie this around your mouth," he ordered Kara before doing it himself. "Is that all right?"

She nodded, wisely not wasting air to talk before slipping a pair of tinted goggles from her pocket. They were an ancient pair meant for swimming. It was a brilliant way to keep her eyes from tearing, but he didn't have time to stop and praise her ingenuity —not with the roof threatening to fall around them.

"Come." He tugged them down the hall, throwing doors open to look for workers overcome with smoke.

Halfway down, they came upon a woman, presumably one of the seamstresses. She had collapsed next to a window that appeared painted shut. Using two fingers, he dug into the wood, crumpling it to give himself a place to grip. The next second, the sash was slapping against the upper part of the sill.

Ash turned to find Kara propping the woman up. He reached out to help, but she took hold of the seamstress and began heaving her out the window.

"What are you doing?" he shouted in normal human tones.

"Relax, flyboy. It's the first floor," she said before giving the woman one last shove out the window.

Someone will find her, he told himself, and he turned to follow Kara as she ran on to the next room. This one was locked.

He pushed Kara behind him, and lifted his foot to kick the door open. When it didn't budge, he realized something had fallen against it.

"What are you waiting for?" Kara asked over the roar of the flames.

"It's blocked," he answered.

"So kick *harder*."

"But what if it's a beam from the floor above or the roof?" He squinted at the ceiling, trying to discern from the sound of the fire whether the roof had come down beyond the door.

"Then we should go out the window and come around," Kara said.

"Wait," he told her, tugging her into the next room.

He touched the wall, feeling for hotspots.

"What are you doing? We need to get outside."

Ash reared back, punching the wall with a hard strike. Plaster and brick collapsed behind his fist.

"Or bust through like an elephant," Kara muttered under her breath. He ignored her, continuing to hit the wall until there was a hole big enough to fit through.

The scene on the other side was a veritable inferno. It looked like Hell itself.

The ceiling above had collapsed. Part of the second floor had landed inside, transforming it into a maze of burning desks and ceiling joists with smaller debris interspersed between like flaming mileposts.

"You have to stay here," Ash snapped, his innate authoritarianism making him curt. "I'll pass along anybody I pull out. You'll have to push them out that window," he said, pointing behind her. "Call out first. The fire brigade should be here by now. They'll help you evacuate anyone I find."

He didn't waste more time. Rushing into the flames, he dug around, moving burning timbers and smoldering desks to look for bodies. He found two. Not stopping to check if they were still breathing, he tucked one under each arm before taking a running leap back through the hole in the wall.

Kara took each burden from his arms, both women. He went back and kept looking, finding a finely dressed man crushed and impaled by a wooden ceiling support.

The man had been killed instantly. Turning away, Ash focused on searching for the living, pulling out three more women before Kara shouted that there should only be one more.

"The first lady you pulled out recovered consciousness! She

says the manager and the youngest apprentice are the only ones left."

"Manager's dead," he yelled back through the opening.

"Then there's just one, a girl named Clara." He could barely hear her reply above the roar of the flames. "She was near the shredders!"

"The what?" What was a shredder doing in a textile mill?

"They were in the second story. *Get your feathered ass up there.*"

Ash scowled and waved to the window. "I'll go look. You get out now. And I mean *now*, Kara. If she's here, I'll get her out."

He turned around, taking a running leap for the hole gaping in the ceiling.

The smoke was thicker on the second floor. His eyes watered so badly he was forced to shift the rhythm of his wings to drive the haze and fumes from his face. Trying not to breathe too deeply, he stayed aloft to keep from destabilizing the floor any further.

"Clara," he called.

He didn't really expect an answer, but it wasn't a large house. If the girl was still alive, she might respond. Pumping his wings, he flew forward, catching a glimpse of faded blue linen in the corner.

A girl no older than fourteen was lying prone near the window. She resembled a rag doll tossed in the corner. Lying all around her were dozens of cylinders studded with sharp, glittering blades.

What the hell? Flying over, he assessed the damage. To his relief, he didn't see any blood. Whatever had happened here, she hadn't been cut to ribbons. Now he just needed to make sure she stayed that way.

Crap. Ash continued to beat his wings. Gingerly pushing a cylinder aside, he carefully lifted another off the girl's booted leg. He plucked her out without slicing off any limbs.

A sickening crack sounded overhead. Reacting on instinct, he tossed his wings higher, forming a canopy over them in case the ceiling came down on top of them both.

He braced himself to be crushed, but the ceiling above him stayed intact. Ash took a tentative peek out.

Fallen supports blocked the only exit. *Damn it.* He could force his way through, but the girl in his arms might be seriously injured in the process. He looked down, reassured to see her chest moving.

That wouldn't be the case for long if he didn't get them out of here. Scanning the floor beneath him, he picked a likely spot and jumped. Using the precarious support as a springboard, he leaped into the air with his burden tucked in his arms. He pushed the girl's face against his chest and spread his wings to shield them as he burst through the damaged roof of the manor house.

Wood splintered, exploding outward with the force of the impact.

Fresh air rushed into the fiery attic behind him. The influx of oxygen fed the beast, stoking the flames until they roared.

Smoke obscured his vision, so he beat it away with his wings. When he could see again, he was over the dirt track that used to be the lawn around the house. It was covered with people. The fire brigade was there, as was Marcus and a few of his lieutenants.

Smoke-inhalation victims stretched out on the lawn. Some were moving. A few weren't.

"Get some nurses down here," he barked at the first man he saw.

"Is that little Clara?" the man asked, holding out his arms before suddenly drawing back.

Ash could see it happening—the transmutation from sympathy and concern to doubt and suspicion. It was always this way now. Everyone was a suspect.

He tucked the unconscious girl deeper into his embrace, like keeping her out of sight would shield her from getting branded as a Firehorse. "Never mind. Go get my aide Marcus and bring him to me."

He turned his back, walking around the flaming wreckage, saluting the fire brigade along the way. The team was setting up their manual crank and pump tank, one of four in the city.

"The house is a loss," he said. "Concentrate on keeping the fire from spreading to the neighboring buildings."

At least the muck from the Seine was finally clean enough to put out the flames now. In the not-so-distant past, adding a bucket from the river would have been adding fuel to the fire. It was nowhere near potable, but at least the muddy swirl could be used as a fire suppressant.

The crowd parted as he carried his burden to the rear of the manor house. Kara was still there. She was directing the survivors, arranging them to help each other with the expertise and discipline of a general in the field.

It didn't seem to matter that no one knew her. They automatically bowed to her innate authority. *The woman could teach the archangel Michael a thing or two about leadership.*

She turned and saw him. If he wasn't mistaken, there was relief in her eyes, but his cynical side told him it wasn't concern for him.

Kara rushed over to him, stopping him some distance from the nearest people. "Is she alive?"

"Yes," he answered, glancing down. The child was starting to stir.

"I need to get her out of here." Kara's dark eyes were darting back and forth as if she expected the crowd to turn on them at any moment. "It's not safe for her."

He could taste her fear like tin on his tongue. "I know all survivors are suspect, but you don't really think she's a Firehorse, do you? She's just a child."

"She wouldn't be the first, now would she?" Kara snapped, giving him a quick glare.

Ash's head drew back. There was something in her eyes he didn't understand. "I know it's happened before. Believe me, I've tried to forget. But it's rare for someone so young—"

"Theo was only a few years older than this," she interrupted. "And if your theory is correct that talent is what gets you marked, then this girl has a giant bull's-eye on her back."

He glanced down at his burden. Clara seemed so small and young. Was there some earth-shaking discovery in this girl's future?

"Isn't she an apprentice seamstress? What has she done?"

Kara looked around again, apparently deciding the nearby smoke-inhalation victims were too close. She motioned for him to follow her to the edge of a scrubby brush line—the kind that should have been cleared as part of Bastille's fire-prevention regimen.

Ash turned his back to the crowd, spreading his wings as if stretching them. The move effectively blocked them from view.

Kara checked behind them one more time before continuing. "Look, I got a quick rundown on this kid from the others. They said she was figuring out a way to recycle cloth—shredding the fibers, mashing them together, and pulling them into new threads. Except the brand-new cord to the machine sparked when she plugged it into a generator, and somehow the whole thing caught fire."

He rocked on his heels. The way the fire started had curse written all over it, but it was the invention she was describing that caught his attention. "People wouldn't have to wear their clothing until it was in rags. Just think of the acres of arable land we could open for crops that currently go to hemp and cotton. It's the bare minimum right now, but what if—"

"What if, what if, what if?" Kara interrupted. "We've all heard that song before. We can't stand here all day debating whether she's a Firehorse. She needs to come with me *now*. Before she sets off an earthquake or a meteor falls on us where we stand. That's what you wanted, isn't it?"

"Yes," he murmured, staring at her as the dots began to connect. She seemed so certain about this...

Merde. He leaned closer. "You can see them, can't you? The Firehorses are marked in your eyes. That's how you knew to get Didier and all the others."

Something in her expression gave her away, even as she scoffed. "Of course I can see them. Everyone can see them. They're not invisible."

"That's not what I meant, and you know it. You can see the taint of the curse on them, can't you?"

She hesitated. "Is that what you do?"

"No, not exactly."

Kara ran her teeth over her lower lip. "So their souls aren't black in your eyes?"

His heart ached. How damaged had she been by that lie? Ash shook his head emphatically. "No. I meant what I said before. The cursed aren't evil."

Her eyes were hard. "How do *you* know you have the right person? If it's not some sort of divine finger pointing from on high, then what is it?"

It was a good question. "I can only identify a Firehorse in the later stages. I see the disturbances they cause, and I don't mean the disasters. There are...vibrations."

"From the cursed?"

"From every living thing. Animal, plants, fungi, people... Everything has a specific vibration, but all the variation falls within a specific range. It's subtle and usually unimportant. A Firehorse's pattern is disturbed. But the curse itself is usually enough of an indicator. Amducious' gift doesn't get an extra kick operating in the dark. It creates more havoc by acting in the open."

"Yeah, I am more than familiar with the mob," she muttered, but then looked down. "Hey, there sweetheart."

He glanced at his burden. The girl was fully conscious now, her eyes wide as saucers as she cringed in his arms.

"Yes, you've been struck down by the curse," Kara said in a matter-of-fact tone. "And no, you're not going to die—not if you come with me."

Terrified, the girl trembled in his arms. She glanced at his face before quickly looking away. "I-I'm not a F-f-fire..."

The poor thing couldn't get the words out. "Shh. Don't say it aloud," he advised, glancing behind him. No others were close enough to hear them, but he didn't trust anyone.

"I'll meet you in a couple of days with some rations," he said.

Kara waved that away. "Don't worry about it. We'll scavenge what we need."

"And if you end up taking the former prisoners?" he asked, frustrated with her stubbornness. "You can't feed them all."

Kara didn't even blink. "I said don't worry about it. We'll just scavenge farther."

Merde. She couldn't give an inch—an admirable trait if it hadn't been so damn frustrating.

"Take her and go." He set the girl on her feet. Kara held her arm out for the girl. They'd only gotten a few steps away before he stopped them.

"Oh, and Kara? The next time I see you, we are going to have a long talk about how you manage to grow food in the wasteland."

It had been a shot in the dark, but her hesitation was all the answer he needed. Kara whirled around, flipping him off.

Next to her, Clara's eyes widened into saucers. The young girl snapped her head to the sky as if she expected Kara to be struck down by lightning for her show of disrespect.

"Don't worry, kid," he called with a rueful sigh. "God's not watching."

18

A sh was bleeding all over the cloth sack. He swore, shifting the supply of ration bars to his other arm.

He hadn't heard from Kara in a few days, and he was starting to get nervous.

After she had left with Clara, Ash decided to let the mansion ruins cool down before beginning the clean-up. Funerals for the dead took place as the embers died, including Clara's. He'd told her coworkers she had succumbed to smoke inhalation after her rescue. Only her brother knew the truth. With luck, he'd be able to resurrect her soon.

Curious about the machine the girl had been building, Ash had salvaged the parts in the hope others could reconstruct it. He ended up slicing his hand open on one of the razor-sharp cylinders spared by the flames.

It could have been worse. His hand would heal. And at least he wouldn't have to regrow any fingers. That would have taken forever.

No further disaster had struck the city, which meant Kara had been correct. Clara had been their Firehorse.

Kara needs to tell me how she does that. And how she grows food in the wasteland. But his miracle maker was like an absentee fairy godmother. No wishes would be granted until she was damn well good and ready.

Reminding himself Kara had almost as many responsibilities as he did, he crossed the catacomb entrance threshold, jogging inside a few hundred meters to deposit the sack. One of their scavengers would find it. Ash would deliver it himself, but he'd vowed to wait until Kara came to collect the prisoners. It would be better if she came to him. Then he might have some leverage to bargain with her.

Meanwhile, he had a city to run.

Ash spent the next few hours flying all over town. He loaded grain in the field onto carts and oversaw the delivery to the mill. Then he helped one of the schools repair their roof.

The perfunctory tasks didn't bother him as much as they usually did. Having hope again did wonders for his attitude. Ash even caught himself whistling once or twice.

His last task of the day was actually his favorite—overseeing the night men. There were dozens of them. Night men carried the city's waste out to the fields to act as fertilizer. It was meant to be a temporary fix to compensate for the lack of plumbing in town. Temporary had become an institution, though he was still hoping to remedy that.

When the axle on one of the waste carts broke, he held up the bed of the foul transport so they could fix it without having to dump the load.

"I don't think anyone would believe me if I said the city's warden visits in person every month, has for years," one of the men told him.

"The night men and women provide an invaluable service, one the city needs," Ash replied, clapping the man on the back. "It's Samuel, right? How is the family?"

"Not bad, not bad. Better since Klein is out of office in this district. He was an ass."

This was news. "I thought he was popular in these parts."

Klein had taken his cue from Mazarin, doing a lot of bragging about his accomplishments, shaking hands, greasing palms. Whatever it took to make it look like he was doing a great job without actually lifting a finger.

Samuel scoffed. "He wasn't popular with me. Not with a lot of people. Totally spit on the night men just because we haul people's shit away."

The man cackled, showing some missing teeth. "Good rule of thumb, you can't judge a leader by how he treats the other nobs. You have to look at how they treat the dirt," he said, spreading his arms wide.

Ash huffed. Now he remembered why this was his favorite task. Samuel and his ilk were such a refreshing change from having to deal with politicians. "Maybe you should think about running to take Klein's place."

Samuel's peal of laughter could be heard across three blocks. The other night men ahead of them on the track to the fields turned around, but kept going with their laden carts when Ash waved them on.

He was warming to the idea. Samuel would make a much better councilman than Klein had ever been. "Think about it. Night men know the city and its people. They even have a good idea of whose eating and what houses aren't getting their fair share," he said, nodding at the loaded car. "And personally speaking, an intelligent night man on the council would be preferable than the last lot."

Ash wasn't exaggerating. He'd feel cleaner after shaking Samuel's hand than Mazarin's.

"I thought there would be no more council," Samuel said, wrinkling his bulbous nose as they walked along.

Ash shrugged. "I haven't decided. Maybe temporary appointments or a lottery would be better. But no one serves indefinitely anymore. That was a big mistake."

Samuel tilted his head as if thinking it over. "Temporary sounds good. Not sure about a lottery. Definitely not sure about me being a councilman. That's a right stupid idea."

"I disagree," Ash echoed, deciding then and there Samuel should be one of the men taking one of those short-term appointments. "Although I'm starting to think the people I want to serve are the least likely to volunteer. Still, why don't you come see me in Belleville and we can talk more about it?"

Samuel laughed again, but agreed when pressed.

Ash could tell the man didn't take the offer seriously, but he would eventually. *I'll have Marcus talk him into it*, he decided. His aide was much better at that sort of thing than he was.

He returned to his apartments in Belleville just before dawn.

Someone is here. Ash could feel the small disturbance in the air caused by someone breathing. It wasn't Marcus. His aide was asleep downstairs. Ash could always tell because the vibrations of the man's snoring traveled up the stairs.

Had a council member hired an assassin? He wouldn't put it past them. He drew his weapon from its scabbard and stalked into his bedroom, ready to strike—only to be hit by a shoe. Judging from the impact, it was one of his boots.

"*Ow.* What the hell?" he asked, throwing the offending article aside.

"Where have you been?" Kara hissed. "I've been all over this rotten town."

Ash brightened. "Searching for me?"

Kara threw her arms up in the air, looking as if she wanted to throw something else at him. "No, you ass! I've been looking for Theo. You need to help me find him."

"What's he doing inside the city?" Ash rubbed his nose. She'd managed to catch him with the heel of his boot. "Of all your band, Theo seemed the most at ease in the wasteland. Why would he come here?"

Kara started pacing. "It has to do with the girl from the fire,

Clara. When she first arrived, she was shell-shocked and kept coughing from all the smoke. I left her with Madeleine so she could be examined. I thought it was safe to lead a scavenger team. I didn't think she was going to be any trouble!"

"And was she?" Kara's concern was infectious and a bit confusing. Clara was such a little thing. What could she have possibly done? Had he handed over some sort of spy or typhoid Mary to Kara's band?

Kara held up a hand. "It wasn't intentional."

"What happened?"

"I didn't know Theo knew Claire's family. She has a brother named George. He and Theo were childhood friends. Claire was going on and on about George getting killed because of her. Theo got all worked up, and came here looking for him. Now I can't find him."

She broke off, wringing her hands. "I can't believe he did this. He knows it's forbidden—"

Ash patted her back. "He'll be fine. We'll find him."

She waved a hand in front of his face. "*Hello!* Did you forget Theo's a Firehorse?"

"But you found a way to neutralize the curse."

She kicked him. "*It's temporary, you dolt!*"

"What?"

Kara released a shaky breath. "I mean, what you think is a cure is not a cure. It's more like a band-aid."

"But it stops," he said, his stomach twisting with nausea angels weren't supposed to feel. The hope that had been fueling him the last few days was taking a hit.

"If it didn't, the wasteland would be nothing more than a crater right now. Theo, Madeleine, and little Clara are alive because of you," he added.

Kara fisted her hands. She rolled her eyes to the ceiling, as if praying for patience. "It's a hack, one that doesn't work in the city as well as it does in the wasteland. Sooner or later, the curse will reassert itself, and Theo won't be able to hold it off for long. He doesn't—he has to be *with me.*"

Ash could feel his blood pumping faster. Frustration warred with anger. "We are going to find Theo, and then *you are going to tell me everything.* I need to know how the hell this works."

She hesitated, jaw tight. "Yes, *after* we find Theo."

"Let's go. We'll start in Place Léon-Blum. It's where Clara lived."

"I tried there already."

"You didn't try with me. If there's a trail, I will find it."

Clara's small neat home was simple and clean, full of efficient and innovative touches made by someone who worked and thought about textiles a lot.

Despite being repurposed from rags, the patchwork quilt on the bed was a work of art. The careworn chair cushion had been repaired with enough artistry that it looked better than the original.

There was no sign of either of the young men they were looking for.

"Has Theo been here?" Kara asked.

"I believe so." There was a hint of something in the air, a damp clay smell. "Someone who has spent a lot of time in the catacombs was here recently." He paused, bending next to the table to touch the trace of a shoeprint. It looked to be close to Theo's size.

"Why don't we—" He broke off, dropping to the floor to press his ear against the floorboards.

Kara knelt, tilting her head. "What is it?"

"Shh." He held up a hand. That sound he was hearing...

O putain. Ash jumped to his feet. "We have to get out there."

"Out where?"

"The river. Come on!"

19

The crack that came from deep in the earth was widening with every step he took.

Ash ran out of the house, pulling Kara behind him. They'd just cleared the threshold when he pulled her into the air, flying them the short distance to the Seine.

One of the reinforced concrete banks had collapsed. A huge fissure ran along the left bank where a geyser was throwing up a fountain of hot steaming water into the air.

The jet was spilling a torrent of water across the Quai Dorsay where the Assembly Nationale used to be. The few blocks between Rue de Constantine and Rue Bonaparte was now one of the most populated areas in the city.

Where the hell was the emergency klaxon? The only sound was the rushing water. Without the alarm bells, people might sleep through it.

"Get over to those houses," Ash shouted, pointing to the cluster of dwellings directly in the path of the water. "Help them evacuate. I have to try to close this crack!"

Kara ran alongside him. "How the hell are you going to do that?"

"I don't know! I'll figure it out," he snapped. "Just go! People live in those basement rooms." There were entire families about to be submerged.

She didn't leave. Instead, she fiddled with her holster, taking out her knife. The blade flashed in the moonlight as she scored a long, thin gash across her palm.

"What are you doing?"

She whirled on him, planting her bloody palm on his breast-plate, just over his heart.

"Now you can go," she said, turning to the houses. She took off at a run, leaving a trail of blood drops in her wake.

What the hell? Stupefied, Ash stared after her like a moron until the klaxon sounded, belatedly kicking in to rouse the popu-lace from their beds.

Refocusing, he leapt into action.

The crack in the riverbed was now the size of a small wagon, and it was getting larger.

I need a plug.

Whipping his head around, he scanned his surroundings. Something caught the corner of his eye. *No. Don't let that be the only thing I can use.*

Ash flew up high, searching for alternatives. There was none. He would have to tear down a building, and all the ones nearby were occupied.

Swearing viciously, Ash streaked forward, intent on destroying the most recognizable symbol of the old Paris he knew and loved, the Luxor obelisk.

The nearly three-and-a-half-thousand-year-old granite column had been brought from Egypt in the early eighteen hundreds—a gift from the ruling pasha. It had been given a place of pride in the center of the city, stretching into the sky for years. The demon horde had enjoyed writing obscenities on it, sparing it the fate of most other human monuments torn down after the Collision.

Flying at top speed, he hit the obelisk with everything he had. It didn't budge. Circling around, he tried again, and again. Nothing worked.

Shit. He was going to need a whole crew out here with chisels and ropes. It would take them hours, if not days, to topple the thing. In the meantime, the left bank was flooding.

Kara was evacuating them. The basement dwellers wouldn't die unawares.

Wait—the demons' target practice. During the demon king's reign, a few of the horde had repaired the old canons from *Les Invalides.* They'd wanted to shoot at the obelisk for fun. The cannonballs had gone wide, hitting the buildings around the obelisk instead, but that had pleased them more since people were hurt.

I won't miss, he vowed.

It took a few minutes find ammunition and fuses, and even longer to drag the cannon into the Place de la Concorde. He pointed the barrel at the obelisk, aiming for a point halfway up before lighting the fuse.

Don't blow up in the barrel, he prayed, covering his ears, squeezing his eyes shut as the blast went off.

He opened them as a chunk of stone fell. He'd managed a direct hit, but the top of the obelisk hadn't broken off completely. Praying it was enough of a start, he flew up and began to kick and punch. He beat it as hard as he could, targeting the fissure made with the cannon.

Bruised and bleeding, he reared back a final time, putting everything he had in his last strike. A snap loud enough to vibrate his eardrums told him the job was done. He'd managed to break off the tip seven feet from the top of the obelisk.

Now comes the hard part.

Ash's hands were wet with blood as he gripped the stone. His hold was tenuous, but with a chunk of stone this size, it wasn't going to get any better. Shoving until the thing came off, he held it tightly enough to avoid sending it crashing to the ground.

Flying was out of the question. The weight of the stone was too much, even for him. He was going to drag it out to the river, and he needed to move fast.

Ash grunted aloud as he pushed the stone. Muscles strained and tore, but he managed to heave the rock to the bank just across from the gaping hole. Just pushing it on top of the geyser wasn't going to cut it.

Half-pushing and half-shoving, Ash positioned the obelisk fragment at the river's edge. He counted to a beat of three before reaching down and throwing the stone up in the air. It only cleared the ground by a few inches, but he made the most of them. He sprang behind it, pushing with lightning reflexes and as much speed as he could muster.

He splashed into the Seine, the tip of the obelisk cutting through the turbulent water like a spear. Holding his breath, he aimed the tip at the fissure in the riverbed, stuffing it into the opening like he was corking a bottle.

He worked by feel under the water. The obelisk tip wasn't a perfect fit, but after he hammered on the flared end enough, pieces broke off to shove into the gaps.

The torrent stopped. Ash looked up, bending his knees to push up from the riverbed. He broke the surface of the water, taking a deep breath. Now that the subterranean geyser was closed, the river's level was dropping back to normal.

He shored up what was left of the crumbling bank with whatever debris he could find. It wasn't a permanent fix, but it would hold until morning. He needed to get to the houses downstream of the flood. Maybe Kara had found Theo somewhere nearby.

The basement of the house Kara had entered first was empty. She'd managed to clear it in time. He hoped the occupants of the neighboring dwellings had fared as well.

When he climbed from the basement, there was a crowd milling outside.

"I need you all to count your neighbors. Account for all the missing," Ash instructed in a loud voice, just shy of angelic timbre. The mumbling ceased, and they scattered before he could add that a clean-up and reconstruction crew would be sent at first light.

It was redundant information, anyway. Bastille's people had been through enough disasters. They knew the drill by heart. He didn't have to coddle them, which was just as well. He needed to find Kara and Theo before the boy set off another disaster.

The water made tracking harder, but this time around, Kara wasn't trying to hide from him. In the end, she was easy to find. All he had to do was follow the scent of death.

ASH LANDED next to a tomb depicting a weeping angel at the Montparnasse cemetery. Her face was forever buried in her stone hands. He wondered if she was mourning the loss of man's innocence.

Kara was lying a few feet away, cradling Theo's body. His face was white and still above the bloody mess that was his neck. It was almost as if he were asleep. He held a stained shard of pottery clutched in his hands, his face peaceful in repose.

It's almost as if the maker wipes the slate clean when He calls you home. Ash hoped that was the case.

The moon was bright enough for him to cast a shadow. When it passed over her, Kara looked up. Twin tear tracks sparkled on her cheeks.

"What happened?" he asked softly.

She shrugged, her face crumpling. "I don't know. I found him like this."

Ash knelt, putting his arms around her as she wept. Kara

opened her hand, showing him the vial all the survivors wore around their neck. Theo's was broken and empty. "My blood wasn't enough."

He stilled, his heart skipping a beat. "He wore your blood?"

"Yes. Sometimes it works, but in the city, the pull of the curse is too strong." Kara turned back, looking down at Theo's face.

That's why she cut herself, marking me.

A shudder wracked her body. "Do you think you can find his killers? Maybe they have his blood on them," she suggested.

Ash drew back, his lips parting.

Kara frowned. "What is it?"

He winced. "Kara, love, this doesn't look like murder to me."

She shook her head in confusion. "What? Of course it does; look at him."

Already regretting opening his mouth, he stayed silent. She leaned forward and pushed him, shoving his arms away. "Tell me what this looks like!"

He closed his eyes, an ache of sympathy welling up. "There are no other footprints save the two of yours," he said, nodding at Theo's body. "He must have run here after the river began to flood. He knew the disasters would keep coming until he was gone."

Kara sprang to her feet. "No. He is *not* a suicide. Suicides don't get to Heaven!" She wiped her eyes with the heels of her hands. The move left a bloody trace on one cheek.

He stood as well, mirroring her movement. "He's not a suicide. He's a martyr."

"But he could have just waited for me!" She sobbed, falling to her knees to grab Theo's cold hand. "Why didn't he wait for me?"

Ash didn't know what to say. Theo had probably realized he'd miscalculated, and he'd done what he thought was best to stop the chain reaction before it got worse. If he hadn't, the destruction might have followed him all the way back to the wasteland.

Ash let her weep a little longer, hoping she would cry herself out. "Let me have him," he said after a few minutes. "We can bury him here."

Most of the cemetery was still consecrated ground, despite the horde's best efforts to make it otherwise.

Ash quickly dug a shallow grave. He lay Theo inside, blessing him and covering him with soil. Kara sat next to the grave, hugging her knees throughout the burial. When he was done, he touched her cheek.

"I have to get back to the others," she whispered, but didn't move.

"That can wait," he said. She was in no shape to get to the wasteland. Kara needed rest, and he needed answers. "Right now, you're coming with me."

He expected her to argue, but she was still in shock. He wrapped one arm around her back and the other under her knees, lifting her into his arms.

His apartments were cold, so he laid Kara down on the bed and covered her with a blanket before lighting the logs prepared in the fireplace. When he was done, he sat on the bed next to her.

The glow of firelight lit her face. Kara's beauty rivaled any angel in Heaven. "You want to know how it works, the blood?"

"Later. I want you to sleep now."

Her eyes were wider than normal. She shook her head. "I can't...what if...can you come lie down with me?"

Ash hesitated, caught off guard by the simple request.

Humans sometimes need physical comfort. It never occurred to him that he did, too.

"Of course," he said, taking off his armor and pulling on softer cotton clothing. He walked up to the bed, climbing between her and the wall. He lay there awkwardly on his side, wondering what to do with his arms.

Put them around her, idiot—like in the old movies.

Every hair on his arm stood on end as he settled it around her waist. Touching someone this closely was the strangest sensory experience of his life. But Kara curled into his embrace as if it was the most natural thing in the world. She faced him, her eyes fixed on his.

Suddenly, holding her was relaxing. He didn't understand how that worked. "There aren't words for what I want to say to you," Ash whispered.

One fine eyebrow rose in the firelight. "You should try, anyway. It's the human thing to do."

"I'm sorry," he said. "For Theo tonight and for everything else you've lost." His heart ached for the boy he'd known so briefly.

She nodded in acknowledgment. "I didn't think you would care so much, but you do, don't you?"

"Theo deserved so much more. They all did. Every Firehorse had a chance to change the world. It was their destiny, and the curse denied them that."

Kara stared at him for a long moment. She lifted a hand, brushing a lock of hair out of his eye. "I hated you for so long."

He nodded. "You had every right."

"Did I?" she asked. "I used to think so. I'm not so sure anymore."

Ash's throat was tight, but he needed to say this. "For what it's worth, I'm sorry." He swore under his breath. "You were just a baby. I used to lie here in this bed and remember. For years, I would see your face, the look in your eyes. Angels don't go to Hell when they die, but dreaming about you, seeing you every night for years—that was my Hell."

Kara started, her lean body tensing against his much harder one. "What? What are you saying?"

"I'm saying I know who you are. You're Katarina Delavordo. Fifteen years ago, I left you in the wasteland to die."

20

Kara stared at him so long, her mouth opening and closing, that he believed she was going to deny it. But in the end, she sealed her lips and said nothing.

"How did you do it?" he asked. "You were a child alone. How in the world did you survive?"

Ash couldn't fathom it. Before seeing that tree earlier this week, he would have said everything in the wasteland was dead, poisoned beyond rehabilitation by the demon horde and Amducious' gift. How had she grown it?

"Please tell me. It could be the key to ending the curse."

She shook her head. "It's not—believe me. I've tried for years, using every occult text I can find. My blood does something, but it doesn't break the curse. It certainly can't end it."

The fact she had tried was news, but it didn't surprise him. Of course she would have made the attempt, just as he would have in her place. "That doesn't mean there's no solution. If we trust each other and work together, we may find a way that neither of us could alone."

The silence stretched. Kara sat up on the bed, wrapping her

arms around her knees. "When you left me, I knew I was going to die…"

He flinched, but rose as well, his arms going around her reflexively. She didn't push him away.

Kara fingered the coverlet. "I was only five, but I knew what happened to people in the wasteland. They starved to death or worse. There was a man who lived on our street named Jonas. He murdered his brother and became a thief. He believed himself to be a great and terrible villain. He called himself the demon's disciple reborn." She broke off to roll her eyes. "Jonas bragged about knowing the wasteland like the back of his hand, but when the thief-takers formed a posse and went after him, he took refuge beyond the fringe. He was dead within the day."

"The wasteland has a way of humbling the most arrogant among us, myself included."

She snorted lightly. "I figured I wouldn't last the day either."

"I know you were frightened. I'm still so sorry."

"I was scared, but more than that—I was furious. *At you.*"

His grimace was almost a smile. "I remember that, too."

Kara raised an eyebrow. "You gave me food and water. You weren't supposed to do that, were you?"

"No. The consensus was that providing supplies just prolonged the inevitable. But you were…different. You were so young."

"I threw it away."

Ash blinked. "*What?*"

The corner of her mouth quirked up, but she wasn't amused. "The food and water. I still remember what was in that bundle you gave me. It was an apple and some stone fruit. There was also a sandwich with some cheese and some sort of grain paste. You said it was your personal rations for the week. You also left me your canteen."

He'd forgotten about the flask. "I swiped that from Raphael

after a healing in Bethesda a long time ago—mainly because he always kept it filled with absinthe."

Her eyes widened. "I threw away an archangel's flask?"

"You tossed it, too?"

Her mouth gaped. "I did. After swearing aloud for the first time in my life. I cursed you and the neighbors who gave me up. Then I threw everything down that hill."

Damn. Even as a child, she'd been fierce.

"What happened next? Did Sij find you?" With satisfaction, he pictured the old crone being knocked in the head by the flask.

"No. I didn't meet her until much later. I was on my own for years—mostly by intent. I didn't trust anyone."

"But what did you do for food?" He still didn't understand.

"The flask spilled open. I slipped on the mud it made at the top of the hill, and then cut myself on a rock sliding down the ravine. I remember being surprised and out of breath when I landed at the bottom. The impact broke through a couple of dry layers of crusted dirt to reveal more mud underneath. It splashed all over my pants."

"I dug and dug until I found a spring coming out between the two boulders. Near it was some kind of wild grass—something close to the onion family. The bulbs at the bottom were bitter but edible. I spent weeks living off that stuff. Slowly, I ventured farther and farther, but I couldn't find anything else to eat. Not until I went back where I'd thrown the food away."

Realization hit home "And you found the fruit you'd thrown away had sprouted into a tree," he finished, connecting the dots.

She nodded. "So, you've seen it?"

"Yes, but only recently. I avoided that particular spot in the wasteland for the last two decades."

"*Oh.*" There was a wealth of meaning in that one word. "Not even a fly-by?"

"No. It hurt too much to remember." He cleared his throat. "So...just like that, you could grow food?"

She let her head drop back. "That's not how it works. By the time I visited the ravine again, the tree had grown. It even had fruit. They're not normal peaches by any stretch of the imagination, but they taste almost good if you cook them first. The grain paste had some intact seeds in it, too. Those had sprouted as well. I tried to replant them, but they didn't take anywhere else."

Kara sighed. "It took me months to put the pattern together."

She had cut herself back then and again today. "You needed to shed your own blood, didn't you?"

"Yes, but not just that. After much trial and error, I realized I need to lean into the curse in a way. If I bled and did something that was actively against my interest, then the effects were nullified or even reversed."

"That's why all the survivors wear a vial around their necks?"

"Yes. If they break it on themselves, it can sometimes stop the curse in its tracks—if they try to make the effects worse like I did. We tested other Firehorse blood. Only mine works. But not always. It depends on how the curse chose to manifest."

He thought back to what happened to Theo. "So if the river sprang a leak because of a tremor or a sinkhole, it won't magically seal up."

"Exactly. But say a tremor started. You wouldn't duck under a doorframe. You'd go stand under a glass window instead."

"Unbelievable," he breathed. "And that really works?"

"Not always. But sometimes...yes, it does. And it's less effective here in town."

He nodded. "That makes sense. Bastille was where the curse was cast—at the demon tower. It must get weaker the farther you get from it."

"Montmeurtre?"

"Yes. The altar was built for that purpose. All the sacrifices were done there. It's the epicenter."

That wasn't a complete surprise to her. "I figured that would be the case. It was the demon kings' seat. I've even tried to get in a few times, but never got past the door."

Err... "Perhaps that's because I warded the structure, blocking access to anyone but me."

Kara looked at him in shock. "You did *what*?"

"At the time, making sure none of the surviving demons took any of those books or objects of power was the priority. I had to make sure none of his acolytes had enough juice to take over. Blocking access was the most expedient way. Over the years, I've pilfered the library, searching for a solution. The books are scattered in caches all over the city. There are even some here in the closet."

Kara smacked him on the arm. "Do you have any idea how many times I tried to get in there?" She smacked him again.

"Sorry," he said, holding up his hands to ward off her blows. "I couldn't risk anyone getting their hands on the things inside."

"Well, at least you didn't burn the books," she grumbled.

"No, I'm not that stupid. But I've read those texts backward and forward, however, and while there were some promising leads, there was nothing that could undo the spell. I've even been back to the altar ruins a few times to search for clues."

The logs in the fireplace shifted, making the light flicker. It caught her lovely face, the sad, distant expression haunting. "What's wrong?"

"Aside from everything?" She laughed, but tears shone in her eyes.

A thought occurred to him. "Is it Theo? The two of you weren't, um..."

How do you ask something like this? In addition to believing theirs to be a master and subordinate-type relationship, Ash assumed Theo had been too young for her. But on a human scale, it wasn't that big a gap—less than a decade.

"*No!*" Kara smacked him on the shoulder. "I can't believe men. You all only think about one thing. Even angels, apparently."

Embarrassed, Ash felt his face growing hot. "I don't usually."

She tilted her head, studying him closely. "But you do with me?"

Breathing became a bit more difficult, enough it seemed wiser to keep his mouth shut.

She took a breath that ended with a little shudder. "Theo was important to me. All my people are, but he was special. I depended on him. I always believed if anything happened to me, he could take over. But it's more than that. Seeing you again and getting to know you has stirred up a lot of stuff for me."

Well, that wasn't hard to understand. "I know. But we need to help each other now. I know I'm the last person you want as an ally, I really do. But we need to get past our past."

Those glittering eyes bored into him. "And is that all you want from me? An alliance?"

He didn't answer.

Something in her expression shifted. If he didn't know any better, he would have said there was a hunger there.

"I can feel it, you know," she said.

"What do you feel?" he whispered.

"You. Watching me. It doesn't feel friendly."

"I'm not your enemy, Kara."

Her eyes gleamed like dark jewels in the dim light. "That's not what I mean, and you know it."

He shifted uncomfortably, keenly aware of her scent and warmth. "I'm not a carnal being, Kara. I didn't fall because of a desire for human women."

"Then why are you still in this bed?"

She knelt on the mattress, getting as close to him as she could without actually touching him. "What do you want to do to me right now?"

Holy heavenly crap. "I... uh..."

Kara leaned back on her heels. "Or are you afraid they won't let you back into Heaven if you touch me?"

His heart was starting to thrum in his chest. "Maybe I'm afraid if I touch you, you'll stab me."

She looked down at his chest—at the expanse of muscle displayed by the open neck of his tunic shirt. Slowly, she raised a finger and traced his collarbone. "I promise not to do that again. Or do you believe God won't forgive you? An angel having sex with a human woman is the heavenly equivalent of a felony, isn't it?"

Ash stared at her, his eyes widening as she reached down for the hem of her shirt. In another moment, it was off, revealing golden brown skin so fine it looked like something out of a Renaissance painting.

Da Vinci couldn't do better. His hands itched. He wanted to touch her so badly.

Kara tilted her head with leonine grace. "Isn't saving the world supposed to earn you a get-out-of-jail-free card? Can't Raphael overlook one little carnal sin, or will it violate the terms of your deal to get back into Heaven?"

His mouth dropped open. "How did you know about that?"

Kara smirked and sat back on her heel. "Everybody knows about that." Pursing her lips, she reached for her shirt. "Well, I guess I've overshot on this one. I'm going to leave."

Moving as fast as lightning, he grabbed her hand before she could pull it back over her head.

"No. *Stay.*"

Ash flipped her over, pinning her to the bed before covering her with his body.

She shivered. "So you do think the big guy upstairs will overlook this?"

"Whether He does or not doesn't matter. You are worth falling for. For you, I would give up Heaven."

21

The sound of a tray hitting the table woke him. Marcus was standing in the antechamber of Ash's apartments. He'd come in to serve him breakfast. He appeared close to a coronary, hopping back and forth from one foot to another as if he couldn't decide whether to run away.

Ash sat up, pulling the sheet to cover Kara's nudity before he turned back to his aide, who was staring at him with his mouth open.

Say something. "I'll need coffee for two this morning, Marcus."

"*Oh.* Of course, my lord." His aide rushed away, pounding down the stairs two at time judging from the racket he made.

When he looked back down at Kara, she was awake, peeking out over the edge of the sheet, which she'd pulled up to her chin.

"I'm naked."

So was he. "Believe me, I haven't forgotten." He stroked her hip under the blanket. "I'd like nothing more than to spend all morning in bed, but I think we shocked ten years off Marcus' life. If we don't want to make it twenty, perhaps we should dress."

Ash stood, pulling on the loose pants he always wore while

alone in his rooms. Kara followed suit, reaching across the bed to her discarded clothing on the floor.

"So...you have a manservant?" she asked, a hint of egalitarian disdain coloring her words.

"Not precisely," he explained, pulling on a clean tunic. "Marcus was my aide-de-camp during the war. Now he's just my aide."

"He calls you 'my lord' and brings you food," she said, a hint of a snicker in her words.

Her teasing stirred feelings of guilt and upper-class privilege. "I've tried to get him to call me Ash, but he's not terribly flexible in that respect. The breakfast routine developed over the years. I stopped thinking about it after the first few. It does save me time," he defended.

"Hmm."

He wanted to say more, but Marcus came in at that moment, bearing a second tray. This one was a feast compared to Ash's more spartan meal. There was fresh fruit and oatmeal, served with cream and a small loaf of crusty bread. A second coffee cup —this one made of dainty porcelain—was in the corner.

Ash stood and waved at each of them in turn. "Kara, this is Marcus, my assistant. Marcus, this is Kara. She's...special."

He could feel Kara's glance turning into a glare. She gave him a surreptitious smack on his backside on her way to shake Marcus' hand.

To his credit, Marcus made an effort at small talk, but his inquiries into her background made Kara clam up immediately. Sensing his blunder, Marcus made a few desultory remarks on the weather before excusing himself.

Kara rounded on him as soon as he was gone. "I'm *special*? Why don't you just hang a sign on me that says Firehorse? You can add that my blood nullifies the curse in small script."

Ash scratched his head. "I wasn't referring to your gift. I meant you are special to *me*." He glanced at the door his aide had just departed from. "I'm pretty sure that's how Marcus understood it, considering the state he found us in this morning."

High dudgeon interrupted, Kara looked down at the floor. "Oh. That's all right then, I guess...I should be leaving now. I have to tell the others about Theo."

"You can delay a half hour. Bad news can wait that long, at least." He gestured to the table, pulling out a chair. "Eat something first. You need to keep up your strength."

She looked askance at the table. "I can't eat all of this and live with myself."

Ash understood, of course. He couldn't stomach a full meal after visiting the poorer districts in his city...and there were a lot of them.

"Then eat some of it and take the rest back to the wasteland. You're welcome to pick up more from the larder on the way downstairs. But you still need something now."

Ash stepped closer to the table, then poured coffee into the two mugs. He held one out to her. "At least have some coffee."

That got her attention. Kara gave the mug a look that echoed the one she'd given him last night. She took the cup without further argument, inhaling the smoky brew with a deep sigh of satisfaction.

"I don't remember the last time I had anything this good," she said after a sip.

"Should I be insulted?" He grinned. "I know I was inexperienced, but judging from the sounds you made, I thought I handled myself reasonably well."

Kara choked on a sip she was drinking. Her face was as red as sunset when she finally spoke. "Well, granted, I don't have a lot of experience to compare to, but yes..." She looked away, adding in a mutter. "Kudos, by the way."

Feeling lighter than he had in an age, he gave her a teasing grin. "Not a lot of experience, you say?" He bit open one of the peaches, swallowing it slowly before speaking again. "Because I would have guessed I wasn't the only virgin in that bed last night."

He took another bite and grinned.

Her eyes fixed on his mouth for a long beat before she gave herself a little shake. "Well, well, well. Look who is a quick study... How annoying."

Ash laughed, stealing a kiss before she could stop him. Blushing, Kara sat at the table, reaching for a bit of the bread. They finished their coffee in silence.

"We should meet later at the demon tower," he suggested when the moment of levity passed. "I want to look around again, and I want you to come with me this time."

"Why don't we start with the books you have?" she asked, turning as if looking for them. "Are they in the closet?"

"No, you can't store that many occult texts in one place. I scattered them all over town. They generate their own tainted aura," he explained. "We can get to those later, once we scour the tower together. I've done it on myself a dozen or so times, but perhaps you'll see something I missed."

She looked skeptical. "All right. I'm willing to try, but I'm not sure what you expect me to find if you've been looking all this time."

It was a grudging acceptance at best. *Of course, it is. People avoid the tower for a reason. It's painted in human blood, you idiot.*

"There's no reason to be afraid to join me there. I'll be with you the whole time."

Kara reached over to smack his arm, then winced when she accidentally hit his armor. "*Damn it.*" She sucked on her fingers. "I'm not afraid of the tower. I live in the catacombs, for crying out loud. Do you know how many dead people are down there?"

"Roughly ten million," he said helpfully.

Her mouth dropped open. "Really? That's a few more million than I thought."

He looked at the table, but didn't really see it. He was lost in memories. Too many bad ones. "Many more were added after the Collision."

Somber now, she nodded and continued to eat.

"Kara, there is something else I'd like to ask you. You can say no if you want."

The crease between her eyebrows deepened. "What is it?"

"I would like a vial of your blood."

She blinked. "I thought you were immune to the curse because of the whole having wings and being an angel thing."

Ash shook his head. "I'm not actually, or at least, I don't believe I am." He snorted. "I guess my presence doesn't move the needle in terms of progress."

And why would it? Human progress was just that...human.

"Move the needle?" she questioned.

"It's an antiquated expression, back from when they used to measure earthquake strengths."

"Hmm." She didn't ask why they had stopped measuring them. What was the point when they had so many, all designed to create maximum damage?

Kara took something out of her pocket. It was an apothecary vial like the ones her band wore. She must have raided an old shop for the stock. "Do you have a knife?"

He held up a hand. "I'll get a syringe." There was one in the med kit downstairs.

Ash performed the blood draw, making sure to clean the area with alcohol first. He filled the vial with it, but hesitated with the little remainder left in the syringe.

"Do you want a second one? Maybe for Marcus?" She lifted her sleeve to offer her arm again.

"*No.*" The answer was immediate and instinctive.

She frowned. "Don't you want to protect him, just in case?"

"I do," he said. "But the more people who know about this," he said, holding up the vial. "The more dangerous it gets."

He could picture the mob now. If they had an inkling what

her blood could do, they'd be baying after her like a pack of wolves. Those animals wouldn't hesitate to tear her apart.

"Your safety is the most important thing."

Kara scowled, snatching the syringe from his hand. She stuck the needle in the crease of her arm, and withdrew another vial's worth of blood.

"Here," she said with a bite in her voice. "You'll need it for the next Firehorse at least."

Ash hesitated before taking the second vial, acknowledging her gift with a bow. Then he took her hand and kissed it. "Come meet me tonight after you talk to your people."

Breaking the news about Theo wouldn't take long, but he'd been a valued member of their gang. They would need Kara's comfort after losing one of their own.

Ash also had his tasks for the day. Making sure Bastille kept running was a full-time job for ten angels, but they only had him.

She agreed and parted with the food he pressed on her. Once she was gone, he held up the vials to the light. The sun shone on them, revealing their color as closer to onyx than ruby.

Which makes sense if it's what you suspect. He pushed the thought away, pocketing the precious vials in his tunic before dressing in his armor and preparing for the day.

Having a spare for the next Firehorse was a good idea, but he wasn't using the other for himself or for Marcus.

No, he had other plans for the blood, ones Kara could never know about.

22

T he moonlight revealed the bleached white bones buried in the blood-soaked cob in stark relief.

I should have burned this place to the ground. Ash would have, too, if he hadn't been concerned he might lose the ability to break the curse. He'd scoured the tower from top to bottom, but there was still a chance the secret was hidden somewhere inside.

A light step alerted him to Kara's approach.

"I have to give you credit," he said without turning around. "That was nearly soundless."

"Apparently, it wasn't close enough since you heard me," Kara growled, coming to stand beside him.

They stared at the abomination in front of them in silence. It said a lot about their daily reality that neither of them flinched or looked away.

"How many bodies in this one?" she asked in a hoarse whisper.

"You don't want to know."

Her glance betrayed mixed emotions—annoyance he wouldn't answer along with a tinge of gratitude.

"Well, let's not waste any more time." She headed for the entrance, but without Ash, there was no way she was going to cross the threshold.

"Here, let me," he said, stepping in front of her.

The door was barred with the thickest steel Bastille could make. He'd carved the sigils on it himself. The angelic wards couldn't be broken by any demon-born, nor the vast majority of humans.

He opened the lock with the key and threw the bar back. The creaking grind of steel on steel reverberated through the night air. He pushed open the door to reveal a yawning darkness.

Assuming it was over, Kara started to walk around him. "Not yet," he said, reaching down to fish his blade out of his boot.

Kara's eyes widened as he held up his arm and cut himself across the forearm. He touched his fingers to the blood, and drew across the air in the threshold. The traces of blood floated in the space before flaring bright and burning out in a shower of golden embers.

She whistled. "Nice."

"Wait. There's four more." More blood, more sigils—one for each of the different species he'd run into onto his time on earth. When he was finished, he turned back to her.

Kara's expression was wry. "You weren't taking any chances, were you?"

"Too much at stake."

"Well, I'm honored to be the first human to cross this threshold."

He frowned. Had she forgotten the human sacrifices killed to fuel spells, or somehow missed the bones poking out of the walls?

Kara wrinkled her nose. "Wait, that came out wrong. Never mind." She waved her gaffe away with an expression of self-disgust and crossed the threshold, slipping into the black darkness beyond.

"I brought a torch," he said, taking out the hand-crank flash-light he'd meticulously repaired. He wound it. The weak light glowed anemically, barely lighting the area around their feet.

"Forget it. Save it for reading—if we find anything." She continued up the stairs, leaving him and the light behind.

Ash hurried after her, concerned she might misstep in the dark. But Kara was way ahead of him, as surefooted up the pitch-black stairs as he was.

The first level was empty. The demon king had used it for meetings and the occasional orgy. The chambers here had been untouched, mainly because there hadn't been much in them to begin with.

Together, they cleared the first and second level within the hour. The third was a far greater challenge.

"This is where most of the books were," he said, gesturing at the empty shelves. He pointed to the left, where he'd inflicted the most damage during the battle with the king. "The altar room was through there."

The broken arch had been haphazardly reconstructed to let him access the room for his various searches. It would hold for now, but he was prepared to fly Kara out if an earthquake started.

The hole he'd made slamming Amducious' body through the wall would make a convenient exit if that was the case.

Kara raised her brows at the breach in the ceiling, but chose not to comment.

A solid grey granite block dominated the center of the room. Its pitted surface was permanently stained black with blood. Human and lower demon both. Here in the altar room, the demon king hadn't much cared which was sacrificed. If any of his followers failed to meet his expectations, they were no safer from his wrath than the humans he spit on.

Kara averted her eyes from the altar. She focused on the walls. Most of the space on them was inscribed with demonic sigils and runes.

"What is this?" she asked, frowning at the long scrawl domi-
nating most of the wall next to the arched entrance.

"It's their language. Surely you've seen the graffiti all
over town?"

"Yes, but...it's not like this," she said, gesturing to the string of
profanity. Her head drew back. "It's a whole bloody paragraph...I
guess I never thought of it as a language of its own, one with rules
and syntax."

Ash sighed. "The demon dialect is a foul tongue. It used to
make my skin crawl just to look at it written like this," he
admitted.

She rubbed her arms, flicking him a troubled glance. For a
human being, witnessing this would be a hundred times worse.
"Does it still?"

"Not anymore," he said truthfully. "After a dozen or so visits, I
suppose I became inured to it."

He wanted to tell her it would be the same for her, but didn't.
With luck, she would only be exposed to this filth this once. If she
didn't see anything this time around, there was little point in
making her come here again and again.

Kara tore her eyes away from a particularly profane impreca-
tion written behind the broken door. She pointed up at the
twisted metal girder worked into the peak of the tower. "Is that
part of the Eiffel tower?"

"Yes, it is."

She stared avidly at the still-recognizable lattice metal frame.
Her brow furrowed as a thought occurred to her. "Were you here
when it went up?"

Glad for the distraction, he smiled in reminiscence. "I was. I
thought it was magnificent, although I was in the minority."

Kara blinked. "Really?"

He nodded. "It was grossly unpopular in the beginning. The
native Parisians thought it was an eyesore. There were petitions
to have it torn down. It was supposed to have been temporary in

any case. The city built it for the Great Exposition of eighteen-eighty-nine. The tower was supposed to come down afterward, but it was a genuine engineering marvel. Plus, it made the city money, so it stayed."

"Hmm." She reached toward the wall where a bit of metal poked through the bloody cob, touching the once much-maligned structure. "I used to wonder why I had the misfortune to be born in this time. But now, I wonder if it would be worse to be you—to have memories of a better world that's long dead."

Ash came up behind her, wrapping his arms and wings around Kara like a protective cocoon. "I can't do anything to restore or change the past, but together we can give Bastille a chance to build a better future."

At least, he hoped they could.

Seeming to understand that his words were about so much more than ending the curse, she nodded before breaking away to resume searching the room.

They piled everything they found in the center. He sat on the floor, sifting through the detritus. There were ritual bowls and mortars along with a few shreds of paper, the remains of scrolls and books he'd left behind.

Kara kept her distance from the altar, doing a complete circuit of the tower room a half dozen times. She dug through the debris for a few hours without rest, handing over everything she found.

Eventually, she gave up and joined him on the floor. "Are there other rooms we can check?"

"There's a basement, but it only has bodies."

Kara shuddered. Ash patted her back absently before plucking a strange object from the pile. It appeared to be a weapon of some kind. It had a Celtic cross-shaped handle paired with a horn made of ivory. Every bit of the surface was intricately carved, but it wasn't in demon tongue. It was in his own.

"This is angelic," he said. "But I don't recognize its construction."

His kind didn't have weapons like this.

"Should you?" She took it from him for a closer look. "It could be from after your time up there. You did fall a long time ago."

"Perhaps," he murmured, wondering why that felt wrong. The strange blade seemed too primitive.

"Maybe it's ceremonial. It doesn't really look functional," she said, slipping her own knife out from its sheath and comparing the two side by side. "What does the writing say?"

"That's the strange part. It just has words, no phrases. There's nothing coherent on it."

She pointed to the altar. "You mean like those?"

There it is, he thought, his heart sinking. "Like what?"

There was nothing written on the altar—nothing his eyes could perceive.

"Can't you see it?" Kara was frowning. "The symbols are like the graffiti on the streets. Just bits and pieces."

He shook his head. "To me, it's completely blank."

She brightened, getting to her feet in a rush. "There's nothing on top, but there's writing on all four sides." Kara bit her lip. "I wish you could see it and tell me what it says."

"You can write it for me," he said, holding out one of the little notebooks Marcus always made sure Ash had tucked into his armor.

He was about to hand it to her when he reconsidered. Sketching rapidly, he drew the symbol for concealment in the filthy demon dialect. "Is there one that looks like this?"

Kara studied the picture, holding it up for comparison as she crouched, crab-walking all around the altar.

"It's here," she called from the other side. "It's small and almost totally covered by others carved on top of it."

He knelt next to her, studying the blank space she'd indicated. "You need to do something... It's not going to be pleasant."

Kara stood. "What is it?"

"Your knife. You need to take it and cut yourself. Put the

wound over the symbol of concealment. I would do it myself, but my blood won't work."

Her nostrils flared. "Is this another thing only humans can see and do?"

Ash looked away. "Yes. Coat it well. Made sure every bit of it is covered."

"*O-kay.*" She took out her knife and drew a thin line across the center of her palm, then touched it to the symbol and moved her hand about.

The hiss was unexpected. Startled, Kara reared back, snatching her hand away as if it had been scalded. However, she hadn't been burned. The symbol flared briefly as the concealment spell was broken, rendering it visible to his eyes.

The center portion of the block blinked out of existence, revealing a small cavity. It was crammed with books and scrolls.

Ash reached in and pulled out a thick volume. It was a rare volume on the creation and control of aquatic monsters, the *Bathra Haeresim*.

Not much use in landlocked Bastille. There were other classics in there as well, Pazuzu's *Codex* and the *Necronomicon*—the real one—to name a few.

He pulled out the scrolls, books, and the other assorted artifacts out, minimizing the amount of skin-to-skin contact as much as possible. Touching the things made him feel unclean.

His hand fell over a small handwritten scroll wrapped around a black enamel rod. It gave him a shock. Ash was about to dismiss it as static electricity when he noticed the decorative flourish on the ends. It was a circle partially bisected with a line.

With a sweep of his arm, he shoved the lot in the knapsack he brought for that purpose. "It's getting late. Let's take this back to my place and get some sleep."

Kara's head drew back. "That's a little presumptuous, isn't it?" She laughed.

"That you'll be coming home with me or that you'll get any sleep?"

She laughed louder, blushing wildly. Kara ducked her head in embarrassment, allowing him to surreptitiously slip the small black scroll into the breastplate of his armor.

"Are you ready to go?" he asked, shouldering the bag and holding out his hand.

Guilt warred with shame as she gave him a beatific smile full of trust. Kara took his hand, and they left the abominable room together. Under his armor, the scroll heated ominously against his chest.

23

Ash traced the pattern the dappled sunlight made on Kara's skin. Making love to her last night had been sublime...and it had kept him from thinking too much about the way he'd deceived her.

Not deceived. Withheld. The scroll he'd taken had been written by the demon king himself. Ash had pored over it for hours after Kara had fallen asleep. But the closely spaced words had been close to gibberish. They would require more study before he could determine whether it had anything to do with the Firehorse curse.

As for the blood Kara had given him, there were things he needed to do, tests he needed to conduct. But those could wait. This morning, he was going to pretend he and Kara were the only two people on earth.

An eternity with her wouldn't be long enough. And without her, it would be Hell.

Don't think about it. *Live in the now.* It had been his strategy for a millennium, a coping mechanism that enabled to get him through the endless series of days.

Taking his own advice, he looked down at Kara. He memorized the lines of her face first with his eyes and then with his fingers. He traced her chin and fragile collarbone, torn between letting her sleep and willing her to wake.

She stirred in his embrace, but didn't open her eyes. Ash pressed a kiss to the soft spot on her cheek next to her ear. He was about to start working his way down her body when a masculine throat clearing stopped him dead in his tracks.

Ash raised his head, sucking in his breath through his teeth. "Do I have to start hanging a tie on the doorknob?"

Except he hadn't actually seen a tie in years. If he wanted one, he'd have to sew it himself.

Marcus' blank expression told him he was unfamiliar with that particular sartorial accessory. He looked from Ash to Kara, a flicker of distaste crossing his features.

Annoyed, Ash rose from the bed. "What is it, Marcus?"

His aide held a piece of paper in his hand. "I...uh." He looked past Ash to Kara. She was blinking at them both from the bed with a sheet wrapped around her.

"Whatever you need to say, you can say in front of Kara," he told Marcus "You can trust her."

I'm the one who can't be trusted, he thought, thinking of the scroll hidden in his armor.

Marcus continued to hesitate, looking down at his report to avoid their eyes. Ash glowered at him.

"It's okay," Kara interrupted before he could reprimand his aide. "I need to get back to check on my people anyway." She glanced at the spot on her arm where he'd drawn her blood. "It may be time to replenish certain supplies," she added.

"All right," he said, wishing she would stay.

Stop being selfish. Making certain the surviving Firehorses had blood to stave of the curse was a hell of a reason for her to go.

"Let me at least get you something to eat or some coffee," Marcus said in a strangled voice. He resembled a turtle trying to crawl back into its shell.

"No, thanks. If you'll excuse me, I'll just get dressed now."

Ash gestured for Marcus to precede him out of the room. He closed the door behind them.

He crossed his arms, staring down at the smaller man.

"I'm sorry, my lord, but this information is very sensitive and your...friend...is still a stranger." He shifted his weight back and forth. "I'm not certain if this information is sound or not. The source was not exactly reliable—"

He held up a hand. "Slow down. Just tell me what it is."

Marcus stepped farther away from his bedroom door to the other side of the room to ensure Kara couldn't overhear them. "I was sent a report late last night from a man in the eighth arrondissement."

He broke off and held up a hand. "Serge is a bit of a drunk, and he can't hold down a job. He can usually be found sucking down rotgut out in one of the empty lots down by the ruins of the Arc de Triomphe. He claims two men passed by late in the evening. They were herding a group of people. He thought the men were bound, that they were holding their hands out in front of them like..."

"Like they were prisoners," Ash finished, a rolling disquiet spreading through him. Could it be? Had someone set up another prison in town despite his warning?

The bedroom door opened. Kara was dressed and ready to leave with her bag in hand.

"Get me an address. I'll take care of it," he said in a low-pitched murmur. Kara didn't need to hear this.

"Right away," Marcus said before excusing himself.

Kara watched him leave out of the corner of her eye. "He does *not* like me."

"Marcus is simply surprised," he said absently. "I don't think he ever expected me to, you know, be with someone."

It was such a weak description for what was between them,

but his mind was racing, trying to figure out who would dare cross him again.

If there was another prison, he'd have no choice but to make examples of the people responsible...

"Are you all right?" she asked. "Can I help with whatever's gone wrong?"

"How do you know anything is wrong?"

Kara scowled, making a move to snatch the report. He held it above his head, conceding defeat to her powers of perception. "It's nothing I can't take care of on my own. If your people need you to refresh their good-luck charms, then that should be your priority."

Kara frowned. "If you're sure."

"I am."

She pointed to the chest he'd used to store the books and scrolls they found in the demon tower. "What about those? Are they going to explode or cause a tsunami to sweep away the city?"

"No. They're not a danger themselves. Objects aren't subject to the Firehorse curse."

"I know *that*," she scoffed. "But didn't you say last night that these things poison the air around them?"

"Don't worry. The wards I've placed on these walls should be enough to hold the corruption these cause at bay—long enough for us to go through them anyway."

She headed for the door, pausing at the threshold. "So I guess I meet you back here tonight?"

He nodded. "Come whenever you are free. I'll inform Marcus you're to be granted access at any time."

"Bet he'll love that."

"He'll deal with it," Ash replied, walking her out. They parted ways downstairs, where Marcus was waiting with the location of their information.

Ash flew out to meet the drunk, who at eight in the morning

was still inebriated—at least when he first arrived. Serge sobered rapidly when he realized who had come calling.

"T-t-they went that way," the drunk told him, pointing to the left where the block ended abruptly in a pile of rubble.

Ash squinted at the derelict buildings in the distance. "What's over there? Anything still standing?"

"Just the old apartment building. Not sturdy to live in so people don't," he said, clutching a half-empty bottle to his chest.

Annoyed his people weren't more productive, Ash dismissed him, heading out in the direction of the building on his own.

Despite the relative prosperity of this district, this particular corner was an island of neglect and ruin. Ash climbed up the first-floor stairs of the derelict building, wondering how many pockets of devastation were left in the city.

Too many. That was damn certain.

The upper levels were empty save for the occasional rat. He was about to give up the report of prisoners as a drunkard's fantasy when he went down to the basement.

Adrenaline pumped through his veins as he saw signs of recent movement. The dust in the room had tracks running throughout with footprints in multiple sizes. And there were voices. They were distant, coming from somewhere below his feet.

Don't kill anyone. Not right away. If the jailers were down there, he'd capture and interrogate them. And whoever was calling the shots would pay.

Ash had left his sword behind in his Belleville room, but he had his dagger. Not that he needed it. For this, his fists would do. He was looking forward to it.

The volume of voices rose as he opened the door to the sub-basement. He couldn't see anything past the threshold. There was a massive curtain blocking the way.

Furious, Ash rushed forward, tossing the fabric aside with

one hand, holding his knife ready with the other. But there was no one there.

The sound of steel clanging boomed in his ears, covering the voices momentarily.

What the hell? He was inside a pentagram, demonic runes written at every point. There was a little box in the center. The voices were coming from it.

"I'm sure you'll be pleased to learn the engineers have finally succeeded in their efforts to repair the radio tower," a voice said.

Titouan appeared from behind a pillar with Kline at his side.

Ash lunged, his wings spreading to close the distance between them in a jump. He was caught short, hitting an unseen barrier with a crash that made his skin pop and sizzle.

Bordelle. He was trapped.

"What is the meaning of this?" he stormed. *"Release me!"*

Klein and Titouan clapped their hands over their ears. But whatever they had drawn on the floor muted his true voice. To his ears, it had full angelic resonance, but the two men weren't falling to the floor, bleeding from their eyes.

When he closed his mouth, they tentatively took their hands off their ears, skirting the edge of the pentagram to get as far from him as possible. This was demon craft—an angel trap.

He'd seen one before. They were unbreakable from the inside.

"How are you doing this?" His eyes narrowed on their sallow faces.

Klein beamed. "We've been watching you for a long time. We knew all those demon volumes you stashed all over the city would come in handy someday."

His mouth dropped open. The little thieves. "How dare you spy on me." Ash spat on the ground. It hit the barrier with a shower of sparks. "And how dare you use this filth to trap me. What the hell are you trying to accomplish?"

Titouan gave him a short bow. "In a word, freedom."

Ash laughed outright. "I think not. You don't know the meaning of the word. What you want is to rule this city in my stead... How the hell do you think to accomplish that with the Firehorse curse unbroken?"

"Well—" Titouan began.

"Oh, shut up," Ash said, cutting him off. "You didn't think of this on your own," he sneered, looking past them. "I know you're here, Mazarin. Show yourself!"

The last councilman slipped from behind the cover of the pillar.

Ash shook his head. "Of course this irresponsible and idiotic scheme could only come from your own twisted head."

Mazarin folded his plump hands primly in front of him. "For what it's worth, I am truly sorry it has come to this. But it's my genuine belief you no longer have Bastille's best interests at heart."

Unbelievable. "I have given everything for this city."

Mazarin feigned surprise. "So the new lover you've taken hasn't distracted you at all? Good to know... Nevertheless, we've decided you must go."

He paused, wiping a sweaty hand on his shirtfront. "It really would have been better if you just let things go on as they had. We were really the best leaders this town could have had. Nobody knows it better than we do." He picked imaginary lift off his sleeve. "But our removal is moot now. Once the people know you're dead, they'll welcome us back. We're familiar. They know us. Even those who don't like us will take comfort in our words."

Ash lowered his chin, glaring at them. "This trap can't kill me."

Titouan grinned. "That's the beauty of it. It doesn't have it. If it works as described—and apparently it does—then you'll be bound here for all eternity."

Incredulous, Ash couldn't help asking. "And just how do you

think to disappear me—the warden of Bastille? Do you really think no one will come looking for me?"

"Oh, we know they will," Mazarin replied. "But they'll never find you. Once we leave this room, the explosions we set will level the upper stories, burying you down here forever."

The man shrugged rounded shoulders. "You're going to be an unfortunate victim of the curse. You've said it yourself in public often enough. Even you aren't immune."

Mazarin looked at the other two, gesturing them to follow him. They stepped over the curtain and were at the door before he turned to look back.

"It's really too bad you can't starve," he said with a tsk. "I don't imagine this will be a pleasant place to spend eternity."

The door shut behind them.

Unbelievable. Ash banged his fists against his forehead, berating himself for his stupidity. *I need to get out of here.*

Still furious, he began to test the trap. He moved with lightning speed, testing the perimeter of the trap with his hands and blade.

The seconds slipped by, rushing away like water, but there was no opening, no weakness for him to exploit. Ash began to count, estimating how much longer it would take for the out-of-shape politicians to safely exit the building.

The explosions went off between ten and eleven.

24

Ash made the mistake of breathing before the dust from the rubble settled. Coughing reflexively, he bent over, wiping the grit from his eyes. Once it cleared, he swore and stood, taking stock of his predicament.

Damn it. The conspirator's explosion had been well-planned. His prison was undisturbed by the building's collapse. No debris disturbed the lines of the pentagram and surrounding runes. The area near the door was impassable. He could have dug himself out with enough effort, but whatever infernal spell was powering the angelic trap had created a protected pocket.

If only the council had managed to mess this up like they did everything else. Why did they have to start doing things correctly *now*?

Furious, he went to kick the radio before checking himself. He picked it up with a rough, choked-off laugh. How long had he been pining for this damn technology to make a comeback? *Now look at me*, he thought, setting it back on the floor. Innovation had come back with a vengeance, only to bite him in the ass.

This was his fault. He should have expected those bastards to pull a stunt like this. But what was really killing him was something Mazarin had said.

How had he known about Kara? Did he know who and what she was?

Gossip was free entertainment. People would have seen him talking to her at the factory fire and made assumptions. Would Mazarin have thrown out the term lover like that unless he was certain?

Politicians lie for a living. The fat little toad had to be bluffing.

Unless those spies had been trained on his apartment...or worse. What if Ash had been set up?

Marcus was the only one who'd known about him and Kara. He was also the one who'd given Ash the information about this supposed prison.

No, it wasn't possible. His aide would never knowingly betray him. Ash knew the man didn't trust Kara yet, but he and Marcus had worked side by side for the better part of two decades. His loyalty was unassailable.

He could have been tricked into revealing something. Someone had obviously fed him false information about the prisoners. Those three must have been planning this for some time.

As long as they don't know the truth about Kara, he thought, clenching his fists. His breath shortened.

Stop it. Angels did not panic. And it didn't matter if they knew about his relationship with Kara. As long as they didn't know about her blood, she would be all right.

Thank God I didn't tell Marcus anything. Paranoia sometimes pays.

And Kara could take care of herself. She'd kept herself and dozens of others alive in the most inhospitable environment on earth. She could probably take on the council singlehandedly.

She certainly wouldn't have fallen into a trap like this. He ground his teeth, cursing his own stupidity.

Refusing to accept there was no way out, he began to test the barrier again. He went over it systematically, even leaping above him in case there was a weakness over his head.

The only thing he got for his trouble was scorched feathers. Hours later, his knuckles and elbows scraped and bloody, he finally gave up. Ash sat in the middle of the pentagram, racking his brain for a solution.

No matter what Mazarin said, people wouldn't accept he had died in the building's collapse. Marcus would look for him. Once she knew he was gone, Kara would, too.

I hope.

He sat back on the floor with the radio, attempting to figure out how to make the primitive device a two-way box. But try as he might, he couldn't make sense of the intricate bundle of wire and transistors. Ash was a warrior, not a creator. Invention wasn't an angel gift.

Time stretched as he waited and waited. Marcus would be looking for him. *No, he won't. Not yet.* Mazarin would have come up with a way to distract him. Kara was his best shot.

If only the engineers had figured out how to recreate cell phones instead of the damn radio. Or if Kara was another angel. Then she'd be able to sense his distress and come after him.

Maybe she'll hear him, anyway.

His connection with Kara was unlike anything he'd ever experienced before. Was it totally beyond the realm of reason that she might hear him if he called?

We just made love this morning. Not to put too fine a point on it, there was still a piece of him with her and vice versa.

Crouching back down, Ash sat in lotus position, making a concerted effort to clear his mind. He focused on her image, drawing the lines of her face until they burned brightly in his mind. He drew on his feelings, balling them up deep inside until he let them out, calling her name silently.

Nothing. At least, he didn't feel an answering echo like he did communicating with his brothers and sisters.

Try again.

The longest twenty minutes of his life later, the silence was still unbroken.

"Putain," he said aloud. He banged his breastplate, wondering if the barrier was muting his connection like it did his voice. What was he going to do?

Enlightenment didn't come with a blaze of light from above the way it did in old cartoons. It was the stinging of his mangled knuckles over his heart...where he'd slipped the demon king's scroll and the vial of Kara's blood.

Ash had a way to strengthen his call, right in a bottle nestled against his heart. Except...it meant answering the question he'd been dreading.

It's time. Putting it off had been a foolish attempt to bury his head in the sand.

Loosening his breastplate, he reached inside for the vial, leaving the scroll where it was.

There was blood on his hand, but he didn't want to do this on his skin. Ash drew his knife, slicing his thumb. He let a large drop accrue on the tip of the blade, staring at it for several heartbeats.

Just do it. Neck corded with tension, he loosened the stopper and tilted the bottle, letting the blood fall onto the flat side of his knife. It landed next to his.

The drop of blood was the darkest possible red, a variant so dark it was almost black. Lips tight, he straightened the knife until the two drops ran together.

The telltale sizzle was small, but it was there. Ash rocked on his heels, taking a shaky breath.

You knew this. This was what he had expected ever since she revealed what her blood could do. Her ability to read the runes in the devil tower had confirmed it.

Yes, Kara was a witch, that much had been obvious for some time. But she wasn't some run-of-the-mill practitioner. Though unschooled in the craft, her gift was stronger than any he'd ever seen. Which made sense, of course—she had demon blood running through her veins.

25

Angel and demon blood didn't mix, not without an explosive reaction. The mix of his and Kara's blood sizzled and burned, but it had died without blowing up in his face.

Which means Kara isn't a full demon. She wasn't even half. But the taint was there.

That wasn't even the worst part. If he was right, then Kara's family had been founded by Amducious himself.

The king had been on earth before the Collision. He'd been part of the sect that warred with Heaven during Lucifer's rebellion. According to rumor, he had raped a beautiful human woman who'd crossed his path. The child that resulted had been born with uncanny abilities, a rare demon-born witch.

Like so many events from that time, the details of the child's life were murky. All Ash knew for certain was his history full of murder and iniquity—and that he'd gone on to have several children. Their family name had never been known to his kind.

He knew it now. It was Delavordo.

He'd believed every witch from that line to be dead—mostly

at the hands of his people. They had made it their mission to wipe out those abominations for centuries.

But Kara wasn't evil. Ash knew it in his bones. No matter what her provenance, her actions were what defined her. Kara was a savior. Nothing would change that—not even a demonic heritage.

Nevertheless, this knowledge was a game changer. So many things now made sense. Now he knew why Kara was so intricately tied to the curse. Her ancestor had been the one to cast it. And she was Ash's best hope for ending it.

Focus on the now. He still needed to get out of here, and he had the means to do it.

There was just one problem. Angels were supposed to be pure of mind and body. That was why sex with humans was forbidden. As transgressions went, it was forgivable. *Probably.* The hard liners in Heaven would disagree.

This spell he was about to cast was another situation entirely. To complete it, he would need to take the blood into his body. Using a human's would have been one thing. Doing this with demon blood would contaminate him, putting him that much farther from Heaven.

It always comes down to this, he thought, fiddling with the vial to swirl the dark ruby liquid around. Nothing was stronger than blood magic. That was what Raphael always told him. Of course, his old commander hadn't mentioned things like this angelic trap.

Ash had discovered these when he was in the field. He'd found his squadron brother Lucien imprisoned in one near the end of the first holy war.

Lucien had been emaciated and nearly demented. Once in Heaven, he'd recovered...eventually. But that angel had been a celibate warrior dedicated to defeating evil. Unlike Ash, Lucien had nothing to lose. That wasn't Ash anymore. All this time on earth had changed him. If something happened to Kara or his city while he was stuck in here, he didn't know what he'd do.

He couldn't think about that anymore. That way lay madness. This angel trap could keep him bound, but it wouldn't stop his call.

Just keep telling yourself that. With a sigh, he picked up his blade again. Cutting deeper, he used the flowing blood to draw a sigil on the floor. His fingers swept in a semicircle, forming a crescent before moving his fingers out in rapid strokes.

Once he was done, he kept his bloody fingers in the center of the sigil he'd drawn, maintaining contact. Using his free hand, he opened the vial and lifted it to his lips.

Should he drink it all or save some for a second attempt? *All,* he decided. Saving some for a second attempt would be pointless. He had one shot at this.

What was it pre-Collision humans had said when taking a shot? "Bottoms up."

Tipping the vial up, he drank the contents in one gulp. The taste of iron and cinnamon exploded in his mouth. Overwhelmed, he swallowed quickly, running his tongue over his lips to ensure it was all down. The aftertaste of bitter ochre lingered.

Using the sacred words for connection, he called for Kara, using her name in between refrains. His spell pulsed out of him, the vibration coming from the very heart of him.

An invisible wave bounced back on him, striking like a body blow. He fell on his side.

Merde. Ash winced and picked himself up. Anxious now, he redoubled his efforts, praying and chanting in the tone and frequency specific to angels. Eventually, his desperation infused the spell. It increased in pitch, battering at the invisible wall generated by the pentagram.

Only some of them ricocheted. He sat there, buffeted by the force of his own spell. The noise generated was so loud he was tempted to cover his ears, but he couldn't risk stopping his chant. He kept his hand on the sigil, breaking off suddenly when he heard stones shift. An ominous crack sounded overhead.

Crap. If he kept going, the subbasement might come down on him completely. Even if she heard him, Kara might not be able to reach him, let alone dig him out.

Wincing, he resumed chanting. It wasn't like he had another option.

You know, now might be an excellent time to pray.

26

H ours passed before Ash finally stopped chanting. The reverberation had stopped, signaling whatever mojo Kara's blood had given the spell was waning.

The subbasement floor had continued to collapse, kicking up a storm of dust that induced a massive coughing fit, but the angel trap was undisturbed.

And Kara still hadn't appeared.

Trying not to lose hope, he lay on the floor, picturing her face. He lost himself in dreams of her. Some were memories of the past, but mostly he fantasized about the future they might never have.

The rock that fell from the ceiling landed a few feet away. Figuring it was just the building settling, he ignored it until he heard his name.

"*Ash.*"

He sat bolt upright, joy and love rushing through him. "Kara!"

"Where the hell are you?" A thin beam of light broke through the darkness. It shone through the ceiling, jerking back and forth as she began to climb down from one of the holes.

"Be careful," he called, watching the progress of the flashlight with his heart in his throat.

The ceiling was ten feet off the ground, but the partial collapse meant there was a pile of rubble for her to land on. Twisting like a gymnast, she landed lightly on top of the stones, dropping the flashlight in the process.

Kara bent to pick it up, waving it in his general direction. "What *happened*? Why are you here? And why in the hell did I feel compelled to come here?"

She held the flashlight under her chin, illuminating her lovely confused face.

"Don't move! Stay right there," he shouted. The trap was generating immense amounts of energy. Crossing the boundary could be dangerous. "It was the council, or rather a damn cabal within the council. They laid a trap for me."

"*Ugh*. Which councilmen?"

"Mazarin, Klein, and Titouan. There may have been more, but those three were the only ones who dared show their faces. They have been spying and plotting against me since I removed them from office."

He gestured to the lines of the pentagram. "I can't cross the boundary."

Her expression was incredulous. "Are you serious?" She pointed the flashlight beam at the ground. "This is all it takes to capture you?" She whistled. "If I'd only known..."

He glowered. "It's demon magic, Kara. They had to sacrifice an animal for this—or worse."

Chastised, she looked down. "Oh, sorry."

"You have to help me deactivate it, but carefully. Don't cross the edge. Don't even put a finger over it," he warned.

Kara looked at the lines of the trap. "How do I undo it?"

"It should be easy from the outside. You just erase the symbols at the edge of each point. That's how I deactivated one a few thousand years ago."

Her expression was dubious. "*O-kay.* I don't suppose you care to explain how the hell I came to be here? Because I'm not sure. I was out gathering roots and tubers for the evening meal when my skin started to itch like crazy, and I couldn't stop thinking about you. The compulsion was so strong I dropped the roots I'd spent over an hour gathering and came straight here."

She wasn't going to like the truth... "Would you believe it was true love calling you to me in my hour of need?"

Kara scowled, swinging the light sharply at him for emphasis. "Didn't you hear me? I dropped *food.*"

He cleared his throat uncomfortably. "All right, I called you to me."

The crease in her brow deepened. "How in the hell did you do that?"

"I...drank your blood."

Kara's nose scrunched in disdain and surprise. "*Eww.*"

"Isn't that how your people use the vials you gave them when they're staving off the curse?"

"*No!*" She laughed, shaking her head. "They just spill it. Some choose to smear it on themselves to be safe."

Ash was skeptical. *I bet Theo drank it.* And Sij looked like the type who would enjoy the taste of blood.

"I needed to take it into my body to strengthen the bond between us," he said. "Drinking it was the most expedient way."

"Whatever," she replied, muttering about vampire angels under her breath.

Taking a few steps to her left, Kara knelt, reaching out to wipe away at the painted symbol on the point closest to her.

"Don't touch it with your hands," he admonished, getting as close to the edge as he could without getting zapped again.

"Got it." Kara rubbed the lip of the torch against the symbol, but the spray-painted symbol didn't budge, so she grabbed a sharp rock and began scratching.

"Is that good enough?" she asked. There was a gouge through the middle.

"Make sure it's completely interrupted," he said craning his neck to see the whole thing.

She nodded and kept at it until the entire thing was bisected in two.

"That should do it," he said, thanking her before she moved on to the next.

Her eyes flicked to his as she began to erase the second symbol. "Are you going to kill the men who put you in here?"

She bit her lip, her face pensive.

Ash hesitated. Would she see him differently if he executed the politicians? How tenuous was their bond?

"Do you think I should spare them?"

Kara took a deep breath and looked up as if she was considering her answer. "Normally, I would say yes...but Titouan would sell his mother if he thought someone would pay. And he's the nice one in the bunch. I know too much about Mazarin and Klein to argue that they deserve leniency. Do whatever you have to do."

Ash's shoulders dropped as he relaxed. "Good. I'm glad we agree. By the way, until I take care of them, you should steer clear of their districts."

She frowned, scratching at another sigil. "Why?"

"They've been spying. That's how they figured out how to do this—they got into the other texts I confiscated from the tower. I should have gone through them more thoroughly. If I'd known this ritual was in there, I would have hidden them better."

Kara glared at him. "I'm not running from those douchebags. If they come at me, I'll make them regret it."

He couldn't help laughing. "Something tells me you would succeed."

"Well, I certainly wouldn't get trapped by such an obvious ruse and a little spray paint."

His lips pressed together hard. "*I know*."

She chortled and kept working on the symbols. The last proved to be a challenge. It had been covered by fallen stones, forcing Kara to perch precariously on them to try and dig it out.

"So...was the part about true love calling me at all true? Is that a factor in your little phone call ritual or did you make that up?"

"Since the only other people I've ever called are my angel brethren, I couldn't say. I don't think it's a factor. I love my brothers and sisters, but I don't *love* my brothers and sisters if you know what I mean."

"Yeah, I think I get it."

He fought the urge to cross the barrier and pull her into his arms. "But I do *love* you."

A cocky grin flashed across her face. "I know," she said, echoing his words.

Damn. He just got Han-Solo'd, and she didn't even know it.

Ash waited for more, but the love of his life just kept smirking and digging away. "Aww, c'mon, Kara, throw a guy a bone."

She giggled. "You're like the most insecure angel I've ever met."

"I'm the only angel you've ever met."

"Thank God for that," she muttered.

"*Kara.*"

"All right, fine—I love you, too, you gigantic winged doofus."

Ash released a breath he hadn't been aware he was holding. "Thank you."

"You're welcome."

She blew the hair out of her eyes, shoving at a chunk of concrete that was blocking the last symbol. Only a fraction of it was cleared, but it was enough for her to start working to interrupt the corner with her rock.

He shifted his weight from foot to foot, impatient to get out of there and hold her.

"Are you—"

He didn't hear the rest of what she said. A tremor shook the building, sending a piece of rebar down the pile of rubble Kara was standing on. It knocked her off balance, propelling her over the line of the pentagram. There was a bright flash of light as her fragile body crossed the barrier threshold.

Ash flew toward her, trying to push her back out of the trap before she got fried.

He failed.

27

T he barrier was down, but it had severely hurt Kara in the process. Somehow, against all odds, she'd scraped the last connecting lines as she fell, granting him freedom.

But she wasn't moving.

Ash cradled her to him tightly. "Don't die," he pleaded, pressing his lips to her hair.

She didn't answer. There was no sign she had heard him—no eyelash flutter, not even a twitch.

"*Damn it,* Kara. Don't do this to me." Fuck saving the world. She couldn't leave *him*.

He checked her pulse. It was weak and thready, but still there. Unsure what else to do, he started performing CPR, rhythmically breathing in and out of her mouth.

Her lips were the first sign of movement. At first, he thought it was his imagination, but the increased pressure of her mouth against his was a real response.

Kara sneezed and blinked, jerking away from him. "I was going to hit you because I couldn't figure out who was kissing me."

"You aren't getting out of this yet."

She sat up, wincing. "Out of what?"

"Life with me."

Kara still appeared to be in pain, but her smile nearly stopped his heart. "You're just a big mushy wuss," she said, punching him weakly in the arm.

The constriction around his heart eased a fraction, but it left a cold spot in his gut. Kara shouldn't have survived that. The fact she was sitting up and talking—or rather mocking him—was nothing short of a miracle. Only Ash didn't believe *his* father had anything to do with her quick recovery. No, her survival was due to Kara's demon heritage.

Demonic blood was acidic with powerful regenerative properties. It was one of the reasons the bastards were so hard to kill. Kara was stronger than a normal human—she knocked him out with a rock. That would be a challenge for a man twice her size. He should have guessed the truth back then.

At least she doesn't have an exoskeleton or diamond-tough scaly skin. "I'm taking you back to my place until you fully recover," he told her, bending to help her stand.

Kara started to speak, but getting up was painful enough to silence any arguments she might have made to reject his help.

Together, they picked their way out of the basement dungeon. Despite the beating the angel trap had given him, he supported Kara the whole way, not letting her bear her own weight except when necessary.

They climbed through the crack in the ceiling before she pulled away again. "I can make it on my own," she insisted when he took her hand.

"Not a chance," he growled, wondering if there was enough room to pick her up again.

There wasn't. In fact, he was forced to bend over double, and then crawl through the narrow space between two fallen walls.

"How in the world did you get to me?" he asked, feeling claustrophobic as they inched along.

"It's just a few more dozen yards, and then there's an opening to another room. There's a hole in the wall leading to a tunnel."

"And to the catacombs after?"

"Yes."

That was a relief. "Once there, I will make my own way," she repeated. "I want you to leave and go after those cabal traitors."

Why did she have to be so bloody independent? "Not until I'm sure you're a hundred percent. You have no idea how much energy was running through that trap."

"*I'm fine.* Now get your tight angel butt through here."

"Through where?" Craning his head to peek around her, Ash spotted a narrow opening in the wall ahead. Once on the other side, he was able to stand.

He immediately pulled Kara into his arms. "If I'd known you were going to get hurt like that, I wouldn't have called you," he whispered into her hair.

Kara leaned back in his embrace to look at his face. "So you would rather have stayed trapped in a hole than see me hurt?" she asked in a *please-be-practical* tone before turning to lead the way.

He followed, his heart heavy as the truth settled in his gut. "I'm not prepared to sacrifice you for myself or for the city—not again... Kara, what if we just left?"

She stopped short in front of him just a few feet from the exit. "What are you talking about?"

"I'm talking about getting the hell out of dodge. Let's forget about the damn council and the fucking curse. We can leave together, eke out a life in the wasteland. Just the two of us."

Kara squeezed her eyes shut before opening them wide, as if she expected to see someone else standing there. "Who are you and what have you done with Ash?"

He sighed, rubbing his hands over his face and leaning against the rough wall of the cave.

She walked up to him, studying his face intently. "You want me to run off with you—to forget everyone else and just leave?"

"*Yes.*"

Now she was starting to look concerned. He broke away from the wall. "I know you can't do that. You don't have to abandon your people, but I don't have to keep trying to rescue this city from itself. We can take your people with us, and we can build a new home somewhere."

She stared at him with wide, disbelieving eyes. "And we're just supposed to leave Bastille to those bastards who tried to imprison you? What about the regular people who have to live under their rule? What happens when the next Firehorse rises? What then?"

He put his hand on his breastplate, just over the scroll she couldn't see. "I...I just don't want you to get hurt again."

Almost losing her just now had shaken him to the core.

Risking his life was one thing. God had created him to serve. Ash had entered the pact with Raphael well aware that breaking the curse might require the ultimate sacrifice. He'd been prepared to die taking down the demon king.

But Kara was just a girl—well, mostly a girl. She had never asked for the burden placed on her shoulders.

But the curse was tied to her. Ash might not have a choice but to let her court danger.

Damn that bastard Amducious. It was too bad the demon king was dead. He'd like to kill him all over again.

Kara stood on her tiptoes and gave him a quick but fiery kiss before breaking into a grin. "Again, I'm not the one who let themselves get snatched by some pudgy pencil pushers. I can take care of myself."

"I don't doubt it," he said after a long pause, guilt flaring. The slight pressure of the scroll under his breastplate burned like a brand, pushing him to act.

Ash put his hand on his breastplate as if to hide it from her sight. Untangling the dark magic tormenting the city could very well cost them her life. Curse or no curse, he couldn't picture a future without her now.

"I guess you're right," he said slowly.

Kara grinned. "Of course I am. Get used to that feeling." She cocked her head. "What brought this on?"

Ash almost reached into the breastplate for the scroll, but caution stayed his hand. Instead, he decided to share a different unpleasant truth.

"If we succeed and break the curse, my banishment ends," he reminded her.

Understanding darkened her eyes. "Of course you'll want to go back to Heaven. It's what you've been working for all this time."

"It's not a question of want. Not anymore," he said.

"Right," Kara scoffed. "You deposed the demon king and took over the wardenship of Bastille to win back a place in Heaven."

"I thought it was where I belonged. But that's no longer true. If I had the choice—if God himself asked me where I belonged today, I would tell him the truth. My place is at your side. I love you."

For a second, he thought Kara was going to punch him in the arm again. But she just gripped his hand. "And you don't think you're going to be given a choice? Is that what you're telling me?"

"I don't really know what's going to happen, but if the curse is broken, I could be recalled without warning. The Host is defined by their service. Being an angel means obeying orders. They might not ask if I want to stay. Unless things have changed, it wouldn't occur to them to do otherwise."

Her expression dimmed. "I see...and if you left, you couldn't come back?"

"I don't know. Passage to this plane is at God's discretion. I could try to fall again, but with a flick of His wrist, I could end up on the other side of the world. I might be trapped in another cursed landscape for the rest of your life. It would be my punishment for defying Him a second time."

If that happened, he'd fight to get back to her, of course, but he'd already failed to fly through the impenetrable barrier the curse had created. It could take years or centuries to get back to Bastille.

Human lives were too damn short.

Kara wrapped her arms around him, her face soft despite the breastplate between them. "This is something I never thought to ask before—do the humans who live good lives here go to Heaven? Or is the curse blocking them from getting there the way it's stopping you?"

"A human soul is energy that can't be measured. As far as I know, it can cross the barrier." At least, he thought so. In all his years since the Collision, he hadn't run into an unusual number of ghosts, just a few here and there. If human souls were trapped here by the curse, he'd have encountered a legion of them.

She put her hands on either side of his face, her expression grave. "If the worst happens and we don't get to live our lives together down here, I don't want you to fall again and risk getting trapped. If God says you can't come back down to earth, sit tight and wait for me upstairs."

"Kara—" he began.

She tugged on his breastplate, a hint of a smile playing on her lips. "What? Are you suddenly afraid of commitment? Haven't you been single for a few thousand years—what's a couple of more decades?"

Tears burned behind his eyes, but Kara was steadfast and fearless. "If things go bad taking down these douchebags and undoing the curse, I have faith we'll meet again in Heaven, so let's just get out there and end this."

It was a sound plan, except for one thing. Heaven had rules. It was pure. Nothing tainted could enter. Which meant Kara's demon heritage barred her from its gates. *Forever.*

But he didn't tell her that. He took her hands. "No matter what happens, nothing—neither Heaven nor Hell—will keep me from you."

He'd war with God himself before he let his fierce warrior princess be damned.

Ignorant of the storm raging in his breast, Kara nodded.

"Nothing will," she promised with a bracing smile. She tugged on his arm to get him moving. "Let's go. We have work to do."

28

Bastille was in chaos. Several fires dotted the skyline, and people were fighting in the street.

Ash and Kara ran into the nearest crowd at the edge of Parc Monceau. Men and women were running back and forth. She pulled aside a random man about to break the door down to a bakery with a rock.

"Looting, *really?* What the hell is going on?" she asked in disgust. "Has another Firehorse risen?"

The man started, his eyes wide as he took in Ash in full armor over her shoulder. "Yes. And the first person to die was him," he said, pointing at Ash.

"The reports of my demise have been greatly exaggerated," Ash drawled, disappointed when the two blinked owlishly at him.

"No Twain fans? Never mind. Obviously, I'm not dead."

Kara wrinkled her nose. "I didn't think the cabal would move this quickly to announce your death."

He turned to her. "Neither did I." They could have at least waited long enough to be sure their trap would hold him.

Mazarin could never count patience as a virtue.

The incredulous man shook his head. "They told everyone over the new PA system. And..." He stopped, clutching at his neck.

"And *what*?"

"They said your aide Marcus caused the building collapse. They're going to execute him as a Firehorse—a real public execution at the Place de Grève. He's to meet Madame Guillotine."

Ash pulled out his blade with his next breath. "*When?*"

The man's eyes skittered to the knife before coming back to his face. "Now, I think. In f-f-fact, he may already be dead."

His stomach dropped as the ground fell away from beneath his feet. Aside from the woman standing in front of him, Marcus was his only friend. "*Kara*—" he began.

She waved him away. "Don't worry about me. Go!"

He stopped just long enough to kiss her before spreading his wings and shooting into the sky. Pumping harder than he ever had before, Ash streaked through the sky, hurtling toward the center of the city.

It wasn't far, but he pushed himself to his very limits. His pecs and scapula were screaming by the time he sighted his destination below.

Place de Grève was mobbed.

It was a flashback straight out of his nightmares. A wooden platform had been erected at one end in front of the Hotel de Ville. Two tiny figures were moving on it, dragging a third figure to what appeared to be an empty doorway, standing in the middle of the stage.

Ash blinked, reliving the nightmare of the revolution in the space between seconds. He'd been in England when the Reign of Terror had started. He'd rushed back to Paris, his goal to save as many of the blameless as possible. His actions had spared a few. The terror had wound down on its own. When the demons had come, they'd rejected the guillotine as too humane.

He could see Marcus' contorted features as the two men forced his aide to lay across the board under the gleaming blade.

Despite being fit, Marcus was no longer a soldier. He strained against their hold, but he was no match for the pair holding him.

Time slowed as he flew down, knife at the ready. The mob was roaring. Some were cheering. Others were screaming, a combined primal shriek that reverberated in his soul.

Ash opened his mouth, his war cry sounding from deep in his core as he plunged down like an avenging angel. But it was too late. The blade whistled as it fell, striking Marcus' head from his body. It hit the platform with a thump.

He was too late.

Red flooded his vision. Raising his blade, he dived, closing the distance as his best friend's head rolled off the stage into the crowd. Slashing wildly, Ash cut down the first man. The force of his blow cut the man in half, spraying ruby-red blood like a mist across the stage.

The screams of the crowd transmuted to terror.

The bewildered audience began to scatter, but Ash had no time to soothe them or explain they had just executed an innocent man. He raised his blade again, caught up in a near-Berserker rage.

The second man to fall was Klein. He stumbled backward when he saw his accomplice cut down, tripping on his feet. Landing on his backside, he crawled away like a worm, but Ash didn't let him get far.

His knife whistled through the air, stabbing down with enough force to drive his blade completely through the man's body, the tip embedding in the wooden stage. Ash pulled it out effortlessly, scanning the crowd at the edge for the fleeing figures of the cabal.

His heart drummed in his ears as he pounced on the first well-dressed man he saw. Reaching out, he snagged the man's collar, flipping him over on his back.

"Please don't!" Titouan screamed. "Have mercy!"

Ash wanted to rail that a murderer didn't deserve mercy, but all that came out of his mouth was an incoherent roar. All around them, the buildings trembled with the violence of the sound.

Titouan clapped his hands over his ears, shrieking in agony. Ash thrust his blade through the man's throat, cutting off the noise with a gurgle.

Blood poured out of the hole in a stream as he withdrew the blade. It was flung from the end as he spun around, looking for the last one.

"Mazarin!" He couldn't pick out the politician's oily scent among the fleeing crowd. The acrid stink of fear overpowered it.

A gurgle made his look down. Titouan was still alive, weakly holding the hole in his neck. In his rage, Ash had failed to sever his spine. He decided to remedy that immediately. Reaching back, he yanked the man by the hair, cutting off Titouan's head in one ruthless stroke.

Carrying the head and knife in one hand, he pulled the first likely looking overweight man roughly to him. The portly man shook and gibbered incoherently. Ash tossed him aside as soon as he realized it wasn't Mazarin.

"Ash!"

Kara was forcing her way against the tide of stampeding humans. She was almost mowed down by a man, but a quick shove gave her enough room to keep her feet.

He met her halfway, his bloodlust too high to think. "I'll kill him," he growled, starting after the man who had knocked into her.

She grabbed his arm. "For fuck's sake, put down the head and leave that poor man alone."

"I need to find Mazarin," Ash said, pulling away.

She ran after him, throwing up her hands. "Look around, Ash. He got away. Taking down random men in the streets won't change that."

Ash blinked, his ardor cooling reflexively in her presence. He dropped Titouan's head, helplessly gesturing to the stage. "I was too late," he said hoarsely.

Kara's eyes flicked to the head lying in front of the platform. She grimaced. "I know. I'm so sorry," she said softly.

She hesitated a beat before walking into his arms. The move forced him to hold his knife away from her, but he was still running hot. He kept his weapon out to ward away any more threats to her.

"Mazarin has to pay for this."

"He will," she soothed, stroking his free arm. "But you can't go running amok with a knife like this and not expect everyone to run away screaming."

"Every second we delay gives him a chance to burrow deeper in some bolt hole."

She held up a hand. "Temporarily. He won't be able to hide without help. And everyone who saw you slice and dice the other two councilmen don't know they deserved it."

He shook his head. "They should. The cabal told everyone I was dead. They killed Marcus!"

"And all they know is you came roaring back from the dead, and you started hacking people to pieces. You need to explain what happened—and not in your terrifying angel voice. Look around you! The buildings can't handle the stress. The people probably can't either."

"How then? The only way the whole town would hear me is if I used my true voice."

Kara stood on her tiptoes, tugging on the top of his breast-plate for emphasis. "*The radio.*"

VIDEL, the engineer at the radio station, knew Ash by sight, but he'd never seen him covered in blood. He fumbled with the microphone, dropping it on the counter of the makeshift radio station before freezing in place.

"I'll get that," Kara volunteered, stepping forward to relieve the panic-stricken attendant.

The short man threw her the most grateful glance Ash had ever seen on a human face. *I should be trying to set Videl at ease. That was what a human would do.*

The thought came from a million miles away. He stared at the microphone, feeling numb and random.

Don't break out into the lyrics of "Video Killed the Radio Star".

"Ash."

He looked up with a start. Kara widened her eyes meaningfully, jerking her head toward the mike.

Go, she mouthed.

Oh. They were ready.

"This is Ash."

Kara waved frantically. She grabbed the skin on her neck, tugging it up and down.

"This is Azazel," he began again, infusing his voice with the peculiar resonance specific to his kind.

He hesitated, wondering what he should say. A description of Mazarin and a threat to anyone harboring would be a good place to start.

But that wasn't how he began. He started with what was in his heart. "I lost my best friend today."

Kara walked to the back of his chair, putting her arms around his shoulders.

He reached up to take her hand. "It happened because of greed and self-importance." He coughed, clearing the roughness in his throat.

"Mazarin and the others lied to you about my death. They blamed a good man for it, murdering him. For that, I executed the two conspirators I found at the scene of the crime. To the other members of the council, I grant clemency. I can't prove their involvement. As long as they stay out of politics, I will leave them be. But not Mazarin. He is still at large. I want him found."

Kara held her hands in front of him, stretching them to indicate she wanted him to speak more.

He took a deep breath. "I was trying to correct the imbalances in our system of government when I removed all the council members. I thought we would benefit from a fresh start, but I forgot human nature. Those who are given advantages without earning them forget they don't always deserve them. They think they are entitled to power, just because they've had it so long.

"I know the politicians have said the same about me." He broke off, glancing up at Kara. "Honestly, all I want is to be able to step down and settle on a small farm, surrounding myself with people I care about. But first, I need to end the Firehorse curse. The good news is we've moved closer to that goal."

Kara stepped around him, hovering anxiously, but he signaled her to calm down. He would never endanger her by revealing her secret. "As little as a month ago, I would have said nothing had changed. Things were about as hopeless as they had ever been. But that's not true anymore. I flew over the wasteland, and I saw something that changed my mind."

He met Kara's eyes. She gave him a nod, no longer worried.

"It was a tree," he continued. "For those of you who have never left the borders of our Bastille, that may not sound like an earth-shattering revelation. Trees grow throughout our city. But thanks to the great Collision and further actions from the demon horde, the wasteland surrounding us is blighted. I believed nothing would ever grow there again. I'm glad I was wrong."

He took a deep breath, dropping the resonance in his voice to speak in a muted human tone. "I think it's a sign from God. Our trials and tribulations will come to an end. It could be tomorrow —or it could be ten years from now. I can't give you a date. But for the first time in a long while, I believe again. I hope you do, too."

Ash reached across the counter, turning off the microphone.

Videl was transfixed. When he looked up, the man had tears in his eyes. He scrambled to turn off the auditory system.

The light in a little bulb on the wall slowly died. "We're off the air," the engineer confirmed.

Kara pounded on Ash's shoulders lightly.

"Was that what you had in mind?"

She hugged him. "It was perfect."

Ash ignored Videl's avid expression and pulled her close to his side, making sure she didn't come into contact with the gore on his breastplate.

"I need to clean up," he said.

She looked down at him "Hell yes, you do," she said, tugging on his hand to lead the way. He had to quicken his step to keep up with her, so eager was she to make an escape. Ash suspected Vidal's curiosity was making her uncomfortable.

Kara threw the door open, stopping short with a low swear. The building was surrounded.

29

P eople were pouring into the streets. The crowd
surrounding the makeshift radio station was almost a
wall, blocking their path.

Ash's feathers bristled as he ushered Kara behind him. He
didn't want to hurt anyone, but if they came at her, more blood
would flow.

"Mr. Angel Sir!" a voice called out. Samuel, the night man,
pushed his way to the front of the crowd. "Is it true, Mr. Angel? Is
there life in the wasteland?"

Ash blinked in surprise. This was not the bloodthirsty crowd
he'd assumed. The waiting faces were open and expectant. He
hadn't seen this auspicious a reaction since the king was first
overthrown.

"Yes," he said, slowly glancing behind him. Kara squeezed his
hand, slipping away to blend into the crowd.

"Can we start planting crops there?" a woman on the left
asked. Ash thought he recognized her as one of the field workers.

"Er... It's a little soon for that. The land is only now starting to
show signs of life," he said, trying to keep an eye on Kara's

retreating form. "The important thing at this moment is to find Mazarin. If you find him, bring him to me."

"When will the curse end?" someone else called out. A hush fell over the crowd.

"As I said earlier, it could be tomorrow, or it could be a year from now," he said. "I don't know. But until we do, the well-being of our city rests in our hands. We must all do our part...so why don't we go to work now?" He held up a hand before they interrupted again. "Now that our announcement system is finally running, I promise to keep you informed of any developments."

After he answered a few more questions, the bulk of the stragglers departed. He looked around for Kara, but she was nowhere to be seen.

"I'm sorry 'bout your friend." Samuel was still there, holding his cap in front of him. "I thought I might help you carry him for burial—I borrowed a clean vegetable cart. Not one of mine."

Ash blinked rapidly. "I hadn't thought of that. Thank you," he admitted. Burials weren't something he'd really had to take care of. Even after the war with the demon king and all the disasters when a new Firehorse rose—Marcus had always handled those details for him.

"I should go get his mother."

Samuel waved that away, pointing his cart in the direction of the Place de Grève. "It's all right. My boy Thomas went to fetch her."

"Does he know where she lives?"

"Someone will tell him. Everyone knew Marcus. We all liked him."

Ash nodded. He followed the cart with an odd detachment, relieved someone else was taking the lead on this.

When they arrived at Place de Grève, the bodies of Titouan and Klein were laying on top of a makeshift pyre.

Kara had taken charge. They had already torn down the scaffold holding the guillotine. The weapon itself was lying on its side, being hacked to pieces by a man under her direction.

A faded blue sheet had been laid over Marcus' body. From the shape of the mound underneath, the head had been returned to the body. Kara hurried up to him. She glanced at Samuel, but despite the night man's presence, she took his hand in an open display of affection.

"Did you do all this?" Ash asked, gesturing to the men dismantling the stage.

"I didn't want you to see him like that," she said, gesturing to the body under the sheet. "You don't have to bury him alone," she added.

"Thank you," he said, rubbing his thumb against the palm of her hand.

"I'll just load him up," Samuel murmured, fingering his cap and nodding at Kara like she was some sort of queen.

Ash washed up while Kara broke the news to Marcus' mother, Noemie. Kara helped Marcus' mother pick out a spot for burial at the top of the hill where Sacré-Coeur once stood.

Ash laid Marcus into the grave himself, holding his burden carefully so his mother wouldn't be able to tell his body wasn't whole.

"I know it isn't nearly enough to commemorate his many years of friendship and service, but this will be his resting place and his alone. No one else will ever be buried here," Ash told Noemie.

"Thank you," she murmured, not meeting his gaze. Samuel doffed his hat and led her away.

"Don't take it personally," Kara said, watching the pair leave. "She doesn't blame you."

He doubted that, but it was kind of her to lie to him.

"It's nothing new," he told her. "Noemie was never comfortable around me. Most people aren't. Only Marcus was at ease in my presence. It's the main reason I made him my aide."

Kara nodded. She didn't speak or try to touch, him. She simply stood at his side as he prayed, wishing Marcus' soul a speedy and safe journey.

Once he was done, he turned and began walking down the hill, making sure to keep his pace slow enough for her to keep up with.

"Marcus deserved so much more," he said with a heavy heart. "He worked tirelessly on the people's behalf, giving everything else up. Now he's gone. The man never even got a chance to marry or adopt children. And it's my fault. If I had only been a little faster—I could have saved him."

Kara veered into him so they were touching as they walked. "You can't think like that. This was Mazarin and the others. Titouan and Klein have paid. And when he's found, Mazarin will, too. Then we're going to break the curse. That's a damn fine legacy for any man if you ask me."

Except they were never going to do that if he didn't hand over the scroll he'd found in the demon tower.

You don't know for sure it is the Firehorse spell. It could have been anything the demon king considered worth writing down—a list of his sexual conquests or instructions to his minions. To him, it was nothing but gibberish.

Kara will see something else. And if she didn't, they were doomed anyway.

"I've been keeping something from you." He stopped and untied the brace at his shoulder, fishing out the simple black scroll and holding it out to her.

"I took this from the records we recovered in Montmeurtre. I think Amducious wrote it himself."

Kara slowed, hesitating before taking the small scroll from his hands. A line appeared between her fine brows.

"Why did you hide it?" She sounded more curious than upset.

"A lot of reasons."

"Pick one," she said, her voice flattening.

"I don't know if it's the Firehorse spell. I can't read it. But if you can…it means you are a witch."

Kara tensed. "I know your people consider witches the enemy, but…you already knew. My blood nullifies the effects of the Firehorse curse. There had to be a reason for that. We just didn't acknowledge the fact aloud."

No, they had tacitly agreed to ignore the blood feud between their people, but there was more to it than that.

He took a deep breath, letting it out with an audible whoosh. "The fact your blood effects the curse doesn't simply mean you're a witch. It means you're part of Amducious' line. He is the founder of your family."

Kara's lips parted, the blood draining from her face. "W-what does that mean?"

Ash wanted to wrap his arms around her, but when he reached out, she backed away.

He let his arms drop to his sides. "His blood runs in your veins. That's the reason it has the effect it does. The Firehorse curse is a very powerful spell. It would have been necessary to add safeguards to make sure he didn't fall victim to it himself. My guess is the demon king worked his blood into the ritual in order to protect himself. As his descendant, his immunity transferred to you. Or at least, part of it has."

"But I'm a Firehorse myself. I'm not immune."

He held up a finger. "You're still human enough to be a victim of the curse. The part of you that makes you such an effective leader beckons it. You were born to change the world, and the curse wants to destroy that. But paradoxically, the demon blood is making it rebound. It confused me at first because you don't work spells, yet I can detect the magic trailing from you. It's like the two forces are constantly at war within you."

Kara started, her mouth opening and closing a few times. "So I'm part demon? I'm evil?" she asked hoarsely.

"No!" Ash hurried to her side. He put his hands on her

cheeks. "This doesn't change what or who you are. Actions define human nature. And everything you've ever done speaks to the goodness and purity of your soul. Against all odds, you turned out amazing."

Even in the face of his abandonment, Kara had become that rare hero who selflessly acted on the behalf of others. In his opinion, she was a walking, talking miracle.

But she didn't seem to be grasping that. "How can you say that? I'm literally demon spawn."

"It's more complicated than that."

"How? What am I? What about the rest of my family? My grandmother?"

He shifted his weight, searching his memory. "I don't believe Simone was evil. But many other members of your family chose to align themselves with Lucifer or other lesser demons."

"That crazy! Why would they do that?"

"Personal gain, or sometimes just for fun. Some people enjoy inflicting pain and misery," he admitted. "But many of your family rejected the legacy. There are some very famous good guys mixed in your lineage, too."

Kara put her hand on her chest, as if she were trying to hold her heart inside. She was breathing too fast, almost panting.

"Demons are not born," he explained, putting his hand on her back. "They are made. Most are human souls twisted beyond recognition. But because you carry their blood in your veins doesn't mean you're evil or that your children will be. Every new generation is a chance to start fresh."

And if he ever got back up to Heaven, it was the first thing he'd be telling God. No matter what happened, Kara deserved a place there, probably more than he did.

Disbelief sharpened her voice. "Are you arguing nurture versus nature? *Seriously*?"

Moving jerkily, she sat on a chunk of concrete littering the path. She turned the scroll over in her hands, tracing the pattern on the decorated ends.

"It's a negative sign, Amducious' personal symbol," he elaborated.

Kara sighed and opened the scroll with a snap. Her head drew back. "It's nonsense. Just a bunch of random letters."

"You may have to sprinkle your blood on it to make the true words visible," he reminded her.

She scowled. "Of course I do. God, demons *suck*."

He was trying not to smile at her reaction when a young girl ran up to them, waving a scrap of paper in his face.

Ash bent to take the note. Assuming it was from one of the city's many managers reporting a problem, he scanned it quickly, but then frowned. "This is addressed to you, but I can't read anything but your name. It's in code."

Kara put the demon scroll in her pocket, buttoning it securely before reaching for the note. "We write in cypher for our safety."

She scanned the note and then scowled. "It's from Claire, the new girl."

"How did she get a note to you here in the city?" Had Claire broken the rules and entered Bastille?

Kara looked back down at the closely packed scrawl. "She's sending this with Mimi, Dr. Brès' daughter. Wait, was that her?"

She snapped up, craning her neck to look for the child.

Ash hadn't recognized her, but the girl had been close to thirteen or so. Old enough to know her way around. "I'm sure she's fine. What does the note say?"

Kara lifted the note and squinted. "Um... Oh, it's about Sij. Claire was supposed to be on a special hunting trip—just Firehorses."

She looked up, her face flushed. "That's not a good idea. We always mix up our teams. Too many Firehorses in one place is a bad idea, even if I'm there..." She turned back to the note. "Claire tried to catch up with them, but they weren't heading out to

Gentilly. She saw them in the north-east tunnel, the one that connects to the old metro and RER lines. Her light blew out before she could catch up, and she was too nervous to go on."

Kara shook her head. "I don't know why Sij would be in that tunnel with so many Firehorses. According to this, it's seven of them."

"That sounds like way too many," he muttered, disquiet spreading through his chests.

"Agreed." She looked confused. "We never have that many cursed people in the same place at the same time. And this tunnel doesn't go to the fields where we hunt."

"Where does it go?"

"Here. It ends in the Tuilleries, in the center of Bastille."

30

T he body was lying just off the road near Val de Grace a few yards away from one of the entrances to the cata-comb and tunnel system.

Kara was trembling as he knelt to examine the corpse, a young man Ash recognized from the desert band.

"I don't understand," she kept repeating. "What happened? Why is he here? He shouldn't be here."

"Who is he?"

"It's Pablo. He's a Firehorse from Rennes." She tugged on Ash's shoulder plate. "It is some sort of accident, right?"

"No, love… his throat is slit," he said, pulling up the man's shirt to reveal an intricately designed Amarisk.

Kara reared back in disgust. "What the hell is that?"

"It's a demon symbol, a kind of calling card." He'd seen it drawn by Amducious' followers many times during the first holy war, but over the years, it had faded in prominence. Only true acolytes of the dead king would even know it.

"Something's very wrong," he whispered, looking up to meet her confused gaze. "Kara…how old is Sij?"

Her head drew back. "I don't know. Who cares? She's old!"

"Yes, but how old? Did she tell you? Has she aged since you met her?"

"She never said. As for whether she looks older, I guess not, but she was ancient when I met her."

"Exactly my point. Sij appears to be in her seventies, at least. She's old in a land where most people die in their forties or fifties."

"That's not unheard of," Kara said, her cheeks tightly drawn. "Before the Collision, people lived to be a hundred."

"That was then. It's different now. But I'm beginning to believe Sij is far older than that."

"What are you saying?"

He gestured to the corpse. "Poor Pablo probably fought, but he was overpowered. And he's not a small man. For Sij to have done this—in front of six other people she somehow subdued—then she would have to be part demon."

Things he hadn't understood were starting to make sense. Sij had hated him on sight. He'd chalked up her instant dislike of him to the fact he was a stranger, but it wasn't that. Their band welcomed strangers in distress on a regular basis.

She must have recognized me. Under normal circumstances, angels and demons knew each other instinctively. The foul stench of a full-blooded demon was unmistakable, but those of mixed blood were harder to spot. If she was half-blood or less, she might not have needed a masking spell.

On the other hand, he would have been unmistakable to her. It was why he lived in hiding during demon rule.

Kara rubbed her arms. They had goose bumps all over them. "So Sij is like me? Is she...related to me?" Her tone was filled with disgust—for herself.

"I don't know. Does her blood work like yours against the curse?"

She shook her head. "She needs mine. I know for sure."

Okay, that was something. "Then she's just likely another

demon acolyte. Hell, she could just be another witch with enough knowledge of black magic to extend her own life. We need to find her. The others are in great danger."

So was the whole damn city. One Firehorse in the city could spell disaster. If Claire had counted right, then there were six others loose in the city.

Kara was already on her feet. "We don't have time to bury Pablo. We need to find the rest of the Firehorses. If the curse gets reactivated, it will be like a bomb going off—" She broke off. "*Oh, God.* That's her plan, isn't it? She wants to finish the city off."

He knew she was right before the words finished leaving her mouth. Hurrying, Ash put Pablo in the tunnel. Most of the denizens of Bastille avoided them, so the body would be safe until they could come back to take care of him.

He drew a quick cross on Pablo's forehead before rushing back out into the open. "Where would she go?" he asked.

Kara wrapped her arms around her middle and squeezed. "I don't know. Is there a location that would cause the most damage?"

It was his turn to stare blankly at her. "Everywhere?"

Bastille was a badly balanced runaway train, one he was forced to repair on the fly almost every other day. He didn't have a clue where to start.

"Could her target be the radio station?" As of today, it was the most advanced technology in town.

Kara shifted her weight, the crease between her brows deepening. "It's not essential for life," she said. "Think bigger."

"It could be one of the refineries or a granary. Or it could be the water-purification plant on the Ile de la Cite. We haven't succeeded in keeping the alternates up and running for longer than a few weeks at a time."

Kara snapped her fingers. "It must be that one...maybe."

She buried her hands in her hair, pulling it hard. "Ugh, I don't know! We can second-guess this till Hell freezes over."

Merde. He did not want to do this. "We need to split up. With all the effort we've made to decentralize critical services, there are too many potential targets."

Ash slipped the angel blade he'd found in Montmeurtre from his pocket, and handed it to Kara. In her hands, it was the length of a short sword. "Take this. It will kill her no matter how much demon blood is in her."

Kara swished the knife experimentally. Like his sword, it had a preternaturally sharp edge—the kind that made it sing when slicing the air. "What about you?"

"If I find her, I won't need a weapon to take her out," he said, enfolding Kara in his arms. He pressed her close, taking the opportunity to draw a protective symbol on her back with his finger.

The ward would have been stronger if he drew it in his blood, but he didn't know how it would react to the bit of demon in her.

He flew her to the water plant on the banks of the Seine, dropping her outside the door. Then he beat his wings twice as hard, heading east in the direction of the main refinery.

Don't look back, he repeated over and over. Kara was a capable woman. If she found Sij first, she'd be able to handle her.

I should have been teaching her defensive spells all this time, not making love. Next time they had an hour to themselves, he'd begin training her in the craft, he promised himself.

Only, there might not be a next time. If they didn't stop Sij now, Bastille was finished.

31

All the mills and refineries were vulnerable. He didn't know which one Sij would target.

Without the wheat and maize stored in the granary, a quarter or more of the population would starve. But attacking one of the refineries would have a larger and more immediate destructive impact.

He flew north, wondering which one to check first.

A hint of something caught his eye as he flew. A black aura was gathering over one of the buildings along the old concourse, where the Moulin Rouge had been repurposed into a manufacturing district. The darkness was concentrated over the steel factory.

It was as if Sij had hung a huge arrow in the sky to attract his attention. *The fiend is calling me out.*

She wasn't trying to hide from him. *Good.* He didn't want to put off this fight either, but he needed to be ready. The old bitch was up to something diabolical.

His hands were tight fists as he shouldered his way inside the main doors.

A blast of heat greeted him as he stepped inside. Ash blinked, his eyes adjusting to the dimmer light. This place always reminded him of Hell. Despite the lights, the room was dark. Most of the illumination came from the molten metal pouring into a clay molds. Today, they were laying out the pieces for a construction truss.

Ash winced, his retinas burning as he watched the white-hot liquid spill down just a few feet away from a worker in an asbestos-lined suit. He scanned the factory floor. Nothing looked out of place. All the refinery workers were going about their business, completely unaware that at this moment a cursed time bomb was about to go off. Whatever Sij was up to, she had stayed away from the main operation room.

"We're closing up for today!" he shouted in a loud voice, before pulling the nearest workman aside. "Tell Christophe, the manager. I need you to wind up operations as soon as possible."

"Is there a new Firehorse? I didn't hear the klaxon," the man said. Ash could hear the panic in his voice.

"This is preventative," he assured him. "But don't waste time. Turn this off and go home. *Now.*"

The man hurried to obey. He scrambled to the catwalk above the manually powered conveyer belt. Fixed to the handrail was a hand-crank attached to a siren. The workman climbed up the rail next to it, turning the handle.

A sonorous wail filled the room. On cue, all the workman began to shut down operations, pouring what was left of the hot metal into thin clay molds. Those cooled faster and could be re-melted easily.

Ash made a mental note to commend Christophe for the internal siren addition. Without it, the noise in the factory could drown out the city-wide alarm. He waited until the men finished covering the cooling metal before reaching for a pry bar from the tool shelf.

On impulse, he dipped the bar into the liquid metal, shaking off the excess into the mold.

A crawling sensation on the back of his neck signaled he wasn't alone anymore. He began to pivot, only to feel a blow to the back of his neck. Someone had jumped on to his back.

He felt a blade rebound off his armor as he flipped the creature off his back. Sij landed on the floor, rolling on her feet with the grace of a cat. She smirked from her crouched position on the floor.

No crone that age should move like that. And how had she caught him unawares? He should have sensed her presence from a mile away.

"Where were you hiding, you demon-loving bitch?"

Sij tsked and straightened. "Do all angels have such terrible potty mouths?"

The rotten stench that came from her mouth had a hint of brimstone.

Ash's lip curled. The thought of this creature being on such intimate terms with Kara turned his stomach. "You *are* a full-blooded demon. How did you hide that from me?"

Nothing about her was reading right. The crone's nose wrinkled as she cackled, exposing a mouth full of half-rotting teeth. "Are all angels such idiots?"

She hopped up on the table, indicated her body with an all-encompassing gesture. "How quickly your kind forget that a demon can possess a human. We didn't all choose to take our physical forms back after the Collision. There are many advantages to staying in a human host. The anonymity for one. Those mewling, clueless humans were so fun to tease."

To tease? Ash couldn't believe what he was hearing. "You socialized with them?"

"So the fallen are the only ones who can mix it up with the meatsacks?" She sneered. "My favorite thing in the world was to join them in a bar or brasserie for drinks after I'd murdered one of their nearest and dearest. I would keep a bit of the victim's blood in a flask, and spike my glass of wine. How I loved it when they would toast with me! It made the taste so much richer."

Ash pictured driving the pry bar straight through her rotten mouth. It was the only thing that kept him calm enough to ask his questions. "That doesn't explain how you could mask your true nature from me. A human possessed is like a beacon."

An angel couldn't see a human soul, but they could certainly see a demonic one, no matter what kind of shell it wore.

Sij was almost jiggering with glee. "True, true...unless, of course, that human is a witch."

Merde. That was too much of a coincidence. "Let me guess...a Delavordo witch?"

"So you're not a stupid as you look," she said, beaming at him like he'd won a prize. "I took this old crone back before the Collision. She was a beautiful young thing back then. Fancied herself a real black witch. But she was an inexperienced pea-brain, one with untapped resources. Even she didn't know the power she had...not until I showed her. I offered to possess her, to teach her all my secrets. She jumped at the chance, and truly enjoyed our partnership, at least up to the point she realized she wasn't getting control of her body back. Her spirit still wanders purgatory as a wraith."

He shook his head. "I don't believe you. Demons can't possess a human for so long."

Those poor unfortunates always died quickly. The human form simply couldn't handle the strain.

Sij preened. "But a witch lasts so much longer if you're careful. This body was the last in an extensive line of practitioners I burned through. Once I used her up, I was going to go out and get another, but then you angel scum labeled witches the enemy, hunting them all down. The ones your lot missed went into hiding." She broke off to spit in his direction. "The few who remained were so much harder to find."

This explained why she attached herself to the band of survivors. "You were going to possess Kara."

Sij rolled her eyes as if she couldn't believe his stupidity. "Kara wasn't even born when I first came to Bastille! I was trapped here after the Collision, just like you were. If I'd been warned, I could have reclaimed my true form first. But since the powers that be did not deign to share the information with the lower ranks, I didn't get a chance to make the necessary preparations."

"And so you were stuck."

She shrugged her bony shoulders. "I presented myself to Amducious, as was his due as king. He accepted my claim to serve him, and history was made. I became a great favorite of his," she bragged.

"But you didn't serve him openly." If she had, he would have known her face or heard some tale of her—a demon possessing a human. There were no new cases after the Collision. Why when a demon could walk openly and at full strength in their true forms?

He'd forgotten the ones that had been here before the Collision. Never in his wildest dreams would he have guessed one would survive in their vessel for so long.

"And after I killed him, you sought out the only surviving Delavordo witch."

"Unlike Amducious, I always knew where the family was. He had lost track of them long ago, but I had a much closer starting point from which to search. As long as one of the members lived, I didn't worry about it. And I never told him in case the rumors were true—that they were of his blood."

"You didn't find confirmation of that until he was gone, and you joined Kara in the wasteland."

"True again, winged freak," she jeered, her claylike hands tapping a staccato beat on the wooden table. "I saw what her blood could do, and I realized I could never take her as my host."

"What?" That wasn't what he'd expected to hear.

Sij rolled her eyes. "Amducious wasn't my sire, but as my liege, he earned my respect. He rewarded my service and relied on my counsel. After he was gone, I couldn't kill or possess Kara without undoing our greatest work together."

His stomach twisted. "The Firehorse curse."

The bitch actually started clapping. "Finally caught up, poor boy. Yes, I helped him cast the spell. My knowledge of the craft was greater than his own. Together, we created something truly diabolical. It made Lucifer so proud."

"No doubt," he muttered, wishing he could smash his older brother's face in. "What the hell did you mean about undoing the work?"

The crone was almost vibrating with excitement. "You know when I first saw you, I feared you would learn the truth and act. But now I know that either way, I will win, so I've decided to tell you!"

Ash felt ill. He knew what Sij was going to say. He'd always known. "Kara has to die to break the enchantment."

Sij hooted, hugging herself to keep her bony body together against the spasms of harsh guttural laughter. "She doesn't just have to die—she has to willingly sacrifice herself on the altar over runes drawn in demon blood. So you can see why I wanted you as far from her as possible in the beginning. I thought you would order her to do it, and to end the curse—selfless idiot she is—she *would* do it. And then to my shock, you fell in love with her. The whole town is talking about it. If the rumors are true, you even bedded her, sacrificing your place in Heaven for a mortal. It's just too perfect. Now you can't end the curse without ripping out your own heart!"

She got up on the table, throwing her arms into the air. "Kara kills herself and ends the curse, but you are doomed to an eternity without her. Or she lives... and the two of spend the rest of your lives in a Bastille that continues to topple around you. Even if I lose, I win!"

She laughed again, brown spittle flying from her foul mouth.

"What's to stop us from continuing as we are, holding off the curse with Kara's blood?" he asked. It wasn't a perfect solution, but with enough preparation, they could mitigate the worst of the curse's effects—as long as Kara never learned how to end it for real.

Sij held up a finger. "You could try that, but I don't think the good citizens of Bastille will go along with it. You see, after a lifetime of lying, I finally discovered how powerful the truth can be. I've made certain interested parties privy to the secret of how to end the curse permanently."

Putain. "The cabal learned the angel trap spell from you," he spat.

She shrugged. "It would be more correct to say I led them to it. Too bad they screwed it up. But having failed that, the surviving council members will be good for something—telling the citizens of Bastille the truth. And I don't think the people will thank you for sparing Kara, not after today's destruction."

His grip tightened on the pry bar tightened. "The curse bomb."

"So you figured that part out on your own..." She pulled something out of her pocket. It was a bundle of leather thongs, with empty vials at the end. The blood had been poured out.

Sij swung the vials in a circle. "I've been planning this for a long time. I admit it was fun watching the curse do its work. Even watching Kara occasionally hold it off was fascinating in a way— it's certainly something Amducious never planned for. But this body is decaying faster and faster, and my time is running out. Once you broke free of the council's trap, I knew the time had come. I even sent you and Kara the message tipping you to my plan."

His head was spinning now. "The note wasn't from Claire?"

The crone rolled her eyes. "The child can't even write. But Kara doesn't know that." She stopped to tap an imaginary watch on her wrist. "By my calculations, you have mere minutes to stop the curse bomb, but since you have to kill me, you won't have time."

This was too much. "You *want* me to kill you?" What the hell was she thinking?

Sij bowed with a little flourish. "Of course. You kill me, and my spirit returns to Hell. One of the perks of possession."

Was she kidding or just stupid? "If I kill you, your evil soul dies here. It's the end of the line," he corrected.

Sij waved that away. "Not without a true angel sword, like the one you used to kill my liege. And that one is rusting away at the bottom of the Seine. You'll never find it."

Unbelievable. Also wrong. "You forget I was one of Heaven's first swordsmiths. Any sword in my hands *is* an angel sword." He flicked his wrist, mouthing a quick incantation.

A network of glowing lines appeared on the pry bar just below his fist. They raced down the metal lengths, forming runes and holy sigils.

The spell polished the dull metal as it went. By the time it reached the tip, it was gleaming silver white. The end was still blunt without a hammer to hone it, but that didn't matter.

The demon's head drew back, and she smiled manically. "Oh, well...you can't win them all. That's why I planted dynamite in the basement."

She did what?

Ash lunged for the demon, but Sij hopped over the table.

She moved faster than that body had any right to. He threw the table aside, running full speed after her, but she didn't try to get away. Instead, she made for the crawlspace under the stairs.

He only caught a glimpse of the twisted, rotting grin on her face when she lifted a box and twisted a dial on it.

The roar of the explosion was deafening. All around him, walls began to buckle. He lost his sight, his head pounding as it reverberated with the force of the blast.

Ash squeezed his eyes shut, using his wings as a shield. He wrapped them around his torso, protecting himself from the flying rubble.

Small bits of molten metal shrapnel peppered the length of his wingspan. It stuck to his back and feathers, drying into misshapen clusters as it cooled on the spot. Swearing viciously, he pushed at the trestle crossbar that had landed on his wing, only to realize the damn thing had pierced it. He'd been pinioned.

Ash tried to tuck his wings in, but with the broken joint, he couldn't magically meld them to his body. Swearing, he let the broken wing drag across the uneven floor, digging below the stairs to find Sij half-buried in a pile of rubble.

The bitch may have been an expert in spells, but she didn't know dynamite or old-world construction. The explosion hadn't been as well planned as the one by the politicians. The blast should have killed her, but the thickness of the floor had weakened its intensity.

Heaving a rock aside, he reached over and pulled the demon imp toward him.

"Just let me die," she gurgled, black ochre blood oozing from her mouth.

"Not without my help," he said, lifting his weapon.

It hurt like the devil. His arm muscles were screaming. Every move exacerbated the pain of the broken joint in his wing, but he didn't stop. Using both hands, he lifted the bar, burying it in Sij's middle with a grunt of pain and frustration.

She died without a whimper. All he heard was the snap and crack of the demon's soul. It burned in the holy fire created by the runes on the metal.

Ash pulled out the makeshift sword, turning for the exit, but the door had been obliterated. Forced to climb and push his way out of the mess, he made for the exit, dragging his broken wing behind him.

He reached open air just in time to see a bolt of lightning streak across the sky. It was followed by three more in quick succession.

Merde. Negative ionization. Ash turned, tracking the lightning to its target.

It was all hitting the same place—Montmeurtre. The demon tower was the tallest point in the city, and despite his best efforts, the heart of Bastille. As he watched, three lightning bolts converged, striking the top of the tower all at once.

It was starting.

32

S hock held him immobile as the ground in front of Montmeurtre opened, swallowing a swath of land an entire city block in length.

Fait chier.

With his broken wing, Ash couldn't fly to the sinkhole. Forced to go on foot, he leapt, running and jumping across the cobblestone roads between him and the demon tower.

He ignored the pain, bounding as high as he could using his good wing to balance him as he landed. It was painful, and he was probably scaring the crap out of anyone who saw him, but he couldn't stop.

All hell was breaking loose.

The ground was rolling under his feet. A series of warning tremors was building in intensity as he went. Somewhere, the sound of running water rushed, the roar too loud to be anything except a break in the Seine's banks. A smaller explosion came from the direction of the Trocadero, most likely from a gas pocket igniting.

Every type of disaster that plagued the city was back, hammering each corner of Bastille with renewed force.

It made sense. Six Firehorses were powering this storm. The city had never had to contend with more than one disaster at a time before.

Shrieks and screams filled his ears as he ran. He put his hands over them, trying to shut out the cries for help. This was only the first wave of destruction. If he didn't get the cursed out of the city, the carnage and ruination would continue. He had to plug the leak at the source.

He made it down to the sinkhole a few minutes later. Sirens wailed in the distance, but the emergency response teams were keeping a wide berth from Montmeurtre.

Ash was prepared to scale the pit. His goal was the demon tower, where he assumed the kidnapped Firehorses were being held captive, but he was hailed by a familiar voice.

"Ash!" Kara yelled.

He couldn't see her at first. He ran around, trying to catch sight of her dark hair. She called out again, drawing him to the edge of the pit. There she was at the bottom, dust covering her hair and face like a brown veil.

She had her arm around a blonde woman who was covered in even more dirt and blood. "*Madeleine*?" he asked.

Dr. Brès looked terrible. Her face was swollen and bruised, with purple and green discolorations under the caked-on dirt. She was holding her arm against her chest as if it was broken.

"Did Sij do this to you?" he asked, jumping down to lift the wounded woman in his arms.

Madeleine blinked at him, her eyes zeroing in on his bloody wing. "Did she do that to you?" She craned her neck to get a better view of the damage.

"Later, Doctor," he said, urging her back down. His injury could wait. "We have to focus on getting the Firehorses out of the city.

"*Damn it*. How hurt are you?" Kara broke off, running behind him to check the damage.

He turned and nudged her forward. "Where are the others?"

"Pablo and Demetria are dead," Madeleine said. "Pablo wouldn't cooperate with Sij after we arrived in the city, so she cut his throat—almost took his head clean off. The rest scattered after Kara cut us loose. We thought the tower was going to come down on top of us because it was shaking so violently. I think I saw Didier clear the field before the pit opened, but Demetria was buried under me. She was crushed."

Madeleine shook her head, blinking back tears. "It was crazy. I didn't know Sij could move like that. And the way she got us here—she told us she had found a colony of wild geese, and we were going hunting. It wasn't until we were almost in the city that we realized something was wrong. But then, she pulled out a knife and said she'd find all our relatives and friends and kill them if we didn't come with her."

Tears streamed down her face freely now. "Pablo didn't believe her. He tried to fight, but she was so fast. And then Roget tried to run away, back to the tunnels, and she caught him like that," the doctor said, snapping her fingers. She shuddered. "After they were dead, she carved them up and tossed them into the road like they were trash."

"Sij wanted them found," he said. If they hadn't, then she couldn't confront them and make her last stand.

Kara was muttering a blue streak under her breath. "I can't believe Sij turned on us like that. She's been with us for years. True, she wasn't always pleasant to be around. Sometimes, she was a downright pain in the ass, but she was skilled and reliable. And it turns out it was just to sabotage us all along. I swear, I'm going to kill that bitch if it's the last thing I do."

"Already done," he admitted. "Let's just get the others back to the wasteland. The destruction will calm down once they are out of the city and as far from the demon tower as we can get them."

Madeleine threw him a troubled glance. "I think it's too late.

Sij said there was only one way to stop it once the chain reaction started."

He tensed. "Did she tell you what it was?"

The doctor blinked, looking behind him to Kara and then back again. "No." She shook her head, meeting his eyes steadily.

Ash heaved a sigh of relief. *Good.* That meant he still had time to find another solution. He glanced back at Kara as they hurried along the edge of the pit, scanning for survivors.

"Anything she said would have been a fabrication," he said, continuing the uneven path. "Demons always lie," he added for good measure.

They found another Firehorse a little farther on. Thierry had been one of the oldest. He'd been impaled in the leg by a large splinter of wood. He was unconscious, but still breathing.

"I think I can stop the bleeding," Madeleine said. "It hasn't pierced an artery. The splinter went through muscle."

"Do it," Ash agreed, gesturing for Kara to follow him. They threw a litter together, so they could drag the wounded out of town.

Kara knelt in front of him, tying a length of fabric they'd found to two scraps of wood. "You'll have to go overland," he told her. "The tunnels will be too unstable, and there may be more tremors or worse."

"*I* have to go?" Kara asked. "But you need me. I have to stop this."

"I don't think you can," he said, glancing at Montmeurtre, turning just in time to see another stroke of lightning hit it. The smell of ozone stung his nostrils. "We're too close to the tower for your blood to make a difference this time."

Her face was white as she squinted at the top of the tower. "It all started here, didn't it?"

He didn't answer. *Sometime in the future, Kara and I will come back here and we will end this—without anyone having to sacrifice themselves.*

Ash cleared his throat. "How many others are left unaccounted for?"

Kara and Madeleine looked at each other, counted on their fingers. "There are two more."

Madeleine finished bandaging Thierry's leg. "It's Adele and Didier."

"*Didier?*" Kara looked worriedly at their dust-covered hands and clothes. "He has asthma."

The doctor straightened, annoyance flicking across her face. "Why didn't he come see me?"

"Okay, let's not get sidetracked," he said, holding up his hands. "I'll find those last two. Just get Thierry as far from here as fast as you can."

Kara's expression was mutinous. "But—"

He held up his hands. "*Please, my love.*"

She pursed her lips, her eyes going from him to Thierry and Madeleine. "All right. But *hurry,*" she grumbled, refocusing on the litter.

Ash didn't watch them go. He began to search for the last two Firehorses, searching the area around the tower in an expanding circle.

Smoke was rising from several places in the city. The klaxon was wailing non-stop. In the distance, people poured into the streets.

It shredded his heart turn his back on the chaos, but his mission was clear. He kept up the search alone. No one ventured close enough to the tower, which was probably the only reason he found the pair hiding in a hole.

Adele took one look at him and screamed her head off. *Merde*, she was one of the Firehorses he'd left in the wasteland a few years ago.

"Adele, stop it," he called out, snagging her with one hand. "Sij is dead. I'm just taking you back to Kara, damn it."

The girl continued to struggle in his grasp.

"She still has nightmares about you," Didier wheezed, limping after them.

Ash held Adele with one hand while he bent to examine Didier's ankle. "Can you walk on it?"

"More like hop," Didier replied.

Ash nodded and began to speak when Adele bit him. "*Damn it,* woman. Don't make me drag you the whole way," he snapped, losing his patience. "You know you need to leave town. You can walk with Didier on your own—he needs the help."

Adele stopped whimpering. Chastised, she kept her lips sealed shut as he shoved her gently in Didier's direction.

"Do you think you two can make your own way back to your base in the desert? Kara's heading overland with Madeleine and Thierry."

"Kara's alive? Does that mean she's not going to save us?" Adele was sobbing now. She turned to Didier. "Why didn't Madeleine tell her?"

"How could Kara save you?" Ash frowned.

"Sij said she could. There's this ritual..."

He didn't hear the rest of what she said. His ears were ringing with a high-frequency buzz that overwhelmed all other sound.

Sij *had* told them. Madeleine had known the whole time.

Kara wasn't going to the wasteland. She was in the demon tower.

"Get to the wasteland," he said, shoving the pair forward before starting to run toward the tower.

"Please don't stop her!" Didier called after him. "It's the only way to end this!"

ASH SPRINTED up the winding staircase of Montmeurtre, his wing dragging behind him.

Please don't, he pleaded silently, unsure if he was pleading with an absent Kara or God.

He burst into the altar room, his chest pumping and adrenaline screaming as if he was preparing for battle. But this wasn't a fight he could win with his fists or his strength.

He was too late.

Kara was sitting upright on the altar, covered in blood. She turned to him, her lips as white as the skin on her cheeks.

Her dark eyes shone like coals against her pale face. They lit in recognition when she saw him. The bloodstained knife clattered to the floor.

Ash was at her side before she could speak. "Kara, no! What did you do?"

Her hand landed weakly on his arm under his shoulder plate. She'd lost too much blood to grip with any strength.

"I found the right spell runes in the scroll." Her voice was a ragged whisper.

Ash had never cried before, but tears were obscuring his vision, making it hard to see her. He swept Kara up in his arms, pressing her face against his.

"Don't leave me," he pleaded.

"We have to end it," she said, touching his face with her hands. "But it's going to be all right. I promise. When I see your face again, it will be in Heaven...forever," she promised.

Except that would never happen. Not with her demon blood.

"Kara, I love you," he cried, his hot tears spilling into her sable hair.

There was no answer.

33

H e pressed Kara's head to his chest. Her blood was all over him, still warm but cooling rapidly. All of her was growing cold. Her lips were ice as he pressed a desperate last kiss to them.

"Don't," he kept repeating incoherently. His throat was too swollen to say more, but it didn't matter.

She couldn't hear him anymore.

A warm hand on his arm forced him to turn. His brother was there, standing in sparkling white robes, his hair and face immaculately clean.

Ash stared at Raphael blankly. The Seraph's face was more solemn than he'd ever seen.

"I'm so sorry," the angel said in a low voice.

"What the hell are you doing here?"

"The curse is broken. I've come to take you home."

"No!" The vise squeezing Ash's chest crushed his heart, making it impossible to breathe. He hugged Kara closer. "I won't leave her."

Raphael winced. "Azazel...Ash, she's gone." He looked down at the woman lying cold and still in Ash's arms. "I couldn't see everything from up there—not until the curse was broken. Who is she?"

"Our savior."

The Seraph nodded, keeping his eyes downcast respectfully. "I think I understand. The curse was too strong to break without the catalytic power of martyrdom. I'm so sorry it was someone you cared for." He inhaled deeply, putting a comforting hand on Ash's back.

Ash couldn't feel it through his armor.

"You need to take comfort in the fact this woman—" Raphael began.

"Her name is Kara," Ash interrupted.

Raphael coughed and nodded again. "You need to take comfort in the fact that Kara's sacrifice has saved an entire city and countless generations to come. Her soul is most likely already in Heaven. If we leave now, you can see her again before she even has time to settle in."

The Seraph really didn't know anything. "Promise me she's there."

Raphael's head drew back. "Why wouldn't she be?"

"If she's not there, promise me you will find her soul, wherever it is, and *you will take her there*."

Raphael frowned. "What am I missing?"

Ash turned back to Kara. He stroked her dark head, laying her down on the altar. "She took her life to save ours."

"Yes, that part I understand." Raphael's unlined face looked wrong with a scowl.

Ash took a shaky breath. "Her sacrifice wouldn't have worked without her demon heritage. Amducious was the primogenitor of her family line."

"*Shit.*"

Ash had never seen that expression on his old commander's face. "Promise me."

Raphael winced. "Azazel, you know I can't do that."

The Seraph didn't see the punch coming. He landed on the floor, holding his nose.

"Bloody hell, Azazel."

Ash hauled Raphael to his feet. "There is no one on earth who deserves a place at His side more than her." He punctuated his sentence with another punch, and then another.

"I know...that...but I don't...make the rules," Raphael spit out between blows. His hands were up, but he wasn't defending himself.

Ash didn't care. The injustice of it all was just too much. "Make it happen!" he yelled, hitting him again.

His brother continued to take the beating. He didn't even try to defend himself.

Ash was a good fighter, better than any human on earth, but his brother was a Seraph, one of God's fiercest warriors. He had seen Raphael charge a legion of demons with nothing but a sharp stick. He was more skilled than Ash at hand-to-hand combat. The fact he wasn't fighting back only made Ash feel worse.

Raphael squinted at him from a rapidly swelling eye. "I can't go up and ask Him something like this. You know that! There are rules about this sort of thing. Ever since Lucifer was thrown out, nothing demon can enter. I'm not even sure there's a way to get around the wards they set up to prevent an invasion from Hell. Those sigils were drawn by God himself."

Panting for breath, Ash pulled back abruptly. "There has to be a way. She's mostly human."

Raphael straightened, spitting a mouthful of blood on the floor. "Az...you know that doesn't matter. Even a drop of demon blood is enough to condemn her to purgatory or worse."

These rules were fucking impossible. He turned away from Raphael, moving to stand next to Kara. "This isn't fair."

"I know, but...it's not our place to question His decisions."

Ash took a deep breath. "You'll have to...because I'm not going back without her."

"Azazel—"

He held up a hand. "Just go."

Raphael's black scowl was mixed with pity. "I'll try. That's all I can promise." He paused, glancing at Kara's still form. "What's it like?"

He frowned at the Seraph. "What's what like?"

"Love."

Ash wanted to tell him it was the best thing in the world, but at this moment, it was also the worst.

Raphael gave up on getting an answer. "Well, it's probably different for everyone." He cleared his throat. "Little brother, even if by some miracle she's granted a place in Heaven, you might not be. If you did what I think you did—Azazel, you know a relationship like that is forbidden."

Ash covered Kara's small hand with his much-larger one. The cold brick in his gut was radiating out. He could barely feel his fingers now. "I don't care. It was worth it. She was worth everything."

"I hope that's true," Raphael muttered, waving a hand over his own face. Instantly, the bruises and cuts disappeared.

Ash glowered, and the other angel shrugged. "I can't go back looking like that. Not if I'm going to be arguing your case for you." He leaned over and embraced Ash.

Ash stood stiffly in his older brother's arms. Angels didn't hug anyone, let alone each other.

"Sit tight. I'll be back." The Seraph disappeared in a blaze of light.

It was the last bit of illumination the room saw until morning.

Ash had stood next to Kara, an unmoving sentinel, all night. Dawn broke, lighting the room with a soft golden glow.

He could barely look at her, which was why he refused to avert his eyes, even when Raphael came back. Ash could feel the Seraph behind him, waiting patiently for him to turn and face him.

He didn't. There was no point. He already knew what Raphael was going to say.

"I'm sorry, Ash. The answer is no."

34

R aphael was pacing as he explained, the way he always did when he felt guilty. Justifying one of their Father's more brutal orders always made him contrite, but he obeyed without question.

Seraphs were the mouthpieces of God. They wouldn't hesitate to carry out His will, no matter how painful it was.

"The wards can't be taken down to make an exception. It would leave the entire Host and billions of human souls at risk."

Each word sounded as if it were coming from miles away. Ash didn't pay them any mind. He was drifting, the part of him that cared what happened next lost. It was as if his mind had become unmoored from the rest of him.

"Ash, please listen." Raphael waved a hand in front of Ash's face, his lips drawn down in concern.

Ash blinked, his mind snapping to attention. He began to form a series of desperate plans. One involved witchcraft and trickery, and the other a one-man war with Heaven.

"But our Father did recognize the heroism of Kara's selfless act."

Ash snapped his gaze up, meeting his brother's eyes. "What?" he asked hoarsely.

Raphael walked around the altar to stand on Kara's other side. He put his hand on her forehead, and then nodded as if he'd just confirmed something important.

He held up his hands. "Father is prepared to offer you a deal, or more specifically, a trade, one that will restore life to Kara. She'll be healed, and will get to live her life out—"

Hope flooded his breast. Ash leaned forward. "I'll take it. Whatever I have to do, I accept."

Raphael rolled his eyes. "Let me finish."

Merde, he was so annoying. "*Fine.* Finish," he said from behind gritted teeth.

The Seraph huffed. "Kara will be restored. She will get to live a normal human life. When it's over, she will be reborn in another time and place."

Ash held up a hand. "Good enough. Do it now."

The Seraph pursed his lips. "*Again,* let me finish. Because you need to think about this carefully."

If Raphael didn't get to the point, Ash was going to kill him. "What is it?"

"God is willing to restore Kara from the veil if you give up your life in trade—"

"Stop! Shut up," he ordered, waving his brother into silence. "I'll do it."

Raphael's face fell. "Are you certain? You have to be sure because it means you'll abdicate your place in Heaven—"

"Just do it. *Save her.*"

The Seraph dropped his hands and sighed. He moved like molasses, coming around the altar until he was standing between Ash and Kara, settling one hand on each of them.

The angel leaned over to whisper in Ash's ear. "I will miss you, little brother."

A lump formed in Ash's throat. He swallowed hard. "I...will

miss you, too." The grudging words were practically torn from him, but Raphael didn't care. He threw his arms around him in an all-engulfing hug.

Ash rolled his eyes to the ceiling, working one hand free to awkwardly pat him on the shoulder. After a minute, he prodded the angel. "Raph, get on with it."

Huffing, Raphael straightened, moving to stand between him and Kara. He fished out his jar of oil, opening it and dropping a few drops on the tip of his fingers.

"This may feel a little tingly," he said, drawing a sigil on Ash's forehead.

The oil burned like dry ice. His skin throbbed wherever Raphael touched him, but it was nothing compared to the anguish he felt when his brother repeated the process on Kara's cold skin.

"Give me your hand." Raphael reached out, closing his eyes. He put the other hand on her.

Heat began to fill Ash, pouring out of the Seraph's hand. It blazed through him, filling him with liquid fire.

It was like walking out in the sun. Ash squeezed his eyes shut as his vision whitened out. Gasping, he took one last long breath. He hadn't expected his long years of exile to end this way. It was okay, though. After all this time, the end was welcome. He could embrace it content in the knowledge that Kara would live.

Dying was painful, of course, but not as bad as he thought it would be. The flare of white light dulled to orange and yellow behind his lids.

Little by little, his strength ebbed away like a golden thread being pulled out of a tapestry. The feathers on the tips of his wings began to scorch and crumple until his wings completely burned away.

Ash's breathing shortened. Burning heat shot through him. He nearly dropped from crushing fatigue, a new and disturbing sensation.

This is dying. He had only one regret. Trading his life for Kara's meant he wouldn't be able to speak to her or see her made whole again.

The intense fire faded. Raphael backed away, removing his hand.

Ash blinked, surprised he could still see. "What the hell, Raph!" Had his brother gone back on their deal?

Raphael smiled, reading his mind. "Don't worry. I didn't go back on my word."

A female voice broke in. "I don't know who you are, but if you don't get your damn hand off me right now, you're not getting it back."

The Seraph snatched his hand away, moving to reveal a beautiful—and *not* dead—Kara.

Ash shoved Raphael to the side before pulling her into his arms in a tight hug.

Her arms squeezed back hesitantly before she snatched them away. She patted her stomach, now intact. Kara lifted her shirt and started, disappointment marring her otherwise-perfect face. "Did I fail?"

Raphael poked his head into her line of sight. "No, you succeeded. The Firehorse curse has been broken. Now you get your reward—an average human life."

Ash didn't understand what was going on. "What about our deal? I'm supposed to be dead."

Kara's mouth dropped open. She smacked him on the arm... and it actually stung a bit. "You're supposed to be *what*?"

"I'll explain later, my love," he promised, gesturing at Raphael to get on with it.

"Well...because of the complications that we discussed earlier," he said, glancing at Kara from the corner of his eye. "God, in his infinite wisdom, came up with a compromise that will balance the scales, metaphorically speaking. You traded your life for hers."

"I know that part. But here I am—alive," he hissed.

Raphael's smirk was back in place. "Alive and *mortal*."

Ash frowned. "What did you say?"

"What you gave up was your immortal life. God stripped it from you. You're not an angel anymore." The Seraph checked Ash up and down. He didn't look all that impressed. "Now you're just a man, Well, mostly. You'll still be stronger, faster, and smarter than most. Not all men, of course, but then, you never really were all that bright as an angel ei—"

Kara reached over and pinched the Seraph, making him jump in the air. "Finish that sentence and I'll slap you."

Raphael wrinkled his nose. "I begin to see why you like this one. She reminds me of you." The tone wasn't complimentary, but Kara beamed at him anyway.

"But I was dying," Ash protested. "I could feel it. I *still* feel it."

"No, you weren't. That's just what mortality feels like," Raphael corrected. "Like everyone else on earth, you'll die a little every day. Don't worry. You'll get used to it."

The Seraph began to back away. "All right then. My job is done here. Enjoy your happily ever after." He disappeared in a blaze of light.

Kara's eyes widened. "Wow. Is that guy always such a toerag?"

Ash laughed, the rumble tickling his chest. It was a new and strange sensation, but not an unpleasant one. "It's sort of an angel trait. Believe it or not, he's actually one of the least annoying ones."

"*Really?*" Kara's eyes widened and then she blinked, her eyes clouding. "Are you really mortal now?" she whispered.

He ran his hands down his chest and over his arms. Even his skin felt different—thinner and more sensitive. "I think so."

Her cheeks quivered. "*No*. That's not right. You can't give up your immortality for me."

He pulled her off the altar. Not only was the blood gone from her clothes, but they were also intact again. "I would do anything for you."

She continued to shake her head. "But all you've wanted for thousands of years was to go home. What if you regret this someday?"

"Don't worry about that. Not ever. I'm *exactly* where I'm supposed to be."

EPILOGUE

Ten Years Later

Ash finished tightening the last bolt on the new antenna array with a satisfied sigh. He slipped the wrench into his tool belt, and then walked along the narrow metal beam surrounding the topmost level of Heaven's Spire. The new monument stood in place of the Montmeurtre, a gleaming blue and white metal spire that served double duty. It was both the new communications tower as well as a monument to Bastille's liberation.

A few kilometers away, a dirigible was departing from the Montparnasse station. The red-colored balloon marked it as the new long-distance airship. The engineers had even added some decorative rivets to the ribbing, giving it a distinctive steampunk flair.

Satisfaction welled in his breast. It was such beautiful sight, one he got to see three times a week now. The airship tracked across the city, disappearing south as it began its journey to New Toulouse.

Many things had changed in the years since the Firehorse

curse was broken. No longer subject to regular bouts of destruction and disaster, Bastille had slowly recovered.

The earthquake and fire damage had been repaired. The Seine's banks had been reinforced and equipped with extra drainage to handle the elevated levels during the rainy reason. The sewer and water purification systems were also up and running. Most of the condemned buildings had been torn down. They were in the process of being replaced, but the mayor's office was still working on clearing the ring of rubble and derelict vehicles that once circled the city. New construction had laid out a city plan in the shape of Triquetra, a simple sigil design that would help ward Bastille from future demon attack.

Mazarin was dead. His bones had been found in the wasteland a few weeks after the city's emancipation. He was identified by the gold jewelry he always wore.

Ash was officially retired. He'd turned over stewardship of the city to Samuel a few years ago after a hard-won election against Madeleine Brès. Ash's instincts about the former night man had been proven correct. Though initially a bit overcautious, Samuel had developed into a capable and compassionate leader—not as good as Kara would have been—but effective nonetheless. Dr. Brès had accepted defeat with good grace. She'd started a flourishing medical school instead.

The council was no more. It had been abandoned in favor of a traditional representative republic with a single head. The mayor would serve five years, and no more.

Kara had turned down the job of mayor in favor of many others. His extremely busy wife refused to settle into any one profession. Finally able to explore her passions, she had started as a community organizer before deciding to spearhead the reconstruction effort. Kara had later served as a demolitions expert, which had sparked an interest in architecture. She had retrofitted the Grand and Petit Palais before laying the groundwork for the new university. Her last project had been designing Heaven's Spire.

The sun dipped in the sky, reminding Ash he was expected home for the evening meal. He climbed down the balustrade, circumventing the stairwell in favor of descending the length of the structure freehand.

When he reached the ground, a little boy about four years old was staring at him openmouthed. "Weren't you scared?"

Ash's lips quirked. "I like heights," he told the child, patting him on the head. Humming, he waved goodbye before turning down Avenue Duquesne to catch the streetcar home. He and Kara had built a micro-farm over the ruins of the Luxembourg gardens.

Before he'd lost his wings, the trip would have taken a few minutes. But Ash didn't mind the commute. Crossing the city was a pleasure again.

Thanks to his and Kara's insistence on using steam and solar power, the city's air was crisp and clean, and the trees and bushes were lush and healthy. He loved how the city smelled after it rained, and welcomed the bite in the air that heralded the arrival of autumn.

Ash was a few hundred yards away from his house when the high-pitched babble of children's voices reached him.

His son was being forcibly removed from the roof of their home by his irate mother again. More amused than he should have been, Ash stopped to watch the fracas from behind a tree. He'd learned from experience that showing his delight over his children's antics was a big mistake.

"I don't wanna!" Little Marcus wailed as Kara reached up to snag him with one arm. Foiled, the boy howled, just as Renée, Marcus' twin sister, ran across the roof. His daughter neatly avoided capture, launching herself into the open air wearing nothing but a cloth diaper and a makeshift white cape.

Ash caught her easily before she landed in the bushes.

"Hello, love." He grinned at his fuming wife.

Kara rolled her eyes. "Take this," she said, thrusting little Marcus into his arms. She turned her back on them all, stomping inside as he juggled their children in his arms, bouncing them high between kisses hello. "I'm serious this time—I'm going to line the roof with spikes. Maybe that will finally keep their feet on the ground."

He wrinkled his nose. "I doubt that would do any good. Their love of heights is probably genetic," he apologized before chastising the children in his best dad voice.

"We're sorry, Mommy and Daddy," the twins chorused with their hands pressed together in front of them in their best imitation of praying cherubs.

"Sure you are," Kara said, her eyes narrowed skeptically on their sweet little faces.

Ash hoisted the twins higher, so they could apologize to their mother properly.

Kara managed to keep the annoyed facade up for a whole minute more before she crumbled under the assault of the twin's sticky kisses. Satisfied with their act of contrition, Ash put them back down on the ground.

"Go wash up for dinner," he ordered benevolently, swatting each on the bottom gently to get them moving.

"I swear those two will be the death of me," Kara muttered, crossing to the dining room to set the table.

He followed, waiting until the patter of little feet had died down in the distance before taking her in his arms and kissing her passionately. When he was done, he was fairly certain she didn't remember the roof incident anymore.

Pressed close together, they chatted about the coming meal before she got around to asking him about his day. "How was the meeting with the Mexico City envoy?"

He lifted his head, reluctantly interrupting his nibbling on her neck. "Ambassador Rebekah postponed until tomorrow, so I moved up the antennae array installation to today," he said.

"*Ah.*" She tsked. "So the children weren't the only ones playing daredevil this afternoon."

"I was careful," he protested, deciding not to mention his method of descent.

"Mmm-hmm," Kara murmured noncommittally. "Does this mean the antique television you have gathering dust in the attic will soon be gracing the salon? Or is it another false start?"

"I think we've cracked it this time, but I'm more excited about this," he confessed with a grin. He pulled out the steam-powered mobile phone prototype he'd picked up at the *Ecole Polytechnique* earlier that morning.

Kara stopped to examine the device. The phone was a simple box with a dial and a flat round combination speaker-microphone affixed to the top. In terms of innovation, it paled in comparison to the smartphones of the pre-Collision era, but he didn't care. He was intensely proud of the thing and the people who had built it, much in the way he was of his wife and her accomplishments.

"Once the network is up, we'll make sure every city head in France has one of these," he enthused. "Bastille will never be cut off again."

"What about you?"

"Hmm?" he murmured, distracted. He didn't look up until the silence registered.

Kara was watching him with an adorable line puckering her brows. "Don't you miss it?"

He blanked. "Miss what?"

"*Heaven,*" she said, her eyes tight at the corners. "I know you miss flying. How can our lives compare with being an all-powerful angel?"

This again. "I don't need wings to fly when I'm with you," he promised, his heart welling with love and pride.

She wrinkled her nose. "So cheesy."

"Guilty." He brushed his lips against her forehead, and then pulled back to stare deeply into her eyes. "I wouldn't want to go back. Any place that doesn't let you in is not somewhere I want to be."

Kara bit her lip, still pensive. She knew her blood forever barred her from Heaven. He'd told her the truth years ago.

His heart ached to see her so distressed. "Please don't let this bother you. I know it's unfair. Of all the people in the universe, you deserve to know the joy of being in His sight and vice versa. If He could but see you, I know He would change his mind and make an exception, because no one in this universe could ever deny your spirit."

A tear slipped past Kara's thick lashes. "I know you find this hard to believe, but I really don't care about that." She squeezed him tighter. "My Heaven is here with you."

He gripped her hand tightly and deepened their embrace until she pushed him away to catch her breath.

Kara was flushed and still breathing fast when a mischievous glint appeared in her eye. She coughed and pulled away. "I do have one request—more of a challenge really. And I'm afraid it may prove more difficult than any of the challenges we've faced before."

Ash pulled himself up to his full height. "Whatever it is, consider it done."

She put her hand on his shoulders, her face grave. "Be certain. This is nothing short of a trial by fire."

Confused and concerned, he nodded. "As long as it doesn't require an angel's powers, I'll slay whatever dragons you set in front of me."

"This is not far off..." She pushed his shoulder and pointed to the stairs. "Go and make sure those children are washed up for dinner. They're probably back on the roof again."

Ash laughed, the sound filling the room. "I will not fail you," he promised, remembering the Seraph's parting advice when he challenged him to liberate Bastille.

Ash much preferred this mission, but Kara had a point. Saving the city might prove easier...

He stooped to steal another kiss before leaving to carry out his lady's quest, whistling as he went.

The End.

* * *

WANT MORE fantastic fantasy from L.B. Gilbert? Check out her award-winning Elementals series.

ALSO BY L.B. GILBERT

"A hot-tempered heroine and the charmingly undead prove a winning combination." - - *Kirkus Reviews*

A 2017 READERS' FAVORITE SILVER MEDAL WINNER

A kick-ass heroine with pyrokinetic abilities and a license to kill. Enter Alec...vampire, scholar, and worst of all--*fan*. What could possibly go wrong?

Diana, the fire Elemental, is nearly burned out. Tired of traveling the world and losing innocent lives, she's slowly slipping into a depression that may consume her. But when she discovers that a child's life is in danger, she feels compelled to help. However, teaming up with one of the most powerful vampires in North America is the last thing she wants to do.

Academic scion, Alec Broussard prefers his studies over the opulent and vicious lifestyles of vampires. And when he learns of another missing child, Alec can't shake the suspicion that his coven may be to blame. Joining forces with an Elemental may be his only hope to save the child and clear his coven's name.

As Diana and Alec work together to save the children, they must relinquish their prejudices and trust one another. In time, Alec is wearing down the walls around her. But just when their friendship intensifies, Alec's future is threatened. Now, it's up to Diana to save him before it's too late. Can this Elemental find the fire within her to protect him once and for all?

Grab Your Copy Today!

ABOUT THE AUTHOR

USA Today bestselling author L.B. Gilbert spent years getting degrees from the most prestigious universities in America, including a PhD that she is not using at all. She moved to France for work and found love. She's married now and living in Toulouse with one adorable half-French baby.

She has always enjoyed reading books as far from her reality as possible, but eventually the voices in her head told her to write her own. And, so far, the voices are enjoying them. You can check out the geeky things she likes on twitter or Facebook.

And if you like a little more steam with your Fire, check out the author's romance erotica titles under her married name Lucy Leroux...

Subscribe to L.B. Gilbert's Newsletter for deals and free reads!

Connect with L.B. Gilbert

www.elementalauthor.com